GOLDEN HANDCUFFS

T. DeWayne Pearson

iUniverse, Inc.
New York   Bloomington

Golden Handcuffs

iUniverse books may be ordered through booksellers or by contacting:

iUniverse
1663 Liberty Drive
Bloomington, IN 47403
www.iuniverse.com
1-800-Authors (1-800-288-4677)

ISBN: 978-1-4401-5132-3 (pbk)
ISBN: 978-1-4401-5133-0 (ebook)

Printed in the United States of America

iUniverse rev. date: 7/01/09

The steady pounding dragged Jennifer from oblivion. She felt groggy, unable to lift her head from her luxurious down pillow. There was no way she could gather enough energy to make it to the door. Much to her chagrin, the knocking continued. It was a practiced pattern, two short raps followed by three hard knocks. As her head began to throb in tune with the knocking, she became acutely aware of the room's sweltering heat. Her mouth was dry and the sheets were soaked with her sweat. Her arm felt like it weighed a ton, but she managed to use it to push her hair from her face. She could feel her roots swelling from the humidity and cringed as she thought of the extra time she'd have to spend in the stylist's chair.

She wasn't exactly sure where she was, but that was of no particular concern to her. Every city tended to blend together when she was touring; last week she thanked all her Milwaukee fans when she was on stage in Indianapolis. She vaguely remembered something about going to the beach earlier in the day. The only domestic beach she bothered to visit was South Beach, so she must be in Miami. She tried to block out the banging noise by covering her head with the pillow.

She tried yelling for someone to get the door, but all she could manage was a croaked whisper. She hoped that one of her assistants was somewhere in the suite, but the renewed knocking let her know that they had all left for the night. She slowly rolled over underneath the covers. As she did, she felt her chemise stick uncomfortably to her body. She was dripping with sweat and her silken lingerie was not helping. She would have preferred to sleep in one of Felix's old T-shirts, but even when there were no cameras around he was very particular about what she wore. As she pulled the fabric away from her skin, she realized that it wasn't just her sweat making it stick. In the dim moonlight filtering through the curtains, she could make out Felix's outline under the sheets next to her.

"Felix!" she hissed. "If you spilled something and didn't clean it up again, I'm going to kill you."

The lump under the covers didn't move. She couldn't tell if he was really asleep, or just pretending to be. He wouldn't want to get out of bed to answer the door any more than she did.

"Felix! Get up and answer the door, I'm not dressed! Get up!" She tried kicking him, but her legs were as heavy as the rest of her body. She doubted he felt her strike at all.

Felix showed no sign of stirring, and Jennifer resigned herself to the fact that he had passed out again. It had been the same story nearly every night for the past three weeks. Jennifer wondered how long he could function this way. He had always liked to party, but lately he was flirting with becoming a full-blown alcoholic. Tonight must have been especially raucous, because she didn't remember any of it.

Jennifer gathered her strength and rolled to the edge of the bed. The hotel had been specifically instructed that she and Felix were not to be disturbed, so she figured Clarence must have come up with one of his asinine questions that required a middle of the night answer. Jennifer thought he was the worst road manager she'd ever seen, but Felix would never fire him, they had been friends since they were six.

The shades were open and the pale glow of the moon cast a faint light. Jennifer could make out a hotel robe hanging on the back of the chair next to the bed. She pulled it on as she stumbled out of the bedroom and into the darkened hallway. She couldn't remember what the suite looked like and she certainly didn't know where to find the light switch. She placed her palm against the wall and let it guide her wobbly legs out into the front room. The light from the hallway shone like a halo around the door. Her head exploded with pain as her visitor again banged loudly.

"I'm coming!" she croaked. The dull throb in her head felt different than her usual hangover. It was much worse tonight. She tried not to drink much when she was out in public. The paparazzi were everywhere and tabloids paid premiums for pictures of sloshed celebrities. She felt awful and she was sure that it was somehow Felix's fault.

Jennifer peered through the peephole and saw a short, balding man in a red hotel blazer standing between two dour police officers. The balding man was wearing a silver nametag that identified him as the night manager. She watched as he raised his fist and rapped on the door again. Jennifer sighed as she wondered what Felix had gotten himself into while she was sleeping.

The tour had been a great success thus far, just as her label predicted. She and Felix, or Optimus, as his fans knew him, were selling out arenas with such frequency that they had added six more dates. Still, trouble dogged Felix everywhere they went. In Denver, he had been arrested in the hotel lobby for marijuana possession. In Newark, several members of his entourage had been arrested for assault in an incident outside a strip club. Just last week in San Antonio, he had narrowly avoided picking up a weapons charge by shoving his pistol into Clarence's pocket when the police arrived.

She opened the door, but left the safety chain connected.

"I'm sure my manager left word that we weren't to be

disturbed," she said, hoping that her attitude might scare them away.

"Ahhh, yes Ms. Stevens," the night manager said. "We've gotten several complaints about… strange noises coming from this room." Her real last name was Weston, but she had learned long ago never to stay in any hotel under her God given name. Fans could be very crafty about getting into places where they weren't allowed.

"Someone must be mistaken," she replied. "There haven't been any strange noises coming from this room. I've been here asleep all evening. So if you'll excuse me, I'm going back to bed."

"We still have to check it out. I'm Officer Wallace," the larger of the two policemen interrupted. "And this is Officer Carter." The smaller policeman nodded his head. "Are you in here alone ma'am?"

"What business is it of yours?" she asked. "How do I know you're even police officers? You could be from Celebrity Eye magazine or something."

"Ma'am," Officer Carter answered as they both pulled out Miami Police Department identification cards to go along with the shields attached to their chests, "Feel free to take a look at our credentials."

"I don't know who called you," Jennifer said, eyeing the men warily, "but you can see that there isn't anything happing here now, so good night." Jennifer began closing the door.

"All the same ma'am," Officer Wallace said as he slid his foot between the door and its frame, "the hotel did receive several calls. Would you mind if we came in and looked around, just to make sure."

"Yes, I would mind," she answered. "It's late, I'm not dressed and I don't think that I'd be comfortable with three men coming in here with me."

"We could call and get a female officer if it would put your fears to rest," Officer Wallace replied.

"Or we could make you stand here at the door while we got a search warrant to go through all of your stuff. I'm certain we'd find some contraband," Officer Carter added. "That would take quite awhile, but my shift doesn't end until seven, so it's all the same to me."

"I'm sure it would just be a couple of minutes," the manager soothed. "Then we would be out of your hair. We value your patronage, but we really do have to check out all complaints."

Jennifer sighed again and decided to open the door. She got the distinct impression that they wouldn't be satisfied until they poked around awhile. She guessed that these two didn't get the chance to hassle celebrities all that often and it probably gave them a little bit of a thrill. Besides, she felt confident that Felix wouldn't be dumb enough to keep anything incriminating in their room.

"Fine," she said as she removed the safety chain. "My boyfriend Felix is in the bedroom, try not to wake him okay?"

The three men crossed the threshold and the manager reached to Jennifer's left to flip on the light switch. She turned around to lead the officers inside and was shocked at what she saw. The living quarter of the suite was a mess. A table and several chairs were overturned. The couch cushions were torn and stuffing from them was strewn all over the room. A bottle of champagne had been shattered, leaving a stain on the thick carpet and the television had a wide crack across the screen. The hotel manager looked horrified as he surveyed the damage.

"No strange noises?" Officer Carter scoffed. "It looks like you've had yourself quite a little party to me."

"I don't care what it looks like to you," Jennifer said as she spun around. "We have more than enough money to cover the damages and there isn't anyone here making noise now, so like I said, you can leave." Despite her brash attitude, she was confused. She had no idea how any of this could have happened. Trashing hotel rooms wasn't the kind of thing she normally did.

She knew that Felix wasn't above doing it, but she wouldn't have slept through a party loud enough to leave this kind of mess.

Jennifer noticed Officer Wallace staring at her face. He gazed intently, as if trying to solve a puzzle. She supposed that he was trying to figure out how he recognized her.

"Ma'am, are you okay?" Officer Wallace finally asked.

"I'm fine," Jennifer answered. She was becoming agitated and she didn't like the tone of his voice.

"Are you sure?" Officer Carter asked. "You look like you've had a pretty rough time."

"What are you…" Jennifer stopped mid-sentence as she raised her hand to her left cheek. It felt sore and puffy. She quickly ran her tongue over her bottom lip and discovered that it too was sore and puffy. Jennifer looked across the room and caught a glimpse of herself in the cracked television screen. Her lip and cheek were swollen, and the flesh above her right eye was dark and discolored.

"Do you need medical attention?" Officer Wallace asked.

"No," Jennifer answered. "I must have… I must have fallen and hurt myself." It sounded as much like a lie to her as it did to the two policemen.

"What is that on your robe?" Officer Carter added.

She looked down and saw that whatever had been in the bed had seeped through the white terry cloth robe, causing a dark red stain.

"Oh, that. Felix spilled something in the bed," she answered, becoming even more troubled. Why couldn't she remember what happened that night?

"Really? What leaves that kind of stain?" asked Officer Wallace. "There's some on your hands and a little on your neck too." She rubbed the back of her neck: It was slick.

"I'm not sure what it was. I was sleeping when he did it," she answered. Her feeling of uneasiness increased when she saw Officer Carter unlatch his holster strap.

"Is your boyfriend in here?" asked Officer Carter suspiciously as he craned his neck attempting to peer into the bedroom.

"Yes, I told you, he's asleep in the bedroom," Jennifer answered.

"Is there anything you need to tell us before we go in there?" Officer Wallace asked cautiously.

"I don't think so," Jennifer responded.

"So you're telling me that you slept through all this," Officer Wallace motioned at the mess surrounding them, "but you woke up when we knocked on the door?"

Jennifer didn't say anything as she rubbed her injured cheek. Her head was killing her and she had no idea how she'd smashed her face. She and Felix were going to have a serious talk once the police left.

"Maybe we should just ask you boyfriend what happened," Officer Wallace said. The friendly tone that he had been using dropped from his voice. "Vick, why don't you go in there and wake him up."

Officer Carter's hand moved cautiously down to his pistol as he disappeared down the short hall leading to the bedroom. A tense moment passed before Officer Carter's voice boomed from the other room.

"Chris! Bring Ms. Stevens with you. I think this is something you need to see."

Terrell Banks had always thought that elated and exhausted were mutually exclusive feelings, but he was learning that he was wrong. He had been working from six in the morning until just before midnight, seven days a week, for eight straight weeks. The billing requirements at Bragg & Shuttlesworth were infamously high but he had annihilated all expectations over the past two months. He had just finished a motion to compel discovery on behalf one of the firm's major clients an entire day early. Mr. Foster had only made him re-write the motion twice, a personal best for him.

Terrell couldn't help smiling as he plunged his key into the deadbolt. He dropped his briefcase next to the refrigerator and lost his tie somewhere between the back door and his bedroom. He kicked his black wingtips into the closet and allowed the cool draft of the house to blow across his feet. Then he stepped out of his pants and tossed his shirt on the floor beside them. He was certain that his mother would frown on his sloppiness, but at the moment, he didn't care. He had more important things on his mind than making sure his bedroom was presentable. After months apart, he was finally going to visit Alicia.

A plum first job was par for the course to anyone graduating in the top 3% of their law school class. Still, Terrell had considered himself more than fortunate when Bragg & Shuttlesworth offered him a job. They weren't the largest firm, but they paid the most. With his considerable base salary and bonuses he'd earned for bringing in two new high worth clients, he figured that he'd bring home close to a quarter million dollars. He had done all this in his first two years out of school. He had even begun to entertain thoughts of making partner in six years instead of the usual seven.

As much as Terrell loved the money, and he did love the money, the perks of the job were even more valuable. The firm paid his country club membership, got him a low interest mortgage on his new home and the insider deal on the six series BMW in his garage. The firm furnished him with a legion of minions to take care of his day-to-day drudgery like collecting his dry-cleaning and picking up his dinner. He had once complained that he didn't have enough time to clean his house before his parents' visit. He was awakened the next day by a housekeeper. She stopped by every Monday and Thursday since. He longed for the day that he had the use of the firm's ultra-plush Gulfstream for business.

Terrell was bright enough to know that none of the perks were free. Prestige and power at Bragg & Shuttlesworth did not lie in your ability as an attorney; greatness was expected from everyone. Rather, the firm was most concerned about how great you were you at billing your time. Associates were expected to bill a minimum of 2850 hours a year. It took Terrell 70 hours of real time per week to meet the 55 hours of billable time. Those 55 hours only satisfied the minimum level of expectation so usually worked from seven in the morning until at least nine or ten at night, Monday through Saturday. On Sunday, he tried to enjoy some of the money he made, but typically he had to go in for at least a couple of hours to stay on his torrid pace.

Much like Santa Claus or the Easter Bunny, vacation time was a myth at Bragg & Shuttlesworth. Technically, every associate was offered two weeks of paid vacation a year, but no associate was foolish enough to actually take it. There was no possible way to keep up with the billing requirements in the remaining 50 weeks. That was why Terrell has spent so much extra time at work lately. He had to visit Alicia and the only way to make that happen was to take four precious days of vacation.

Alicia was the love of Terrell's life, but their mutual success caused them to spend a lot of time apart. Pegasus Athletic, the number one manufacture of athletic shoes and equipment in the country, hired Alicia right out of business school. As a part of her executive training, she had to take a yearlong trip to Barcelona to work in the Euro-Pegasus office.

Terrell really was happy for Alicia, but the distance between them was killing their relationship. The time differential between Florida and Spain made telephone conversations very inconvenient. She was sleeping when he was at work and when she was at work he was sleeping.

He looked at the clock on his nightstand and quickly did the math. It was nearly the time for siesta, but she should have a couple of minutes. He dialed her office number from memory. On the third ring, a female's voice answered.

"Hola," said her assistant.

"Great," muttered Terrell. His Spanish was terrible, so he struggled to find the right words.

"Uhhh…," he stammered into the phone. "Desear… uhhh, bronca, ummm… la senorita Alicia Lawrence?"

The woman answering the phone answered with a fast stream of words Terrell couldn't identify. He hoped she was asking him who he was.

"Umm, Terrell Banks?" There was an audible click as Terrell was transferred to a different phone.

"Hola," said Alicia.

"Alicia," Terrell said excitedly, "It's me Terrell."

"I know what you sound like," she laughed.

"Just wanted to make sure you haven't forgotten," Terrell said. "Why can't I have your direct line?"

"I already told you, it's a trunk system. There isn't a dedicated number for any of the office phones."

"I feel stupid when I talk to that receptionist. I wish I spoke better Spanish."

"Yeah, she makes fun of you."

"Very funny. I'm sure you don't speak it much better than I do. You've only been over there three months."

"He aprendido mucho desde que he estado aquí," Alicia responded.

"What?"

"I said that I've learned a lot since I've been here. I speak well enough to get around anyway. Doesn't really matter though, most everyone at work speaks English."

"Does your assistant?" asked Terrell.

"Yes," she answered.

"Then why does she always make me jabber like an idiot when I call?"

"I told you, she thinks its funny. Last time you called you said something like I want to eat her foot when you asked for me."

"I meant to say that," said Terrell defensively. "At least, I might want to nibble on your toes when I get there. Maybe I'll even nibble on some other body parts too."

"That sounds good," Alicia purred. "Do you promise?"

"Only if you're good," said Terrell. "I miss you."

"I miss you too," Alicia said sadly. "I can't wait until you get here."

"My flight leaves at eight in the morning, but I have a layover in New York. I won't get to Barcelona until Saturday," explained Terrell.

"That's okay, just as long as you get here. Send your flight schedule to my Blackberry. I'll pick you up from the airport."

"Since when do you have a car over there?" he asked.

"We have a service. Your little law firm isn't the only business with perks. Did you look at that furniture I e-mailed you yet?"

"I haven't had the time." Most of the rooms in Terrell's house were bare. He thought of it as Spartan, but it seemed to bother Alicia.

"In a year and a half?" she asked. "You need to take some time off for yourself. That job is going to kill you."

"I am taking time off," he responded. "I'm coming to see you aren't I?"

"When did you leave work today?"

"I don't know, maybe seven."

"Liar. I bet you just got home."

"No, I came back early and read a book."

"Sure you did. And what did you eat for dinner?"

"Chicken salad." By chicken salad, he meant a fried chicken sandwich with lettuce and tomato eaten quickly at his desk.

"I'm not even going to start with you about your diet. When I get back, I hope you don't think you're going to be working all times of night like you're doing now."

"Wouldn't dream of it."

"Don't patronize me."

"I know, I know," Terrell interrupted. They had this discussion at least once a month. "I need to take better care of myself and stop working so much."

"I'm serious," she said. "If you give yourself a heart attack, I'm going to beat you up."

"Okay, I got it. I promise to get some rest and eat some vegetables."

"Good, I mean real vegetables and not French fries. A little exercise wouldn't hurt you either. You're starting to get a little chunky around the middle." Terrell could hear her smirk.

"That's just more of me to love."

"Whatever," she laughed.

"Okay, if I don't get a chance to talk to you before I get there, I love you."

"I love you too," she answered. "See you on Saturday."

"Bye," said Terrell as he hung up the phone.

Terrell walked over to his nightstand and retrieved the small black case that he had purchased only a few days earlier. Inside was Tiffany diamond engagement ring. He removed the ring from the box and held it up to the light, fantasizing about her reaction. He knew that she was all he'd ever want in a woman and he didn't see any reason to wait.

The housekeeper had taken the liberty of packing his bags for him. He thought of going through his items to make sure she hadn't forgotten anything, but he decided against it. She had never made any mistakes before, and frankly he was too exhausted to look. His flight to Barcelona left in just shy of seven hours. As he flopped onto his bed, he realized that the four hours of sleep he planned on getting was the most he'd had in two weeks.

***

Terrell leaped from the bed thinking that he had overslept and missed his flight. He was confused because the clock showed that it was only 3:28. It took him a couple of moments to realize that the ringing was coming from his cell phone instead of the alarm. He picked it up, wondering who would call him at this hour.

"Hello," he said.

"Terrell," barked a gruff voice. "You need to meet me at the airport in thirty minutes. Bring a suit, you can get dressed on the plane."

"What?" Terrell asked groggily. "No, you must be mistaken. My flight doesn't leave until eight. Who is this anyway?"

"It's Earnest Bragg," shouted the voice. "My name is on the letterhead where you work. Now get down here, we have a new client to see."

"Sorry sir," Terrell apologized. "I didn't recognize your voice." Earnest Bragg III was the grandson of the firm's founder. He was a portly man in his late fifties and was the lead partner of the firm's litigation team.

"Um, sir?" Terrell asked cautiously. "I'm going to Spain tomorrow to see my girlfriend. I'll be gone for four days. Gene is supposed to cover any emergencies that come up with my clients until I get back."

"I'd rather have you on this than Gene. This is a particularly sensitive set of circumstances and I think that the firm would be best served if you lent your particular talents to it. Don't worry, I already took the liberty of having Brenda cancel your flight reservations."

"But sir," Terrell said as he began to panic. "I've already billed 200 hours this month just so I could get a few days off to take this trip."

"Two hundred?" Mr. Bragg asked. "Not bad for three weeks work, young man. At that rate, you'll be the youngest partner we've ever had. When you add this new case, you'll set a personal record."

"Mr. Bragg," Terrell gathered himself, "with all due respect sir, I just can't do it right now. I'm going to propose this weekend. Is there any way this can wait until I get back? I'll even come back early if I have too." Mr. Bragg was a very crotchety man, but Terrell liked him more than all the other partners because he was usually reasonable.

"Is it that young lady you brought to the Christmas party?"

"Yes sir."

"Congratulations. I'm sure she'll make a fine wife," Mr. Bragg replied nonplussed. "But that doesn't change anything."

"But,"

"Let me ask you something," Mr. Bragg interrupted.

"Alright."

"Does she love you as much as you love her?"

"Yes," Terrell replied. "I think so."

"Good, then she'll understand that an emergency came up and you couldn't make it. These kinds of things happen in a marriage from time to time. If she loves you the way you think she does, then she'll say yes whenever it is that you get the chance to ask her. If she can't deal with it, then you shouldn't be asking her to marry you in the first place. Now stop bellyaching and get down here. Do you know how to get to the municipal airstrip?"

"Yes sir," Terrell sighed. "It's a couple miles down the road from Tampa International right?"

"Yes, our jet's in hangar three. When you pull up to the security gate, show them your firm ID. I expect to see you in twenty five minutes." Mr. Bragg hung up the phone before Terrell could say anything else.

"Wonderful," Terrell mumbled as he turned off the phone. Alicia was going to kill him for this. He'd never worked on any case that required him to fly to away in the middle of the night. If it turned out to be some stupid contract dispute, he'd rip his eyes out of their sockets.

Terrell rolled out of bed and grabbed a pair of jeans from the hamper. He knew from experience that when Mr. Bragg said twenty-five minutes, that's exactly what he meant. He grabbed the duffel bag packed with his personal items and pulled a freshly dry-cleaned suit out of the closet. He'd have to freshen up on the way to wherever they were going. He hurried out of the house and prayed that he would be able to reschedule his flight to Spain.

CHAPTER 2

As Terrell pulled up to the airport's guard station, he reached across the interior panel and turned down the music. He'd turned up the volume as loud as he could and he'd still dozed off twice during the drive to the airport. Luckily for him, traffic was light and he made the short drive from his home to the airport with three minutes to spare. A sleepy looking guard walked around to the driver's side of his vehicle and glanced at him as he lowered the tinted window.

"I'm going to hangar three," Terrell said to him as he passed the guard his Bragg & Shuttlesworth identification card. The guard casually looked at the worn picture on the ID card and compared it to Terrell's face. He secretly hoped the guard wouldn't let him inside. His heart sank along with his last glimmer of hope that he'd make it to Spain when the guard waved him though the gate.

Terrell passed a couple of identical metal hangers before spotting Mr. Bragg's black Mercedes parked in the tight alleyway between hangars three and four. Terrell swung into the parking space next to him. He yawned mightily as his body reminded him that it was still very early in the morning. For the millionth time, he wondered if the job was worth all the aggravation. He gingerly got out of the car and pulled his suit, briefcase and duffel bag from the rear seat. Then he set the alarm and walked toward the metal door on the side of the small hangar.

As soon as Terrell stepped inside, he was greeted by hustle and bustle of the small flight crew making adjustments before takeoff. There were several men in blue overalls checking the engines of the idling jet. He saw that a staircase descending from the plane was open, so he figured that anyone else unfortunate enough to be summoned that morning would be waiting inside the plane.

"Mr. Banks," a flustered voice called. "Yoo-hoo, Mr. Banks!" Terrell turned around to see Brenda flagging him down. Brenda was Mr. Bragg's secretary and personal assistant. She had been working for Bragg & Shuttlesworth for 23 years and knew everything about everything. He was sure that Mr. Bragg wouldn't be able to tie his shoes without her help in scheduling it. She always went out of her way to help Terrell do things and he liked her a lot.

"Mr. Banks," she repeated as she caught up to him, "Is there anything you need taken care of before you leave? I know all of this has been on very short notice."

Terrell always marveled over Brenda's organization and professionalism. It was four in the morning and she was immaculately dressed, not one hair out of place, not one wrinkle in her clothing.

"Yes, Brenda, thank-you," Terrell replied. "I have a flight leaving tomorrow morning at eight…"

"Mr. Bragg already told me to cancel it," she said. I'm sorry, I know you had plans this weekend."

"Yes ma'am. I know." Terrell groaned. "Actually, I was wondering if you could reschedule it for me. Do you know what time we're supposed to be getting back?"

"Mr. Bragg had me cancel all his engagements until 5 o'clock this afternoon. I expect you should be back by then."

"Excellent," Terrell said. He thought that he might be able to make it to Spain after all. "See if you can get a new flight for me. I should be able to make any flight that leaves at six or later."

Brenda slowly shook her head. "You're going to have to discuss that with Mr. Bragg. You'll be back here, but I think he's going to have work for you to do this afternoon. He was very adamant about canceling your flight."

"Do you have any idea what this is all about?" Terrell asked curiously. Brenda always had the scoop.

"Not really. I've only heard bits and pieces. You know how Mr. Bragg can be. He told me to be here and so here I am. Whatever it is, it's big. I haven't seen him this agitated since the Barnett trial."

"Really?" Terrell said, suitably awed. Every marginally interesting story in the firm began with the line, 'Back when we were doing the Barnett trial…'

"Mr. Bragg and Mr. Foster are waiting for you," she continued as she gently shooed him towards the plane. "You can carry those bags with you, or one of the men in the blue jumpsuits can put them in the cargo hold."

"I'll carry them," Terrell answered. "I'm going to have to change on the plane. Are you coming too?"

"No," she replied flatly. "Mr. Bragg and I have a very specific arrangement. I set up the appointments and he flies to them. They don't pay me enough to get into those things," she pointed disgustedly at the small jet.

"I'm surprised Brenda," Terrell smiled. "I wouldn't have thought that you were afraid of anything."

"I'm not afraid," she smiled back. "But if the good Lord wanted us to fly, then he would have given us wings."

"Alright," Terrell replied. He had reached the small ladder extending from the plane. "I guess I should see what the big guys want from me. I'll see you when we get back."

"Not if I see you first," she said as she began making her way back to the far end of the hangar. It was her trademark joke and she told it every opportunity she got.

Terrell had always imagined what the inside of a private jet would look like. He envisioned posh leather seats and luxurious wood grain. He imagined that big screen televisions would be mounted on the wall and maybe even a wet bar in the back. The Bragg & Shuttlesworth jet didn't have any of those amenities. In fact, the interior looked a lot like the drab offices in their building. There were cushioned swivel chairs mounted to the floor. Adjacent to the first two chairs were two computer workstations mounted to the wall. The rest of the chairs were bolted down around a small rectangular table in the middle of the floor.

"It's about time!" Mr. Foster greeted Terrell gruffly from his seat at the table. "I knew we'd be late waiting for him to get here." Peter Foster was the other senior partner on the firm's litigation team. "Earnest, tell the pilot we're ready for takeoff."

"What are you yelling about now?" Mr. Bragg said as he turned in his swivel chair to face Mr. Foster. "Oh, Terrell." He checked his watch. "Right on time." Mr. Bragg arose from his station, eased past Terrell and knocked on the small door separating the cabin from the cockpit.

"We're all set to go," he spoke loudly through the door. "Terrell, put your bags down and have a seat at the other terminal. There are some things we need you to do before we get there."

"Okay," Terrell replied. "Where are we going anyway?"

"You're going over to that computer terminal," Mr. Foster barked. "Start pulling up some case law on what the court might look to in setting a bond on a murder suspect. You should be able to handle that."

"We already know that the court will determine the threat level to the community and risk of flight," Mr. Bragg interjected. "But we need something that discusses a defendant's wealth or means to flee and whether or not that should pay a role in the judge's decision."

"Murder?" Terrell asked as his interest level rose. He laid his suit across one of the empty chairs and switched on the computer. "Did the State Attorney file a pre-trial detention motion?"

"We aren't sure because the clerk's office is closed," Mr. Bragg explained. "But I would guess that they are."

"Okay, I'll see what I can find." He was very curious about who they were representing on a murder, but he knew better than to ask. Partners asked the questions, associates did what they were told.

"Make sure you pull the case histories too. I'd better not find out that any of the cases you find were overturned," Mr. Foster said sharply.

"Yes sir." Terrell turned his head away from Mr. Foster and rolled his eyes as the blank computer screen lit up. He knew that he didn't have the most experience at the firm, but Mr. Foster treated him like a first year law student. Senior Partners were notoriously malicious in their scrutiny of the work of new associates. Terrell expected to have his work corrected from time to time, but Mr. Foster seemed to go out of his way to nit-pick every memo, brief and motion that Terrell wrote.

Mr. Foster's constant criticism of Terrell's work served two equally frustrating purposes. It was a major annoyance for Terrell to have to change around a brief's wording just to have Mr. Foster tell him to change it back the moment he finished the revisions. Second, it hampered his ability to log billing hours. If he spent two hours writing a motion and Mr. Foster made him revise it for another three, he only got to bill the first two. At first, he doubted the quality of his work. Then he noticed that none of the other partners made nearly as many revisions to his work as Mr. Foster.

"We're going to taxi down the runway now," the pilot's voice sounded over the intercom. "I've got clearance for takeoff so I'm going to need you fellas to lock down everything and stay in your seats until we get up into the air."

"Earnest, when does the bond hearing start?" Mr. Foster asked in his usual sour tone.

"Eight." Mr. Bragg answered as he fastened his seatbelt. "I'll call Paul in the morning. I'm sure I can convince him to bump us to the top of the docket. Hopefully, we can get it done before the media figures out what's going on."

"Good," Mr. Foster answered. "The last thing we need is for this thing to turn into a damned circus."

"Terrell," Mr. Bragg said as he swiveled his head. "I wanted to say that I appreciate your professionalism. I called you in the middle of the night, cancelled your vacation and told you to meet me at the airport and you did so without delay."

"Thank you sir," Terrell answered, "but I'd be lying if I said that I didn't wish I were somewhere else."

"So would I, but sometimes emergencies happen. What matters is how you handle them, and you're doing a fine job."

"Mr. Foster doesn't seem to think so," Terrell whispered, hoping Mr. Foster didn't hear him.

"Don't mind him," Mr. Bragg responded, making no such effort to lower his voice. "That man is incapable of being pleased. He hasn't tried to fire you yet, so you're doing okay."

Terrell shrugged his shoulders.

"Do you still want to know where we're going?"

Terrell thought carefully. Things were rarely as they seemed with Mr. Bragg. He was always friendly, but he had a way of testing people to find out how they thought.

"Not really," Terrell answered at last. "The where isn't important. What I'd actually like to know is why you're taking me with you. Why would you take a second year associate with practically no courtroom experience on an emergency trip to do a bond setting for a client?" Terrell glanced carefully at Mr. Foster who was busy reading through a stack of papers. "Especially a client with enough clout to demand two senior partners at four in the morning. I can't imagine that I add any more legal skill to the team of Foster and Bragg, so I'm curious as to why my presence is necessary."

"That's what I like about you Terrell," Mr. Bragg grinned

smugly. "You don't have all the answers, but you're pretty good at figuring out the questions. There is some knowledge about this case that we hope you can add."

"What?"

"How old are you Terrell?"

"I just turned twenty-seven," Terrell answered.

"Really, when?"

"Two weeks ago."

"Oh," Mr. Bragg said thoughtfully. "You're a little younger than I thought. Happy belated birthday then."

"Thank-you."

"What kind of music do you listen to?"

"Um… all kinds I guess," Terrell answered cautiously.

"This isn't a test," Mr. Bragg said flatly. "If I turned the radio in your car on, what kind of station would it be tuned to?"

"R&B and Hip-Hop," Terrell answered. "But sometimes I'm in the mood for…"

"Wait a second," Mr. Bragg interrupted. "I'm getting old and I don't know what that means. Is that the same thing as rap music?"

"Pretty much." Terrell answered.

"Excellent," Mr. Bragg continued. "We're been retained by American Music Incorporated to represent one of their artists on a murder case. We're flying to Miami so that we can convince the judge to set a bond for her in the morning. I was hoping that you might be familiar enough with the principles to give us a little insight into what might have happened."

"Wow," Terrell said, suddenly interested. "Who is it?"

"Her name is Jennifer Weston. From what I can tell, she's some kind of singer."

"Jennifer Weston from Fantasy?" Terrell asked, stunned.

"So you've heard of her." Mr. Bragg stated.

"Of course I have! Everybody has heard of Fantasy. They are one of the most popular female groups ever. I think they won like three Music Awards last year."

"What do you know about her?" Mr. Bragg asked.

"Not anymore than anyone else I guess," Terrell answered. "Just what I read in magazines and see on television."

"Since when do second year associates have time to read magazines and watch television?" Mr. Foster interrupted. "Obviously, we're not giving you enough work to do."

"And Ms. Weston is a part of the group?" Mr. Bragg continued nonplussed.

"I suppose you could say that," Terrell answered. "But it would be more accurate to say that she is the group. The other girls are more like her back up singers."

The small plane suddenly picked up a boost of speed as it cruised down the runway. The whine of the jet engine became a powerful roar and Terrell felt the plane lift from the ground and rise into the sky.

"What kind of reputation does she have?" Mr. Bragg asked.

"Pretty good," Terrell said after some thought. "I can't really think of any scandals where she's been implicated. She models for some cosmetics company and she's had a couple of small roles in movies lately. Frankly sir, she doesn't seem like the type of person that would be involved in something like this."

"We should take advantage of that," Mr. Foster said. "We're going to need to keep the public on our side with this. People are going to want to believe her. We can use that."

"I agree," Mr. Bragg answered. "As soon as we get on the ground, I'll get Bill working on some press releases. As far as the media goes, I'd like to get the jump on the prosecution and have our story straight. If we get a bond, we can have a conference on the steps of the courthouse. We'll talk about a rush to judgment. That always plays well."

"It's a murder?" Terrell asked, unconvinced. "I could see a drunk driving or something like that, but a murder?"

"I wish it were a simple drunk driving case," Mr. Bragg replied. "If it were, we could have taken care of it without leaving Tampa. This will be much more difficult. Preliminary reports indicate that the victim died from multiple stab wounds. Ms. Weston was found in the hotel room with the body, covered in blood."

"That's horrible," Terrell replied.

"You never know what those people are capable of. Rich or famous, they still act like hoodlums," Mr. Foster replied.

Terrell wondered exactly what Mr. Foster meant by 'those people', but he decided that now wasn't the proper time to make an issue of it.

"Who's the victim?" Terrell asked curiously.

"Someone named Felix Caldwell."

"You mean Optimus?"

"Who?

"Optimus, also known as Felix Caldwell, is widely thought of as the best living rapper by people interested in such things. It's public knowledge that he and Jennifer have been dating for a while now. He's the victim?"

"Apparently so. What do you know about him?" Mr. Bragg asked.

"Just a little. I met him once at a nightclub when I was in law school. He seemed like an okay guy."

"That's very nice," Mr. Foster said sarcastically. "We're glad that you liked him, but do you have any helpful information? Anything that we might be able to use?"

"Well, I'm pretty sure he has a criminal record," Terrell tried his best to remain respectful to Mr. Foster, but it was difficult. "Probably some weapons charges and maybe a couple of drug incidents."

"I'll have Brenda pull a rap sheet for him," Mr. Bragg said.

"Any enemies?" Mr. Foster asked.

"I don't know, maybe. I can't recall hearing anyone do a song about killing him or anything."

"Is he in a gang?" Mr. Foster asked while scribbling notes on his pad.

"I have no idea. He talks about stuff like that in his music, but I don't know if any of it is true."

"We should get some of those songs transcribed, maybe we'll be able to pin this on someone other than our client," Mr. Foster added.

"See what kind of info we can get from the record company. They probably know some things that we don't about this guy." Mr. Foster flipped up the screen on his laptop computer and began typing.

"Thanks Terrell," Mr. Bragg said. "You've been very helpful."

"With all due respect sir," Terrell said, "You could have asked me that stuff over the phone. In fact, I could probably have answered that from Spain."

"I suppose you could have," Mr. Bragg reflected. "I'll take that under advisement. Now, get busy on that case research, I want to review it when we land. They are paying us quite a bit of money to ensure that she gets out of jail in the morning, and I intend to make sure that's what happens."

CHAPTER 3

Terrell tugged several times at his tie before giving up and starting again. He wasn't accustomed to dressing in a car, much less one being driven in Miami's hectic morning traffic. He'd managed to put on his suit in the back seat of the taxi, but he'd never been able to tie a Half-Windsor knot without the use of a mirror.

Mr. Bragg sat next to Terrell in the rear seat speaking softly into his cell phone while Mr. Foster sat in the front. Terrell was exhausted and he just wanted to go home. As he untied the knot for the third time, the taxi pulled into a reserved parking space in front of the courthouse.

"Our bond hearing is first on the docket this morning," Mr. Bragg said as he exited the car. "But Judge Keller wants to see us in chambers before the hearing."

"Who's the prosecutor?" Mr. Foster asked as passed the driver a couple of bills. He kept his hand extended to indicate he expected his change.

"Karen Rojas is doing it herself."

"Rojas," Mr. Foster repeated. He didn't sound surprised. "That woman has never met a headline she didn't like."

"Who's Karen Rojas?" Terrell asked.

"Karen has been the Miami-Dade county chief for what, four or five years now?" Mr. Bragg answered

"It's been longer than that. I don't think she's actually tried a case since she took the position. This could be good for us. She's bound to be rusty." Mr. Foster said.

"Don't be too sure," Mr. Bragg replied cautiously. "She's smart. She wouldn't put herself out in front of this thing unless she had a good case."

"Earnest, if it's hers, then there's a good chance that she's already tipped the media about it."

"I know. Bill hasn't finished putting together our initial statement yet."

"Well he better be finished by the time we get out of this interview," Mr. Foster said gruffly. "We could win or lose this thing today depending on how it spins."

"Bill will have it ready, he always does," Mr. Bragg said with confidence. "Now, let's go see our client."

***

"Fairness and equity are hard to find here, yet the city was pretentious enough to call this place the Justice Building," Mr. Bragg said as they entered through the side of the building. "It's almost comical," he continued as he placed his briefcase on the x-ray scanner. Terrell could only half-listen to Mr. Bragg. He was asleep on his feet.

"Sir!" one of the deputies manning the security station shouted, snapping Terrell back to reality. "Sir you have to place your bag on the conveyor belt before walking through the metal detector."

"Oh, I'm sorry, I guess my mind was somewhere else," he apologized sheepishly.

"Somewhere else?" Mr. Foster huffed. "Do I need to remind you that we're paying you far too much to keep what passes for your mind here?"

"No sir," Terrell answered. "It won't happen again."

"It better not," Mr. Foster snapped before walking through the metal detector himself. "We've got a lot of work to do and I don't have time to hold your hand."

Terrell cursed Mr. Foster under his breath while he gathered his briefcase from the conveyor belt.

"Terrell, look at me," Mr. Bragg requested. Terrell looked him squarely in the eyes. "Your eyes are all red and puffy. You look worse than Peter and that's not easy to do."

Mr. Foster shook his head and walked up the hallway.

"Here, take this," he said and passed Terrell a bottle of eyedrops. "We can't have you in the meeting looking like that."

"At least she'd know I was up all night working on her case," Terrell replied as he placed a few of the clear droplets in his eyes.

"I'll let you in on a secret Terrell," Mr. Bragg said as they began following Mr. Foster. "The appearance of success is the precursor to success. We win a lot of cases based on reputation. Other firms fear us because they know we have the resources to bury them. If the perception ever got out there that we get tired too, we'd lose some of that edge. Use the eyedrops, focus, and pretend that you're ready for another 15 hours of work."

The prisoner holding area was in the basement of the courthouse. Mr. Foster pressed the buzzer outside the locked door marked 'holding area'. Terrell glanced upward and saw a small camera trained on the spot where they stood. He resisted the juvenile urge to wave and smile as they waited for someone to disable the powerful magnetic lock.

After an audible pop, Mr. Foster pulled open the door and they walked into a small room. It had the stale smell of a gym locker filled with damp, moldy socks. The drab concrete walls oozed despair and Terrell felt depressed just having to stand inside of it. A husky deputy sheriff with meaty hands sat tapping a pencil on the cluttered desk. His crew cut, thick neck and beady eyes made the deputy look like an ogre. Directly behind the man were two heavy steel doors.

"Phweee!" the deputy whistled. "Three lawyers in expensive suits?" he grinned through a mouthful of yellow teeth. "Let me guess, you must be here to see the superstar."

"If you're referring to Ms. Weston, then yes, we are," Mr. Bragg replied. "Would you please get her for us. We have some matters to discuss before court."

"Sure thing," the deputy said with exaggerated politeness, "Anything to help you fine gentlemen." The sagging chair sighed in relief when the deputy shifted his bulk. He spun his ring of keys on his thick finger before unlocking the door on his right.

"Lance!" he shouted down the narrow corridor. Small cells lined the walls, each with a white number stenciled across the narrow steel doors. "Bring Weston out of six and down to the interview room! Her lawyers are here to see her!" The deputy came back and unlocked the second door.

"You can have a seat in here," he said as he ushered the men into a tiny interview room. The room was furnished only with a small metal table and two plastic chairs. There wasn't enough room to accommodate anything else. Mr. Foster sat down on one of the chairs and Terrell and Mr. Bragg stood behind him. The door on the other side of the room creaked open and Deputy Lance escorted Jennifer Weston into the room.

The morning had been very hectic for Terrell. He hadn't slept, hadn't eaten, and he'd spent the better part of it staring into a computer screen trying to figure out how they were going to get her out of jail. During all that time, he hadn't thought much about the fact that he was about to meet one of the biggest celebrities in the world. He was starstruck as soon as she entered the room. He had to fight back the urge to ask her for an autograph.

She was far from glamorous dressed in the baggy orange jumpsuit and cheap plastic flip-flops. Her hair was a tangled mess and the last remnants of her makeup were smudged across her face. Her cheeks were puffy and her lip was split. Her manicured hands were shackled to her waist using a belly chain. Despite all of that, she was still gorgeous. Jennifer shuffled inside the room, nearly tripping over her heavy leg-restraints.

"Are those really necessary?" Mr. Bragg pointed disgustedly at the chains Jennifer wore.

"Sorry," Deputy Lance shook his apologetically, "All capital offenders must remain in level three security while they're on courthouse premises. It's for your safety."

"She's not a capital offender," Mr. Bragg said in a kindly voice. "She's my client. She's scared and I don't think the three of us have anything to fear from her."

"But," the deputy started.

"Put them back on her when she leaves the room if you have to," Mr. Bragg cut him off. "But have a heart, we won't tell anyone."

Deputy Lance thought about it for a couple of moments, then shrugged his shoulders and unlocked the chains.

"Just knock on this door when you're done," he said as he left.

"Thank-you," Jennifer said as she rubbed the red marks on her wrist.

"Don't thank us. We haven't done anything yet," Mr. Foster answered. "I'm Peter Foster and this is Earnest Bragg. AMI hired our firm, Bragg and Shuttlesworth to represent you in this matter." Terrell couldn't help but notice that Mr. Foster had neglected to introduce him.

"Can you get me out of here?" Jennifer asked, hope creeping into her voice.

"I don't know yet," Mr. Foster answered abruptly. "It depends on several things. We don't have a lot of time, so I'm going to need you to answer some questions for me."

"I'll try," she replied. "But I don't really know anything."

"What do you mean, you don't know anything? What did you tell the officers that arrested you?" Mr. Foster asked.

"I said that I don't remember anything. We were doing a show and the next thing I knew, I was waking up in the room."

"Who do you mean by we?" Mr. Foster asked.

"Me and Felix. I guess you'd call him Optimus. We're touring together."

"And by show, do you mean some kind of music concert?"

"Yeah, like I said, we were doing a show."

"But they found you at the hotel."

"Yeah, I know."

"How did you get from the show to the hotel?" Mr. Foster asked.

"I don't know."

"Did you go anywhere else in between those times?"

"I don't know."

"Was there anyone else in the room with you?"

"I don't know," she said again.

"Did anyone see the two of you go into the hotel room together?"

"I have no idea."

"Think," Mr. Foster said with agitation creeping into his voice. "You have to know something about what happened, something, anything."

"Look," Jennifer replied, becoming flustered, "I don't know okay! You can ask me 500 times 500 different ways but I'm still not going to know. The cops woke me up by knocking on the door. I answered it and the next thing I know, I end up here." She waved her hands around at the concrete walls.

"Young lady," Mr. Foster said in the condescending tone that Terrell thought was reserved only for him. "We are trying to help you. Right now, we're the only ones trying to help you, but you've got give us something to work with."

"How did your face get bruised?" Mr. Bragg interjected.

"I'm not sure," Jennifer answered, hand instinctively rubbing across her split lip.

"Was he hitting you?" Mr. Foster pounced on the idea like a hungry lion. "Is that it?"

"No," she said with conviction. "He didn't hit me. He wasn't like that."

"Are you sure," Mr. Foster pressed. "Maybe it was an accident? He's hitting you, knocks you down. Maybe you picked up a knife to protect yourself and before you knew it, he was dead. A jury would understand that. That's what happened, right?"

"No. That's not what happened."

"How can you be sure," Mr. Foster charged. "You just said that you don't remember."

"Because," she answered, "He didn't hit me."

"Maybe you came into the room and found him dead?" Mr. Bragg tried to help.

"I… don't… know," she said as if explaining it to a mildly retarded caveman. "I woke up and Felix was dead. That's all I know."

"I understand that you've gone through a fairly traumatic experience," Mr. Foster sighed. "I know it's been a rough night but…"

"Traumatic experience!" Jennifer said incredulously. I woke up this morning and my boyfriend had been murdered right next to me while I slept. I had to wash his blood off of me in a cold shower at the jail while one of the deputies watched me like I was some kind of animal. I sat on a steel bench in a holding cell with seven other women for hours. And to top it off, everyone seems to think that I did it. All you can say to me is that it's been a rough night? Go to Hell! She was so angry she began shaking as she folded her arms and turned away from them. Terrell could sense that she was close to hysterics.

"I don't have time for this," Mr. Foster replied, unmoved by her statement. "I've tried to be nice, but if you want to play games, fine. If games are what you want, then games are what you'll get. But know this young lady, Thirty minutes from now, you'll be arraigned on a charge of first-degree murder. If you don't let us help you, the State's Attorney will eventually get you strapped into the electric chair. Don't think that your status will save you. The last time I checked, the electric chair works on celebrities just as good as it does on everyone else. You might want to think about that before you continue on with this I don't know nonsense." Mr. Foster snatched his blank notepad from the table and stormed from the room.

"Peter! Wait!" Mr. Bragg shouted as he followed Mr. Foster out the door. Terrell was unsure if he was supposed to follow them. He leaned towards the door, then decided to sit in the now vacant chair. Jennifer sat across from him, arms folded, staring at the wall.

"So, who are you?" she asked without looking at him. He could tell that she was a woman that was accustomed to life's finer things. He thought that sitting in that holding cell must have been very humbling for her.

"Terrell. Terrell Banks, I work for Bragg & Shuttlesworth."

"Are you one of my lawyers too?"

"Yeah," he answered. "The record company paid for a lot of us."

"Do you guys work with Sydney?"

"Sydney who?"

"Sydney Goldstein, he's usually my lawyer. He works out all my contracts. I figured my manager would call him."

"No," Terrell explained. "We're with a totally different firm. We specialize in things like this."

"Oh. Do you specialize in being jerks too?"

"No, not all of us," Terrell smiled. "I think Mr. Foster pretty well has that covered."

Jennifer pulled her knees into her chest and wrapped her arms around them. She rocked slightly back and forth. Terrell noticed how small and scared she looked. He found it incredibly difficult to believe that this young woman could be guilty of murdering anyone.

"I'm sorry to hear about what happened to Felix," he offered.

"What?" she asked.

"I said, I'm sorry about what happened to Felix. People have probably been asking you questions all night about what happened. I imagine that people haven't thought about the fact that that you lost someone that you obviously care about. I just figured that I'd let you know that I'm sorry to hear that he's gone."

"Thank-you," she nodded before dropping her head. She sat still in the chair for a few moments before continuing, "It hasn't even had a chance for it to sink in yet. It's almost like it's not even real. I keep thinking that any minute, I'm going to wake up and he's going to be lying right next to me."

"I met him once," Terrell revealed.

"You did?" she asked surprised. "Were you one of his lawyers or something?"

"No, it wasn't anything like that," Terrell explained. "I met him a couple of years ago in a nightclub. My girlfriend and I had some VIP passes to this place called Club Millennium. We got the chance to talk to him for a little while."

"I know that place, we go there all the time," She smiled for a moment and then her eyes went wide. "Wait, he didn't drag you up on stage with him, did he?"

"As a matter of fact, he did," Terrell chuckled.

"I'm sorry," she apologized for him. "I told him that it wasn't right for him to bring people up and embarrass them like that."

"Don't worry about it," Terrell said. "It was the most fun I think I've ever had."

She looked at him skeptically.

"Really, it was. For what it's worth, I liked him."

"Yeah," she agreed. "He's a good person." Her words trailed off and her lip began to quiver. "He… he was a good person." Tears streamed from her eyes and she dropped her head to her chest. Terrell rummaged through his briefcase, and found a couple of tissues. He stood up and placed his hand on her shoulder. She felt small and frail through the rough fabric of the jail jumpsuit. Still, he had to fight a surge of idol worship when he realized that he was actually touching Jennifer Weston. She took the tissues and wiped her eyes.

"Are you okay?" he asked, before realizing how silly the question sounded. "I mean, I know you're not okay, does it hurt?"

"It's not as bad as it looks," she replied as she dabbed away another tear. "My cheek is a little sore and I think I lost my contact somewhere. I can hardly see."

"Just stick close to me when we get upstairs," Terrell smiled. "I'll make sure you don't trip over anything."

"Thanks, you're a lot nicer than your friend," she sniffed.

"He's not my friend, we just work together. You said that the two of you have been to Club Millennium before. Do you think you might have went there last night?" he asked.

"I don't remember," she answered. "But I think they were supposed to throw us a party after the show. I vaguely remember going there with Felix, but I don't remember leaving."

"Who else was there?"

"I'm not sure exactly. Probably everyone."

Terrell looked closely at her face. Her cheek was swollen and she had the cut lip, but otherwise she didn't seem to be beaten up. "If Felix didn't hit you, do you have any idea how your face could have gotten bruised?"

"I wish I did," she replied. "Maybe I fell out of bed or something," she said hopefully. Terrell had heard numerous battered women use that line before. For some reason however, he believed Jennifer. It wasn't as if she had anything to gain by lying about whether or not Felix hit her.

"What did you say your name was again?" she asked.

"Terrell Banks."

"What's going to happen today, Mr. Banks?"

"Mr. Banks is my dad. Call me Terrell. You're going to have what's called an arraignment and detention hearing. They will advise you of your charges and the State's Attorney is going to ask the judge to keep you in jail until your trial. Mr. Foster and

Mr. Bragg will be asking for him to release you until your case is called for trial."

"They can keep me in here until the trial?" she asked, alarmed. "How long will that be?"

"It's a murder case," Terrell explained. "My guess is that it will be around a year before it actually gets called."

"A year!" she panicked. "I can't stay in jail for a year! You've got to get me out of here right now!"

"Ms. Weston," Terrell said in a calm voice.

"You've got to do something to get me out of here!" she said, eyes going wide with fear. "I can't stay here! You've just got to help me!"

"Ms. Weston, listen to me," Terrell said firmly and grasped her hand. The fleeting thrill of holding her hand threatened to break his focus, but he pushed on. "I promise that we will do everything in our power to get you out of here today. Trust me, we can do a lot of things. Even though our meeting didn't go well, Mr. Foster and Mr. Bragg are two of the best lawyers in the country. If I ever get in trouble, they'd be the people I'd call. Well, I probably couldn't afford them, but if I could, I'd hire them."

"Do you think you'll win?" she asked hopefully.

"I don't know for sure," he replied honestly. "I think we have a good argument that they should let you go. I might be biased since I'm the one that worked on the brief all night, but I think we've got a good shot."

"What should I do when we get in there?"

"Well, you have the right to speak, but you probably should just let Mr. Foster do the talking. In fact, from here on out you shouldn't say anything to anybody except Mr. Bragg, Mr. Foster or me about this case."

"That'll be easy," she said with a humorless laugh. "I don't have anything to tell anybody. Why can't I remember what happened?"

"I wish I knew, but we'll figure something out, we always

do." The door leading to the cellblock opened slowly and Deputy Lance peered inside the room.

"Sorry," he said, "but I gotta take her upstairs now. The judge called and said he's ready to take the bench."

"Okay," Terrell answered. He wasn't sure if Mr. Foster had planned on coming back, but he guessed that they were out of time. "Jennifer, we'll be waiting for you upstairs. Try and relax as much as you can, okay?"

"I'll try," she said, swinging her legs down to the cement floor. Deputy Lance carefully reattached the leg restraints and refastened the waist chain and handcuffs. Terrell watched closely to make sure that he did not cinch them too tight. Deputy Lance led Jennifer from the room and Terrell gathered his briefcase and left through the other door. He was shocked to see Mr. Bragg and Mr. Foster chatting calmly in the front waiting area.

"Didn't you need to speak with her some more?" he asked curiously.

"No, not really," Mr. Bragg answered. "How'd it go?"

"How'd what go?" Terrell asked.

"With her. How'd it go? Did she tell you what happened?"

"She says she doesn't remember."

"Sure she doesn't," answered Mr. Foster sarcastically. "Did she say anything else?"

"She asked me a couple of questions about what was going to happen today. I explained the hearing and told her some of what we were going to do for her."

"Excellent Terrell," Mr. Bragg replied. "You've done well. Come on, court is about to start." Mr. Bragg said as the headed back out to the elevator.

"Done well with what?" Terrell asked, bewildered.

"Establishing a basis of trust with our new client. That's the most difficult thing to do in a criminal case. It's much harder than arguing the law."

"I'm sorry sir, but I don't understand."

"It's really quite simple," Mr. Bragg explained as he punched the elevator up button. "Criminal defendants don't trust anyone. Trust is not in their nature, they're criminals. They don't trust each other, they don't trust the cops and they certainly don't trust their expensive lawyers. They don't at first anyway. You'll find out that the biggest hurdle to overcome in these cases is the fact that your client won't tell you about some key piece of damaging evidence because he doesn't trust that you can handle it. They think that if they don't mention it, then no one will find out."

"Until the State's Attorney brings it up in trial, and at that point you're screwed," Mr. Foster added.

"Precisely. Most of our criminal clients don't necessarily trust our advice and she doesn't either. She thinks that we're just taking her money. That's why we have to gain her confidence and her trust. That's the only way we'll get through this supposed memory block about what happened last night."

"So you think she'll tell me things that she might not tell you?" Terrell said as the three men climbed aboard the empty elevator.

"Of course she will," Mr. Bragg said confidently. "You've built more trust with her in three minutes than Peter and I could have built in three months. She might tell you something small, something that she doesn't even think is important. And it will break the case wide open."

"Mr. Bragg," Terrell asked, "Was all that back there on purpose? I mean, the whole thing?"

"Don't be naïve," Mr. Foster said. "Of course it was on purpose. Why else would we bother bringing some still wet behind the ears associate on a case this important? Surely you don't think it was for your legal skills."

"I had a feeling that if Peter pushed her buttons, you'd try and smooth everything over." Mr. Bragg explained. "I've noticed that you're very diplomatic that way. Besides, she can relate to you better than she can to me or Peter. It should be easier for her to identify with you, and therefore easier to gain her trust."

"Why didn't you tell me before we saw her?"

"Because then your concern would have been faked. She would have seen through the charade. Better that you not know and express some genuine concern. Peter was rude and mean to her but you came to her rescue. You cared about her, not about her case. She'll remember that, and we'll be better off because of it."

The multi-layers of thought shown by Mr. Bragg never ceased to amaze Terrell. They were absolutely right. He did come to her rescue and she did start opening up to him. He was so deep in his own thoughts that he was totally unprepared for the wave of light that washed over him as the elevator doors opened.

CHAPTER 4

Terrell was immediately disoriented by the strobe effect of the flashing lights. He feared that he was having some kind of seizure. Then he realized that the accompanying roaring he heard was the throng of reporters outside the elevator doors shouting questions at them.

"Will she plea guilty?" one brash woman in the front of the crowd yelled.

"Isn't this a case of being caught red-handed?" a tall reporter challenged.

"Is it true that Ms. Weston is a battered woman?" another shouted.

"Will she claim self defense?" Terrell heard from somewhere in the back.

Mr. Foster and Mr. Bragg stoically pressed through the crowd, ignoring the questions, video cameras and snapping flashbulbs. Terrell followed closely behind them and imitated their non-plussed demeanor. The media swarmed over them like attacking bees, each fighting for the best video shot. Terrell saw crews from every major news network as well as several smaller stations. He heard a man giving a report in Spanish near the railing and another speaking in some Asian language by the far wall. Mr. Foster swung the courtroom door open revealing two burly deputies standing inside.

"Sorry gentlemen," one of the deputies said. "Courtroom's full. You'll have to wait outside."

"Son, we're counsel for the defendant," Mr. Foster said gruffly as he walked right past the deputy without stopping. "I'm certain that we have reserved seats right down front."

"So much for getting out of here before the press finds out," Mr. Bragg muttered as he dropped his briefcase into one of the chairs behind the defense table. Reporters and other assorted gawkers stuffed every available bench in the gallery as they eagerly anticipated the detention hearing.

"Terrell," Mr. Bragg asked.

"Yes sir?"

"We need to get rid of some of these people. It's already enough of a spectacle as it is. How can we get these cameras out of here next time?"

"I'm not sure," Terrell answered truthfully.

"Find out," Mr. Bragg commanded. "I want a plan that will work with supporting case law in my hands by six o'clock."

"Yes sir," Terrell replied. His last hope for flying out that evening evaporated. A tall, slender woman with dark black hair approached the table from the far side of the courtroom and extended her hand.

"How are you doing Earnest?" she said in a pleasant voice. "It's been ages."

"Just fine Karen," Mr. Bragg replied as he shook her hand. "And yourself?" Karen Rojas was not an unattractive woman. She was gracefully moving into her late forties, but her sharp, angular features made her look cold and hard.

"Oh, you know me Earnest," she smiled. "As long as I'm putting the bad guys away, I'm happy. I see that Ms. Weston has already paid for the big guns."

"Why would you say that?" Mr. Bragg asked.

"Because," she pointed out, "I know you don't come out of the office for less than six figures."

"Seven," Mr. Bragg retorted. "She didn't have a choice but to hire us once she found out you were on the other side, Karen. We have to keep the playing field level."

"Flattery? If I didn't know better, I'd think you wanted something from me Earnest," she laughed.

"Maybe," Mr. Bragg replied. "My daddy told me that a teaspoon of sugar will get you farther than a gallon of vinegar. I assume this circus is your handiwork?" He jerked his thumb at the mass of people in the courtroom.

"Oh no," she answered innocently. "I have no idea how the word got out so fast. It's probably someone down at the police station."

"And here I thought we were going to have ourselves a nice quiet little bond hearing. My client deserves to get out of here without the entire process becoming a mockery."

"Bond?" she laughed in disbelief. "You've got to be kidding me Earnest. She's a cold-blooded murderer. She's not going anywhere but back to the Women's Detention Center until trial."

"I wouldn't expect you to say anything different," Mr. Bragg responded. "This time you're wrong though. You know Peter Foster, don't you?"

"Yes," she replied. "We met at the Governor's fundraiser a couple of year ago, right?"

"Yes, good to see you again," Mr. Foster said curtly. He quickly shook her hand and sat back down.

"And who is this young man?" she asked Mr. Bragg.

"Terrell Banks," Terrell replied, shaking her hand.

"Terrell is one of our new associates. He'll be assisting Peter and I today."

"A new associate actually making it into the courtroom? Impressive," she said. "You must be very talented indeed. You should come work in my office. Now we can't pay you what they do, but at least you'll be able to sleep at night."

"I'm sure Mr. Banks sleeps quite well. We gave him a mattress filled with money on his first day. Now stop tampering with my people or I'll report you to the Bar," Mr. Bragg joked. "When does Judge Keller want to see us?"

"He told the bailiffs that he wanted to see us in chambers as soon as you arrived. I think he wants to get this over with as soon as possible."

"He's not the only one," Mr. Bragg responded. Ms. Rojas turned to leave and Mr. Foster rose from his seat to follow. Mr. Bragg leaned forward and whispered to Terrell, "This shouldn't take long. Stay here and prepare the table. Make sure that they don't bring Ms. Weston out before Peter and I get back."

"Yes sir," Terrell answered. He watched as they disappeared through a side door.

Bragg & Shuttlesworth spent a lot of time and money analyzing everything about trials, including what the defense table should look like. It wasn't enough that they were over-prepared to argue the case: it was just as important to look over-prepared. Terrell pulled nearly a ream of paper from his briefcase and arranged it on the table into several stacks. None of the papers contained information pertinent to the hearing. They were simply to give the impression of authority.

After he had carefully arranged the stacks and scattered a few pens across the desk, he sank back into his chair. He swiveled to the left and took a cautionary glance around the room. He was shocked to see that most of the eyes in the courtroom were staring at him. He snapped his chair back to its forward position, sat up straight and pretended to read something on his notepad. He realized that every gesture, every motion, every argument that they raised was going to be scrutinized and picked apart on television by every legal expert in the country. He suddenly wished that he'd had more time to complete his research from the night before.

Suddenly, an excited murmur went through the crowd. Terrell peeked up and saw the hall door begin to creep open.

Deputy Lance was busily trying to remove his key from the bulky lock. Terrell hopped up and walked quickly to the door.

"Deputy Lance, hold on just a second," Terrell said as he pushed his way through the door and into the back hallway. "Why don't we just keep Ms. Weston here until Judge Keller decides to take the bench?" Jennifer was standing behind Deputy Lance, still shackled at the waist and ankles. She looked as though she was trying to remain calm, but Terrell could see that her hold on her nerves was precarious at best.

"The judge doesn't like to wait," Deputy Keller explained. He likes to get started as soon as he sits down, so they told me to bring her inside."

"I know," Terrell replied. "But, today is a little different." He pressed open the door a little wider so that Deputy Lance could get a view of the courtroom. "All these people are here to see this. There are fans and reporters and newspeople all over the place. All those people are out there waiting for something to happen. It's too tense. If you take her out there before the judge is ready, it will be complete pandemonium. There will be all sorts of yelling and screaming. It would be better if we waited until the judge came out of chambers. That way at least, someone will be there to keep order."

Deputy Lance glanced out the door and surveyed the situation. The crowd was moving and surging like a thing alive. People were craning their necks and crawling over one another just for the hope of getting a glimpse of Jennifer.

"I guess it wouldn't hurt to stand back here for a minute," he said finally.

"Thanks, I appreciate it," Terrell said.

On a typical day, the back hall would have contained a couple of bailiffs, maybe a judicial clerk and a couple of deputies milling around. Today, it seemed as if the entire courthouse staff suddenly had important business in that particular hallway. There were extra bailiffs, court reporters, clerks, secretaries, receptionists, janitors and maintenance men all clogging the hallway. Each and every one of them pretended not to stare at Jennifer. Terrell was certain that the most of those people had never been at work this early.

"Is it always like this?" Terrell whispered to Jennifer as he gestured toward the rubbernecks.

"It's not usually this bad," she sighed without looking. "It's only going to get worse, isn't it?"

"Probably," Terrell admitted.

"I'm used to living in a fishbowl," she stated calmly. "But this is different. They all think I did it. I can see it in the way that they stare at me." She looked at Terrell in his eyes. "I didn't. I don't know what happened, but I know that I didn't do it."

"Don't say anything about it now," Terrell said. He motioned to Deputy Lance, whom he was sure was eavesdropping. "We'll talk again in a little while, but don't say anything out here."

"Sorry," she said, biting her lip. "It's just… You have to… I didn't…"

"I believe you," Terrell said earnestly as he cut her off. "I do. We'll figure out something."

Terrell spotted Mr. Bragg and Mr. Foster exiting the door of Judge Keller's chambers. They didn't look pleased. Ms. Rojas followed them, looking quite happy. The two men walked quickly toward Terrell and Jennifer.

"What happened?" Terrell asked curiously.

"Judge Keller is going to screw us somehow. I can feel it," Mr. Bragg answered.

"How?"

"I'm not sure yet, but I'm sure he'll figure out a way to do it. He hasn't liked me since the Barnett trial."

"When they lead you inside," Mr. Foster said to Jennifer, "Walk quickly and sit in the third seat, between Earnest and Terrell. Keep you hands under the table so that they can't videotape your cuffs. Don't look behind you, don't look at the cameras and for God's sake, don't say anything."

Jennifer scowled at Mr. Foster's brusque manner. Terrell

nodded at her to reassure her that it was good advice. Deputy Lance opened the courtroom door and let the group inside. It was difficult for Jennifer to walk to the table in her leg irons, but she managed to do it without stumbling. Mr. Bragg pulled out her chair, and she plopped down into it. She leaned her head forward, letting her hair to hang down and obscure her face from the side. It looked like a maneuver that she had done before.

"All rise!" the bailiff spoke in his practiced voice. "The Honorable Judge Jonathan Keller presiding. Let all who have business before this court step forward and be heard."

"Be seated," Judge Keller said as he took the bench. Judge Keller was short man, in his mid-sixties with thinning, gray hair. He had large ears that served as excellent anchors for the horn-rimmed glasses he wore. His deliberate manner suggested that he was bored. However, the sparkle in his eyes suggested that he didn't miss much. "State, call your first case."

"We would call the case of The State of Florida versus Jennifer Lisa Weston. The charge is murder in the first degree." Ms. Rojas clearly enunciated every word and paused for dramatic effect. "Your honor, this is a pre-trial detention hearing." Terrell was absolutely certain that the judge knew exactly why they were here. He had spent the last ten minutes in chambers discussing the matter. Karen was playing to the audience.

"Is the State seeking detention under Rule 3.132?" Judge Keller asked calmly.

"Yes, your honor," Karen replied.

"What says the defense?" Judge Keller asked Mr. Foster, who was already standing in anticipation.

"We oppose the motion and would request that the court set bail in the case."

"Of course you would," answered Judge Keller. "Madame State Attorney, if you would give the court a brief resuscitation of the facts alleged by the State."

"You honor," she began, "The facts are as follows. The victim, Felix Caldwell was found murdered in the bed of his hotel room at around 1:30 this morning in Miami-Dade County. Preliminary reports indicate that the victim died of exsanguination secondary to being stabbed at least nine times. The defendant was the only other individual at the scene. The police found her covered in the victim's blood and she was subsequently arrested. Your honor, the State contends that the heinousness and sheer brutality of the crime suggests that the community at large would be endangered by the release of the defendant on bond. Furthermore, the defendant has vast financial resources, as exhibited by her ability to retain Mr. Foster and Mr. Bragg."

"Your honor!" Mr. Foster interrupted, but Judge Keller simply held his hand up.

"Madame State Attorney, stick to the facts of what you're alleging. The defendant's choice of counsel has no bearing on this hearing. Do not make another comment like that."

"I apologize your honor," Ms. Rojas said without remorse. "Still, the fact remains that the defendant's financial resources will offer her a great ability to flee the jurisdiction of the State. Therefore, we respectfully request that she be remanded to the Miami-Dade County Women's Detention Center until the resolution of these charges."

"Mr. Foster?"

"Yes, your honor. As the court is well aware, the Constitution of the United States provides that every criminal defendant is entitled to pre-trial release." As Terrell listened to Mr. Foster outline the relevant factors for determining whether or not bond should be granted, he had a brainstorm. He grabbed one of the yellow legal pads on the table and began writing. Terrell had plenty of time to flesh out his argument since Mr. Foster had a tendency to be long winded. He slid the notepad down the desk. Mr. Bragg scanned it and smiled before he passed it to Mr. Foster.

"In conclusion," Mr. Foster said as he glanced down at the pad, "The State's argument that Ms. Weston is a flight risk is patently flawed. While it is true that she has attained a degree of financial success, the State fails to account for the reason she achieved that success. Last year, Ms. Weston's singing group sold over eight million albums worldwide. That equals eight million households with at least one picture of her. She performed during the SuperBowl halftime show broadcast to billions of people across the world. In the past year alone, she has been on the cover of dozens of nationally distributed magazines and has made numerous appearances on television and film. That is far greater coverage than any all points bulletin in the history of law enforcement. As evidenced by the crowd in the courtroom today, the news media will provide more surveillance of her person than she would have to endure even if kept in the detention center."

"Let's not be over-dramatic counselor," Judge Keller warned.

"Yes your honor. I was merely pointing out that Ms. Weston's fame serves as more than an adequate prison. We submit to the court that there is no risk of flight from Ms. Weston as it is impossible for her to go unnoticed. There is no airport, bus station or marina that she could slip through unrecognized. She already lives in a sort of isolation from the same general public that the State claims it is trying to protect. Your honor, we only request that the court set a reasonable bond to allow the release of Ms. Weston."

"Okay, I've heard enough." Judge Keller wrote for what seemed like an eternity to the tense courtroom. Then he addressed the court in his gravely voice.

"The court finds merit in the defendant's argument. The facts that the State has presented at this stage do not rise to a level that would necessitate this court to deny the defendant her right to pre-trial release. The defendant's lack of a prior criminal record strengthens this position. Therefore, bond is hereby set upon the following conditions. The defendant is to be released upon the posting of a three million dollar bond secured by three hundred thousand dollars cash with the remainder to be levied against qualifying property. While on bond, the defendant must appear at the call of the court. Furthermore, the defendant must remain within the physical jurisdiction of Miami-Dade County for the duration of these proceedings."

"Your honor," Mr. Foster said indignantly, "With all due respect, we feel that your conditions are too burdensome. Ms. Weston is not a Florida resident. She has neither family nor close friends in the immediate area. Your honor, she does not even have a roof over her head in Miami."

"Counselor," Judge Keller said in an exasperated tone, "These are the most serious of charges. The nature and circumstances of the offense charged and the penalty provided by law gives this court serious cause for concern. Her lack of ties to the community is exactly why I am imposing these conditions. If she has a problem securing shelter, I'm sure the Women's Detention Center will find a bed for her. The bond may be paid to the clerk of court. This court will stand in recess for 15 minutes." With that announcement, Judge Keller banged his gavel and left the bench.

"What just happened? Jennifer whispered to Terrell. "Can I go home?"

"Not home, but you don't have to stay in jail either. You just can't leave town," Terrell answered.

"Where am I supposed to go?"

"Don't worry about it. We'll figure something out," Mr. Bragg answered. "They're going to take you back to the jail so that you can process you. Then you will be released."

"How long will that take?" she asked.

"An hour, maybe less. We will send someone over for you. Don't talk to anyone".

"I don't think that will be a problem." She answered. "I don't have anything to tell them, remember?"

"Well then, remember that you don't remember okay?" Mr. Bragg said. "The deputy will escort you back. If anyone asks you anything, just keep quiet and tell us who it was later."

Terrell watched as Deputy Lance led her from the courtroom.

Ms. Rojas came over to talk with Mr. Bragg while Mr. Foster barked into his cell phone.

"If she wants to plea, I'll take the death penalty off the table. She'll do 30 to life, but she'll have the chance of seeing the outside of a prison one day."

"As appealing as that is," Mr. Bragg said sarcastically, "I don't think so. Besides, you can't get the death penalty anyway."

"We'll see," she said calmly. "Talk it over with your client and let me know what she wants to do." She left with a confident smirk.

"God, I hate that woman." Mr. Bragg said under his breath.

"AMI is going to wire the three hundred thousand dollars to our trust account immediately." Mr. Foster said as he flipped his phone shut. "They're also sending us the copies of the paperwork to levy her property."

"Good," Mr. Bragg stated. "We'll make sure the bond's paid before we leave. What do we have in terms of somewhere to put Ms. Weston?"

"I was thinking that we could stash her at the house on the canal. There's more than adequate security and I don't think anyone is using it right now."

"That's a good idea," Mr. Bragg said thoughtfully. "We can charge her for renting it too. I'll have someone draw up a lease agreement for her to sign. Now, let's go meet the press."

CHAPTER 5

"I'm sorry, but that's all we have time for right now," Mr. Bragg said. He seemed to genuinely want to end the impromptu press conference, but Terrell knew he had enjoyed every second of it. "If you'll excuse us, we have work to do." Mr. Bragg had spent the last ten minutes providing newsworthy sound bites to the rabid flock of reporters gathered on the courthouse steps. He made sure to accuse the prosecution of rushing to judgment. He spoke with righteous indignation about the shoddy treatment Jennifer had received from the police department and the investigators. He angrily protested the state of the justice system, and made a very convincing argument that Jennifer Weston was the victim in all of this.

Terrell and Mr. Foster hurried down the steps after Mr. Bragg as the reporters hurled additional questions. Awaiting them at the bottom of the steps was a black sedan. The passenger doors popped open and Mr. Foster eased into the front seat while Terrell and Mr. Bragg slid into the rear. Terrell had assumed that a driver had been hired to chauffeur them back to the airport, so he was surprised to see Joe sitting in the driver's seat.

"That went well," Mr. Bragg said of his performance on the

steps. A juror's first impression of the case is very important," he told Terrell. "Always remember that."

"What do you have for us Joe?" Mr. Foster asked. Joe was the firm's investigator. Terrell didn't know Joe's last name and he was fairly certain that Joe wasn't even his first name. All he really knew about Joe was that he was a muscular 6'3" with broad shoulders and a square chin. His powerful frame seemed to burst from the black suits he always wore. He had a clean-shaven head and always wore a pair of dark sunglasses to hide his unnervingly pale blue eyes.

Terrell had only seen Joe a couple of times and gave him a wide berth. It was rumored around the firm that he was some kind of ex-CIA agent, but no one knew for sure. He never spoke to anyone except the senior partners and even then he only came in for the most important cases. The only thing that was really known about Joe was the fact that he always got results. He found documents that no one else knew existed. He convinced witnesses to come forward when no one else could. When he became involved in a case, even the most stubborn plaintiffs settled for much less than they were entitled. All of this made him an invaluable asset to the firm.

"I've got pictures of the scene," Joe said flatly as he pulled the car into traffic. "I haven't been able to examine any of the physical evidence yet."

"You've got the pictures already?" Mr. Foster said in amazement. "How'd you manage that so soon?"

"It's what you pay me for," Joe replied. His tone indicated that it was best not to ask any further questions. He reached inside his coat pocket and pulled out a stack of photographs and handed them over to Mr. Foster. Mr. Foster began shuffling through the images before handing them to Mr. Bragg, who in turn, handed them to Terrell. They were the most horrible images Terrell had ever seen.

The first photos were shapshots of Optimus' body. A large gash was ripped into the left side of his neck. The blood had flowed out and congealed in a pool on his pillow. His eyes bulged and stared blankly out into space. Terrell noticed several other wounds concentrated primarily around his upper torso. There was also one photo showing a close up of another gash across his cheek. The flesh there drooped and had folded over itself, revealing his jawbone and teeth underneath. It locked his face in the grin of a demented clown.

"She stabbed him in the neck and chest," Joe began as he weaved effortlessly in and out of traffic, "the neck wound killed him quickly, but he would have died from any of them."

The next few pictures showed the room itself. There were a couple of bloody towels crumpled on the floor near the body. There was also a large blood smear on the wall directly above the bed.

"My guess is that she was trying to wipe the blood off the wall with the hotel towels when the police arrived. It was stupid, really. All she succeeded in doing was rubbing it into the paint. They found another bloody towel on the bathroom floor. The drain in the tub had traces of blood too."

"Is there evidence that anyone else was there?" Mr. Foster asked.

"It will be at least a couple of weeks before the forensics are done, but it's a hotel room. There's probably going to be evidence of dozens of people being in that room."

"What happened in here?" Mr. Bragg asked, as he looked a picture of the trashed living room.

"They had a fight. The police were there responding to noise complaints. I figure the two of them get in to it in the living room and he smacks her around a couple of times. She waits for him to go to sleep and then perforates him."

"We can work with that," Mr. Bragg said. "I figured we'd want to go with the battered woman defense when I saw her face. This guy is violent. He makes violent music and lives a violent lifestyle. We can play that to a jury."

"I agree," Mr. Foster answered. "We can use her booking

photo as evidence, but I'd rather send someone to take some more pictures of her face."

"Bruises usually look worse on the next day. Joe, take some pictures tonight and a few more in the morning."

Joe nodded affirmatively.

"Do we have a doctor that can testify to this?" Mr. Foster asked.

"We've used Dr. Liotta in the past," Mr. Bragg replied. "He typically sees things our way."

"He ought to," Mr. Foster said thoughtfully. "We pay him enough. I'll set an appointment for him to see Jennifer. Joe, I didn't see any pictures of the murder weapon. Where is it?"

"Cops haven't found it yet. It wasn't in the room with her. She probably dumped it in one of the trash bins. I'll find out what happened to it," he said with confidence.

Terrell's phone rang. He grabbed it from his briefcase and pressed the answer button.

"Hello?"

"I just saw you on TV! Your face is all over the news!" Sean screamed at him over the phone. "You're Jennifer Weston's lawyer?"

"One of them," Terrell answered. "Now's not a good time…"

"Un-freaking-believable!" Sean cut him off. "Did you meet her? Sorry, that's a stupid question, of course you did. Does she look the same in real life as she does in her videos?"

"I guess so. I'll call you back."

"Hold on, this will just take a second. Ebony!" he screamed. "I told you! I told you it was him!"

"Shouldn't you be at work by now?" Terrell said.

"Nah, it's only 6:30 here. I've got at an hour before I have to leave," he answered. Sean had been one of Terrell's best friends since college. He moved to Arizona with his girlfriend Ebony and was doing postgraduate engineering studies while working for an aerospace company. "Ebony didn't think it was you."

Terrell could hear Ebony in the background telling Sean that she did in fact think it was Terrell and that he was the one that doubted it.

"This is all very fascinating," Terrell said, "But I'm kinda in the middle of something and…"

"Hold on! I'll ask him," Sean said. "They're saying she stabbed Optimus to death. Is that true? Did she do it?"

"You know I can't talk to you about anything like that."

"Right, right, I figured as much. She did it though, didn't she? Otherwise, she wouldn't need you right?"

"No!" Terrell answered emphatically. "It doesn't mean that at all. I'm hanging up now, don't call back."

"Wait! Wait!" Sean said frantically as Terrell switched off the cell phone. Mr. Foster was glaring at him through the rear view mirror.

"Friend of yours?" Mr. Bragg asked calmly.

"Yes sir," Terrell answered. "He saw me on the news a few minutes ago."

"You're going to need to get a new cell phone number. Don't give it to anyone or you'll have all kinds of crackpots calling you every minute of the day about this case."

"Alright," Terrell agreed. "I'll do that as soon as I get back in town. Are we going to the airport now, or are there things that we need to do here first?" He still held out hope that he might make a flight to Spain. He'd probably have to come back early, but one day with Alicia was all he needed.

"We," Mr. Bragg emphasized as he gestured to Mr. Foster, "are going back to the airport. Peter and I have a meeting with AMI this afternoon. You are staying here. There are some things we need you to work on for us."

"For how long?" Terrell asked fearfully, "I didn't pack enough for a long stay."

"You will be here for as long as it takes," Mr. Foster said without compassion. "Don't worry, Miami has plenty of stores. I'm sure that you'll be able to find whatever supplies you require."

Terrell bit back a smart remark, folded his arms, and sat back in his seat.

"Fine," Terrell said as he stared out of the window. "What is it that you need me to do?"

"Keep an eye on the client," Mr. Bragg answered. "Make sure she doesn't do or say anything stupid before we get another chance to debrief her. Peter and I will be back in the morning. In the meantime, see if she'll tell you what happened last night."

"Anything else?" Terrell tried to mask his agitation about the situation, but he knew he wasn't doing a good job of it. Mr. Bragg pretended not to notice.

"I don't know if the record company is going to send any of their representatives here or not. They're probably afraid of the bad press. But if they do, be visible to them. For the amount of money they're paying us, they'll want someone available all the time."

"Okay," Terrell said, "Should I find a hotel on my own?"

"Didn't Earnest just tell you that you need to be available at all times," Mr. Foster snapped. "That means all the time. You will be there in the house too."

"Wait, hold on a second. With all due respect sir, I can't be shacked up with that woman. My girlfriend will not tolerate that and I'm in enough trouble as it is."

"Stop being so melodramatic," Mr. Bragg said dismissively. The house has five bedrooms and 6,000 square feet of space. It's practically a hotel. She probably won't even know you're there."

Terrell pouted and stared out the window. Alicia would not like this development one bit. Having his trip cancelled was bad enough. Being stuck in Miami indefinitely was worse.

"Terrell," Mr. Bragg asked, "What is the last thing she says she remembers?"

"Only that she remembers going to a nightclub. After that, everything is blank."

"Did she say which one?"

"Yeah, it's a place called Club Millenium. I know where it is."

"Excellent," Mr. Bragg said. "Joe, drop us off at the airport and then see what you and Terrell can dig up at this Club Millennium."

The three of them continued talking for the remainder of the ride, discussing potential strategy and hazards. Terrell didn't listen. It seemed as though his usefulness had been exhausted for the day and they didn't have any more questions for him. He was content to sit back and be angry that he was here instead of on a plane to see Alicia.

Joe dropped Mr. Foster and Mr. Bragg off at their private gate. He didn't even bother to wait for them to get inside the airstrip before he screeched out into the busy airport traffic. He didn't turn on the radio and made no effort to start a conversation with Terrell. That suited Terrell just fine as he laid his head against the cushy seat and caught up on some needed sleep.

***

The car's deceleration woke him from his nap. He had no idea where they were, but the car was traveling alongside a 10-foot high, peach colored, stucco wall. Joe made a sudden right turn and stopped at a gated entryway. A serious looking guard stared at them until Joe flashed an ID card. The guard nodded and promptly pressed a large red button to his left. The heavy metal gates swung inward and Joe eased the car inside.

The wide street was lined with tall palm trees, but Terrell didn't see any houses. Instead, several small paved paths branched out from the main road at varied intervals. Joe turned down the path marked Bragg. The driveway was narrow, with more palm trees and underbrush lining the way. They drove down several sharp curves before coming to another gated entranceway. Joe rolled down the window, inserted a card into the small metal box next to the road and punched in a code. The gate rolled back and Joe drove the car onto the property.

The massive, Spanish-style house was situated on a small peninsula bordered on three sides by water. A stand-alone garage sat separated from the remainder of the house. Technically, as a member of the firm, Terrell had access to the firm's vacation home. However, as a young associate, he had neither the time to visit, nor the funds to cover its rental. Joe stopped the car in front of the staircase to the main entrance and killed the engine.

Terrell followed Joe as he unlocked the front door. The house had the musty smell of a place that hadn't been lived in for a couple of weeks. The foyer of the house was decorated in marble tile and the far wall had huge bay windows offering a spectacular view of the canal. To the left, Terrell could see a large kitchen and to the right was a den with a huge television. Two spiraling staircases led upstairs to what Terrell assumed were bedrooms. Joe punched a series of numbers into the security system keypad.

"The code is 54287," Joe said as he tossed Terrell an extra set of keys from his pocket.

"You'll be staying on that side," Joe recited his programmed message. He gestured down the left hallway and continued, "There's a small office over there. It's linked to the firm's computer network."

"Great," murmured Terrell to himself. Of course the firm would include a fully functional workstation inside a vacation home.

"I need to check a few things here in the house," Joe explained. "Then we'll go to that nightclub you said she remembered."

"Do I have time to make a phone call?" Terrell asked.

"As long as you keep it short, I'm on a schedule."

Terrell wanted to tell Joe exactly what he could do with his schedule, but decided not to. Joe looked like the kind of man that could kill him with a paper clip and then make his body disappear. Hopefully he could catch up with Alicia. He walked into the kitchen and picked up the phone off the wall. He thought of using his own phone, but if the firm could cancel his trip, then he thought they could absorb the cost of an international telephone call. After being disconnected twice, he finally got her office on the third try.

"Hello?" Alicia's voice came over the phone.

"Alicia!" Terrell said relieved. Just hearing her voice made him feel better.

"I was wondering when you were going to call me," she said disdainfully.

"What?" he asked, confused.

"Let me guess, you called because a huge case has come up and you're not going to be able to come see me because you have to work."

"Uhhh, yeah. How did you know?" he asked.

"Some lady called a little while ago. I think she's one of your secretaries. I can't say I'm surprised. You always have to work." She was more upset than he feared she'd be.

"It's not my fault this time," Terrell explained. "I mean, the hugest thing just came up and..."

"I already know," Alicia responded. "Jennifer Weston was arrested for murdering Optimus this morning in Miami and the prestigious firm of Bragg & Shuttlesworth has been retained for her defense. It's all over the news."

"Even over there?"

"Yeah, even over here."

"But I'm working directly on the case. It's not like I'm stuck at my desk writing useless memos."

"I know. I've seen that clip of you standing behind that guy on the courthouse steps twice already. I watched it on my computer. It's the biggest case ever and you'll probably never have opportunity to work on anything else like it, I know." She spoke to him in the same miffed tone she used when he neglected to call her back.

"Why are you so mad?" Terrell asked.

"I'm not mad."

"Yes you are. You're mad at me. It's not like it's even my choice to be here. Mr. Bragg called me at 3:30 this morning and told me to come to the airport."

"Gee that's funny, I talked to you before he did and told you to come over here. Why did you listen to him instead of me?"

"That's not fair."

"I know," she apologized. "I know it's not your fault. I'm just disappointed. We haven't seen each other in months. I haven't even talked to you much because you were always at work. I was going to take a couple of days off so we could take the train to Paris, and now you're not even coming."

"I'm going to come, I just can't come today." Terrell rationalized.

"Oh really?" she challenged. "When?"

"I don't know exactly, but I'll make time."

"Just like you made time this weekend?" she asked. "And before you can say it, I know that this is a big deal for you. I'm just tired of not being able to see or talk to you. I guess that I'm just selfish that way."

"I miss you too," Terrell said. "This isn't going to last forever."

"I guess," she sighed, "But tell the truth, you're going to have even less free time now than you did before, aren't you?"

"Yeah, at least for the next couple of days. They're making me stay down here in Miami."

"Where? At a hotel?"

"No, the firm has a house down here. It's really nice."

"For how long?"

"I'm not sure. It could be a couple of days or it could be a couple of weeks."

"Terrell," Alicia said in that tone that let him know she was about to give him a lecture. "Just because they pay you a lot of money doesn't give them the right to order you around like some kind of slave."

"Actually it does," Terrell laughed. "At least it does until I make partner. Then I'll get my very own set of associates to order around like slaves."

The silence on the phone let Terrell know that she didn't think his joke was funny.

"I'm sure it won't be for very long," he reassured.

"If you say so. Look, I'm happy for you. I know this is a good opportunity and I'm sorry if I snapped at you."

"Don't worry about it," Terrell smiled. "I know how irresistible I am. Withdrawal from me can be devastating."

"Oh whatever! Get over yourself. Now I have to find something to do with all of this free time I'm going to have. Maybe I'll see if Leonard is busy this weekend."

"Whose Leonard?" Terrell asked.

"Just a guy I work with. He says I'm cute."

"Are you trying to make me jealous?" Terrell asked.

"Now why would I go and do a thing like that?" she answered innocently. "I just need to fill some of that quality time I was going to spend with you."

"What!" Terrell said in mock alarm. "You're giving him my quality time? That's cold."

"Hey, you snooze, you lose mister. You know, Leonard's not that bad looking either, maybe I really should give him a call."

"Okay! I've heard enough! I'll figure out some way to get over there."

"You better," she answered, "or next time I might not be kidding."

"I love you," Terrell said with sincerity.

"I know," she answered.

"Wow. And people think I'm the vain one. I've got to go. When can I call you back?" he asked.

"I'm not sure," she said noncommittally. "It depends on how late I stay out with Leonard."

"You're the devil."

"But you love me anyway, I'll talk to you later."

"Bye." Terrell hung up the phone and sighed. He turned

around trying to think of a way to see her and nearly jumped out of his skin. Joe was standing behind him.

"How long have you been standing there?" Terrell asked, flustered.

"Not long," Joe answered flatly. "Let's go."

CHAPTER 6

Despite the trendy nature of late night entertainment, Millennium was four years old and still one of Miami's hottest nightclubs. Its reputation for hosting Miami's wildest parties attracted celebrities and socialites from all over the country. Luckily for Terrell and Joe, no one was clamoring to get in at eleven o'clock in the morning.

The nightclub itself was partitioned into separate sections. The club used a ten-foot high wall to keep out those people not fabulous enough for entrance. Joe pushed on the door and it creaked opened without interference. The two of them walked through a roofless courtyard area. It was decorated in a beach motif, complete with powdery sand and wooden boardwalks. The glare of the early morning sun reflected brightly off the glassware hanging from the immense bar in the center of the courtyard. A janitorial crew was busy cleaning up after the last night's party. Joe ignored them as he stomped down the center boardwalk towards the main building. He approached the second set of doors and swung them open. A young woman with bleach-blonde hair was inside, arguing with someone over the phone.

"You'd better be here before eight, or else don't bother coming," she said angrily into the phone. "We're already a bartender short and you know how this place is on Fridays." She paused as she listened to the other voice on the phone. "No, Miguel can't cover for you. I don't care how important it is, get here, on time, or find yourself another job." She slammed down the phone and looked up at Terrell and Joe.

"We're closed," she said contemptuously as she eyed their clothing. Two men in drab suits would never make it past the bouncers. "Doors open at ten. Come back then. You'll have to get in line like everyone else."

"I don't think we will," Joe said forcefully. He pulled a leather wallet from his coat pocket and flashed what appeared to be a badge. "Where's the owner of this establishment?" He snapped the wallet closed before giving the woman time to inspect it closely.

"Ahhh," the woman said, taken aback, "He's in the office. May I ask what this is about?"

"No you may not," Joe said coldly. "We need to see him. Now."

"Okay," she said nervously, "Just wait right here, I'll go get him for you."

"If it's all the same," Joe replied, "We'll follow you. We don't have a lot of time." The woman looked as if it wasn't all the same to her, but she didn't seem anxious to tangle with Joe either.

The inside of the club was divided into two separate dance floors, one on each side of a wide partition in the center. Two long bars ran across the entire length of the outside walls. She led them to the far left bar, lifted the counter gate and walked into the drink preparation area. She stopped at a bare space on the wall and pounded on it. A moment later, an audible click was heard and the small section of wall swung inward.

A fat man in a black and red tropical shirt sat inside the posh office eating a Cuban sandwich. He watching news coverage of the Jennifer Weston hearing on a large wall mounted television.

He looked up, obviously surprised to see Terrell and Joe standing in his office.

"Sorry, Mr. Encarnicion," the woman apologized, "These two detectives are here to see you."

"We won't take a lot of your time Mr. Encarnicion," Joe cut her off. "We'd just like to ask you a couple of questions about last night."

"What about it?" Mr. Encarnicion said suspiciously as he wiped mustard from his mouth with one of his beefy hands. "I was here all night. Angelina can vouch for my whereabouts and…"

"Excellent," Joe interrupted. "If you were here last night then you must have seen Jennifer Weston here as well."

A wave of relief washed over Mr. Encarnicion's greasy face. "Oh! You're here about that! I guess I should have figured the cops would show up sooner or later. What can I do for you?" Terrell was skittish about not correcting the man. He had always thought that impersonating the police was a serious crime, but Joe seemed to have no compunction with it.

"You saw Ms. Weston here last night," Joe stated, rather than asked.

"Oh yeah, her and Optimus always come here when they're in Miami. This is there favorite place," Mr. Encarnicion bragged. "I heard what happened. It's a shame what she did to him."

"Yeah," Joe agreed. "Where were they?"

"Up in the VIP room," he said as he rose from his leather chair. "What did you say your name was?"

"Joe," he said smiling. It was the first time Terrell had ever seen Joe smile, fake or otherwise. "Everyone calls me Joe and that's Bobby." Terrell almost turned around to look behind him until he realized that Joe was introducing him.

Terrell shook Mr. Encarnicion's hand. He smelled strongly of onions, mustard and cigars.

"Would you two like a drink?" he asked. "Angelina, please, get these two men something from the bar."

"No, but thanks," Joe answered.

"It's on the house," he smiled.

"Really, no. We're on the clock," Joe explained.

"Of course, but you two have to come back by here one night and have a drink with me when you're off duty.

"Sure," Joe replied. "If you could take us to this VIP room and let us look around, we'd be out of your hair."

"Yeah, about that. The thing of it is that I would," Mr. Encarnicion stalled, "It's just that I've got an awful lot to do and…"

"We're only looking for things relating to Ms. Weston. I'm sure we'll be far too busy looking for evidence in that case to see any other contraband materials that might be up there. It's important that we get a look inside before it gets accidentally disturbed, if you know what I mean. I'd hate for some judge to have to sign a search warrant. That would mean a lot more people would be involved. It could take days or weeks to search a place this big. I'd hate to have to shut this place down for that long."

Mr. Encarnicion stared at Joe, trying to figure out whether he could be trusted at his word.

"Alright," he said warily, "But anything you find up there isn't mine."

"Of course it isn't," Joe said.

Mr. Encarnicion led them back out of the office and into the club. Mr. Encarnicion pressed a hidden panel on the wall and a doorway opened, leading to a narrow stairway. Terrell climbed through the opening at the top of the staircase and emerged into the VIP room.

The room was just as Terrell remembered it. He was surrounded by one-way glass that offered a spectacular view of both dance floors. The janitorial crew hadn't made it to the VIP room as it was still littered with empty champagne bottles, half-eaten hors d'orves and random articles of clothing. The room's scattered coffee tables were covered with an assortment of marijuana roaches and cocaine dusted mirrors.

"Uhh, sorry about the mess," Mr. Encarnicion said as he attempted to use his large frame to block the drug paraphernalia from view.

"Don't be," Joe said in a friendly voice. "I'm glad no one had a chance to tamper with anything." "Where exactly did you see Ms. Weston?"

"I think she was over there on that couch, but there were a lot of people in here last night," he said. "I'm not sure."

"Was she doing anything unusual?" Joe asked as he whipped out a small camera and began taking pictures. "Arguing with anyone? Anything like that?"

"I don't think so," Mr. Encarnicion answered as he frowned at the camera. "At least I didn't notice if she did."

"And how long was she here?" Joe continued to pepper Mr. Encarnicion with questions as he busily snapped pictures. Terrell supposed that he should be paying attention, but he found his mind wandering. The entire situation was just so crazy. Everything was happening so fast that he hadn't had a chance to really wrap his mind around it.

He remembered sitting in this very room with Alicia back when they were telling themselves that they were only friends. He walked slowly over to a couch, remembering how they met Optimus that night. He couldn't believe that he was dead. He took another step and felt something sticking to his foot. He looked down and saw that a condom was tethered between his foot and the thick carpet.

"That's just wonderful," he muttered to himself. He looked around, searching for something that he could use to scrape the soggy latex from his shoe. He spotted a plastic drink stirrer on the floor. As he reached for it, he noticed something shiny in the carpet just under the edge of the couch. He picked it up and examined it. It was a platinum charm engraved with the initials JW. Terrell knew it could have been a coincidence, but he doubted it. He dropped the bracelet into his front shirt pocket and then re-examined the drink stirrer he found. A tiny, white speck clung to the end of the rod. Then he noticed the spot on the carpet where he found the stirrer was wet. A wine glass was tipped over on the table above the spot. He quickly popped open his briefcase and set the glass and stirrer inside of a small pouch within it.

"What are you doing?" Mr. Encarnicion asked curiously.

"Nothing," Terrell said calmly. "My foot got caught on a party favor." He pointed down at the condom that still clung to his foot. He rubbed his shoe quickly across the carpet to dislodge it.

"Oh," Mr. Encarnicion smirked. "Sorry, but sometimes it gets a little wild up here."

"I can imagine," Terrell answered.

"Do you have a guest list of the people in here last night?" Joe asked.

"No, we don't keep that kind of thing. The usher decides who gets in here. My guests like their privacy."

"What's the usher's name?"

"Carlos. Carlos Rentieria."

"I suppose that means that you don't have any security video of this room either," Joe asked as he scribbled down the name.

"Of course I don't."

"Can you tell me what time they left?" Joe asked.

"No, I wasn't here when they left."

"Is there an exit that they would have used to avoid the crowd?"

"Yeah," Mr. Encarnicion answered. "It leads to the back alley. Do you want to see it?"

"Sure," Joe answered. "And by the way, you might want to get the rest of this stuff cleaned up before the cops get here. I'd hate to see you get into trouble."

"I thought you said that you were the cops," Mr. Encarnicion replied, confused.

"Your assistant said that, not me. I only said that we were investigating. It'd be best for everyone if you forgot that we were here. I wouldn't want to have to turn over all my film to the police. Those pictures of the drugs you have stashed up here could cause you some serious problems. They'll be here within the hour, so you'd better hurry if you're going to get this place spic and span. Now if you'd be so kind as to show us outside."

Mr. Encarnicion didn't look particularly happy about it, but he did lead them down the back stairway. It led to an area behind the stage. A dimly lit emergency exit sign hung over the door Mr. Encarnicion opened for them.

"This is how they would have gotten out," He said curtly as he motioned for them to leave.

"Thanks," Joe said as he and Terrell went out the door. The exit door slammed shut and they found themselves in a gritty alleyway. The alley was just wide enough to allow a car to pass through it. A large green dumpster was against the wall of the next building and trash was piled high around it. Joe began poking through some of the garbage and found a cache of empty liquor bottles under a ripped trash bag. His head immediately popped up and he scanned the rest of the alley. Terrell followed his gaze and saw a man squatting against the building at the far end of the alley. Joe walked quietly up behind the man and nudged him.

"Do you stay around here?" he asked.

The man looked up at Joe with deadened eyes and scratched his chin through his long, scraggly beard.

"I asked you a question," Joe said more forcefully. "Do you stay around here?"

The man nodded no and let his eyes drop back down to the pavement.

"Is that a fact?" Joe shrugged. "Well, let's do this the hard way then." He grabbed the filthy backpack that was lying on the ground next to the man.

"That's mine!" he shrieked. "Give it back!" He sprang from the ground and lunged at Joe. In one fluid motion, Joe grabbed the man's wrist, twisted it, and shoved him headfirst into a pile of garbage bags.

Joe yanked open the backpack and pulled out an old shirt, a couple of cans and a blanket before he found what he was looking for. He tossed the bag to the ground and held up a whiskey bottle with a few ounces of brown liquid in the bottom of it.

"I don't like it when people lie to me," Joe began. "It puts me in a bad mood, and I'm not a nice person when I'm in a bad mood. You told me that you don't stay around here, but you do. Would you like to know how I figured that out?"

The man shook his head no.

"You got this liquor from the club. You show up every night and rummage through the trash, collecting bottles that have a few drops in them. You pour what you can scrounge into this one bottle. You do this because you're a drunk. Am I right?"

The man kept quiet.

"Let's try this again. Keep in mind that I will hurt you if you lie to me."

The man glared at him.

"Do you stay around here?"

"Yes," The man mumbled.

"Much better," Joe commented. "Now, I know that you're not the only bum that knows this little trick. I figure that you have to spend a lot of time out here in order to make sure you get the bottles, am I right?"

The man tried to stand. Before he could rise, Joe kicked his left leg out from under him, sending the man sprawling back into the filth.

"I asked you a question. When I ask you a question, you answer it. Do you understand me?"

The man nodded fearfully.

"Were you in this alley last night?"

He nodded yes.

"Good, now, was that so hard? Did you see anyone come out of that door?" Joe pointed to the emergency exit.

"Ahh, no I don't remember seeing anything happen."

"Stand up," Joe sighed. When the man rose, Joe grabbed his

wrist and yanked it behind his back, spinning him 180 degrees. Then he drove the man's face into the wall.

"I didn't ask you if you saw anything happen," Joe said in a calm but menacing voice. "I asked you if you saw anyone come out of the door. Answering questions that I didn't ask makes me think that you're lying to me again and I've already told you how I feel about that."

Terrell had seen enough of Joe's questionable ethics. Pretending to be the police was one thing, but he wasn't about to idly stand by and allow Joe to brutalize a defenseless homeless man.

"I think that's enough," Terrell said as he put a hand on Joe's shoulder. Faster than the blink of an eye, Joe's elbow flew backward and collided with Terrell's sternum. The air exploded from Terrell's lungs in a whoosh as he clutched his chest. He felt his legs buckle and give as he fell to the ground. It felt like his chest had been crushed. He couldn't even make a sound as he rolled on the ground, gasping for breath. He reached out for Joe, but Joe had turned his attention back to the homeless man.

"Did you see anyone come out of that door last night?" Joe asked forcefully as he punched the man in the kidney.

"Yes!" he shouted. "Yeah I saw some people come out late last night!"

"What did they look like?"

"I don't remember!"

Joe released the wrist hold he had on the man and spun him forward. He kneed him once in the belly and then used his forearm to pin the man's neck to the wall, choking him.

"Think harder," he said calmly.

"It was two guys I think," he said in a choked whisper. "No wait, it was two guys and one girl. The girl was out of it. They had to practically carry her to the car. I think she was drunk or something."

"What did they look like?"

"Black. All three were black. They looked young to me. The girl was pretty. I noticed that the guys had on a lot of jewelry."

Joe released his chokehold and allowed the man to slump down to the ground and then kneeled beside him.

"Did any of them look like this?" he said as he pulled a couple of pictures from his pocket.

"Yeah," the man said rubbing his neck. "That looks like one of the guys and the girl."

"What kind of car was it?" Joe asked.

"I don't know. I swear. It was over near the dumpster. I didn't really look at it."

"Why didn't you try to rob them?" Joe asked.

"I don't rob people. I'm not a criminal." The man said in a hurt tone.

"Sure you are. You were probably just to drunk to move," Joe said, disgusted.

Terrell had managed to pull himself up to his hands and knees. His chest ached and he could only breathe in rapid, shallow breaths.

Joe picked up the backpack once more, reached inside and pulled out what looked like an ID. He scanned it before placing it back into the bag.

"You are Henry Tucker," he said flatly.

"Yes sir," the man said meekly.

"Okay Henry Tucker, here," Joe said as he flipped the man two crisp, one hundred dollar bills. "Get out of here. Go smoke crack or get drunk or whatever it is that you do when you find some money. Don't come back here. This alley is off limits for you. If I find out that you've been back in this alley, I will hurt you. Do you understand?"

Henry nodded and Joe turned to leave.

"Get up!" Joe shouted at Terrell. Terrell was still having difficulty breathing and didn't expect to be getting up anytime soon.

"We're on a schedule," Joe exclaimed before grabbing the back of Terrell's collared shirt and yanking him to his feet. Joe shoved him into the passenger seat and got in on the driver's side before pulling the car into the street.

"Don't ever do that again," Joe said as they drove away from the club.

"Excuse me?" Terrell asked in a hushed tone. He could breathe again, but a fire was burning inside his lungs.

"I said don't ever do that again. When I'm asking some bum questions, don't undermine my authority. The next time you get in my way, I will not take it easy on you."

"Take it easy on me? Are you out of your mind?" Terrell asked. He couldn't believe Joe was actually threatening him.

"No, I'm quite sane." Joe said calmly. "I do however have a job to do. And if a bum has to get roughed up a bit to get pertinent information in a timely manner from him, then that's what's going to happen."

Terrell scowled as he rubbed his chest. He wondered how long the bruise was going to last.

"You'd like to kick my ass right now wouldn't you?"

"Yes, that's exactly what I'd like to do," Terrell answered honestly.

"Should I stop the car?"

"No, I'd need some kind of weapon to make it fair."

"It still wouldn't be fair. I'd take the weapon from you before you ever got the chance to use it," Joe answered. It wasn't a joke. "What did you put in your briefcase back at the club?"

"Huh?"

"I saw you open your case and slip something inside when I was talking to Mr. Encarnicion."

"Oh that, I think I found a piece of Jennifer's jewelry. I thought I'd give it back to her". Terrell didn't know what he was going to do with the stirrer, but after seeing Joe in action, he certainly didn't want to tell him about it.

"Oh," Joe looked at him skeptically, but he didn't ask any more questions.

CHAPTER 7

The quiet neighborhood around the firm's house had been totally transformed during Terrell and Joe's absence. The street leading to the entrance gate was choked with news vans and photographers. It took them nearly an hour to reach the guard station. A compliment of sheriff's deputies was assisting in crowd control. The photographers and reporters swarmed like angry ants over the car. They knocked repetitively on the windows shouting questions in the hope that Terrell or Joe had some scrap of information for them.

Joe brandished the car's permit for entrance at the guard while the deputies checked the car for unauthorized people. One of the deputies took off running when he spotted one especially industrious photographer attempting to scale the outer wall to gain access to the neighborhood.

The scene outside the house was no less chaotic than outside the gate. People were scurrying around everywhere. Terrell noted men in jumpsuits performing upgrades to the security system. Some people were taking various items and supplies in and out of the house, while others stood around barking orders. Joe had to park the car at the end of the driveway because several dark

SUVs were blocking the way. Terrell grabbed his briefcase and got out of the car.

A beefy man stood leaning against the front door. He was easily 6'5" and at no less than 300 pounds. He wore baggy jeans and Terrell spotted an earpiece in his left ear. As they approached, he looked at them with mistrust.

"Where do you think you're going?" he asked them rudely as they neared the door.

"Inside," Joe answered.

"I don't think so. Who are you with?" the man asked.

"Bragg & Shuttlesworth," Terrell spoke up. "We represent Ms. Weston. The firm owns this place."

"Do I look stupid you?" the man asked. "I'm supposed to believe that a law firm would hire a skinhead and a teenager to work for them? Who are you really with, the music network or something? I don't know how you got this far, but give it up. She's not doing any interviews. So how about you two just turn around and get out here before I have to hurt you."

Terrell saw the same look in Joe's eyes that he saw before he began beating the homeless guy and he realized that this could turn into a bad situation very quickly. He reached into his pocked and pulled out his firm ID card.

"I know that you have a job to do," Terrell said calmly as he showed the bodyguard the ID. "But so do I. Now, please step aside. I've got work to do if I'm going to keep Ms. Weston out of prison." The bodyguard carefully examined the ID before giving it back to Terrell. He stood aside.

"Here," Terrell said smugly as he passed the man a business card. "You look like the kind of man that might need a defense attorney one day. Remember my number." The man scowled and flipped the card into the bushes. There were several people mulling around the foyer, none of them looked familiar to Terrell. Another mammoth bodyguard stood atop the spiral staircase leading to the upstairs bedroom and a man with a teased hair and manicured fingers stood in the foyer, yelling into his cell phone.

"I don't care how much it costs," he shouted. "I want someone here now!" He noticed Joe and Terrell's entrance as he snapped shut the phone.

"Who are you supposed to be?" he snapped.

"Terrell Banks, Bragg and Shuttlesworth. I'm one of Ms. Weston's attorneys. And you are?" Terrell said as he extended his hand.

"Brian Dunn," the man replied icily as he glared at Terrell. Terrell remembered his name from their representation contract. He was some kind of vice-president for AMI. The small, permanent wrinkles in his forehead indicated that he spent a great portion of his day angry.

"Practically a thousand bucks an hour and you're the one they send? How old are you?" He asked. It wasn't the first time a client questioned Terrell's ability after seeing his face, and he was certain it wouldn't be the last. At least he was prepared for it.

"Sir," Terrell started his practiced monologue, "The question that you need to be asking yourself is not how old I am. The better question is how good am I? You should think about the fact that an outstanding firm like Bragg & Shuttlesworth would trust me with a case of this magnitude. They didn't get to where they are by employing anything less than the best. If it's an old lawyer you want, I'm sure we can dig up some fossil to work on this case. On the other hand, if you want a exceptionally talented and intelligent attorney then I'll suit your needs just fine."

Brian stared at Terrell, still not totally convinced.

"This is our investigator," Terrell turned to introduce Joe, but he wasn't there. He looked around, but Joe had seemingly melted into the house.

"You're the only one here?" Brian asked, irritated.

"For right now," Terrell answered. "Our private investigator is looking into some things as we speak. I will stay here on the premises to work on the case and to answer any questions Ms. Weston might have."

"I want status reports twice a day," Brian interrupted. "You're going to keep me up to speed on everything that's on in this case. I want to make it clear that all decisions need to go through me."

"Hold on just a moment," Terrell cut him off. "Our firm works solely for the benefit and at the discretion of our client. That client is Jennifer Weston, not you. While this firm will be more than willing to address your concerns, we will be doing what is best for Ms. Weston. We will make legal decisions whether or not you agree with our course of action. I will be providing her with updates, not you. If she decides to provide you with the information, that is her prerogative."

Brian's face looked as if it might melt away from his skull in anger. He certainly was not the type of man who was used to people telling him no.

"In the morning, Mr. Bragg and Mr. Foster will return," Terrell continued. "They are the lead attorneys on this case and you can address your concerns with them if you like. I am quite sure they will tell you the same thing I am."

"Yeah, well we'll see. I spoke with Mr. Bragg a little while ago," Brian said, stroking his chin. "He said someone would be along to explain what happened this morning in court. I guess that's you. Why didn't you wait for me?"

"Mr. Dunn," Terrell said. "We are being paid a tremendous amount of money for our legal advice."

"I know, AMI is footing the bill."

"Be that as it may, I'm sure that a man that has been as successful as you have didn't get there by wasting money on bad advice. I must implore you to trust our decisions. We successfully secured a bond. I am sure she would like to be able to leave the county and we will be working on that next."

Terrell spent the better part of an hour standing in the foyer with Brian smoothing his ruffled feathers. He asked pointed questions and slung half-baked accusations while Terrell deftly sidestepped and deflected his anger. By the time Brian concluded their conversation by rudely storming off to the upstairs bedroom,

Terrell was exhausted. His eyes felt like dry marbles rolling around in the sockets and his feet throbbed from standing up for so long. He needed a good night's sleep, but he had no time for that. He had research to do.

***

Terrell had been staring at the glass and stirrer from his briefcase for quite awhile. He didn't know what to make of them, but he did know someone who might. He picked up his cell phone and dialed a familiar number.

"Hello?" a cheery voice spoke into the phone.

"Hi Tammy," Terrell answered. "This is Terrell, how are you doing?" Tammy was married to Wesley, another one of Terrell's long time friends. Wesley worked in product development for Wellspring Chemical and was an adjunct chemistry professor.

"I'm doing fine, Terrell. It's been so long since we've seen you! When are you going to get back up here for a visit? Wesley always complains that everyone left him here all by himself."

"Soon," Terrell promised. "I've just been real busy. Is Wesley around?"

"Yeah, he just got home. I'll get him for you."

"Thanks." Terrell waited as he heard muffled voices on the other end of the phone. Soon he heard Wesley's voice.

"What's up Terrell?" Wesley said.

"A couple of things," Terrell answered. "What about you?"

"Same old stuff," he answered. "My wife has been trying to convince me that we need another kid." The couple had a three-year-old boy named Will. Seeing Wesley struggle through a year without a good night's sleep convinced Terrell that it would be a long time before he was ready for children.

"Good," Terrell said. "Will needs to have a little playmate."

"That's why we send him to school. There are plenty of kids to play with there. Besides, he can play with you and Alicia's kid," Wesley said sarcastically.

"That's not funny," Terrell said. "Why would you even say anything like that?"

"Because everyone knows you and her are going to get married. I don't know what you're waiting for. You're making all that money, you need at least one kid to help you spend it."

"Whatever man," Terrell laughed. "I'll leave the baby making to the professionals like yourself."

"So, why the call? I know you want something."

"You probably know about Jennifer Weston," Terrell started.

"That's the girl from Fantasy right?" he asked. "What about her?"

"You haven't heard?" Terrell asked, surprised. He expected that by now everyone knew about murder. Terrell quickly gave him the condensed version of the morning's events.

"I can't believe that you haven't heard by now. It's on every television station from here to Bucharest," Terrell said. "Alicia knew about it and she's in a whole different continent."

"What do you want from me? I've been in the lab all morning. Tammy!" he shouted. "Did you know that Jennifer Weston stabbed Optimus to death!"

"I didn't say that!" Terrell quickly responded. "I said she's accused of stabbing him."

"Sorry," he said sarcastically before shouting, "She allegedly stabbed Optimus to death!"

"Much better," Terrell replied.

"If she's using your firm, she did it. Why else would she need the most expensive lawyers in the world to help her beat the charge?"

Terrell had once mistakenly told Wesley how much the firm charged its clients. Now, he brought it up every chance he got.

"We're expensive because we're good," Terrell answered. "Innocent people want good lawyers too. But I didn't call to talk about that. I need your help."

"Really," Wesley said. "What could you possibly need from me?"

"You can analyze stuff in that chemistry lab where you work, right?"

"What kind of stuff?" Wesley asked curiously. "I work at a taste lab. I spend my days trying to make a more authentic lemon flavor."

"I know," Terrell said, "but you have equipment that can tell you what's in something right?"

"Yeah," Wesley said thoughtfully. "It's not a forensics lab, but I can do deconstructions with a spectrometer."

"Good," Terrell sighed in relief. "I've got some dried liquid and little fleck of something that I need to know about."

"Where did you get them from?"

"A nightclub. I think they might have something to do with the case. I can't be more specific than that."

"What do you think they are?" Wesley asked suspiciously.

"I don't know. That's why I called you. How long do you think it will take you to find out?"

"Depends on how complex it is," Wesley answered. "I'll have to do it after work when most of the staff is gone if you want me to keep it a secret. If I can't do it there, I'll have to take it over to the university. Either way, it shouldn't take longer than a week or two."

"So I can send it to you?" Terrell asked.

"Yeah, go ahead. How much of it do you have?"

"It's not a lot," Terrell said as he looked at the inside of the glass.

"Seal the glass in multiple layers of cling wrap and then put it into a plastic bag with a seal so nothing else gets into it."

"Okay. What else?"

"What does the other thing look like?"

"It's a very small, white speck," Terrell answered. "It was on the end of a stirrer that I found near the glass."

"Is it crack?" Wesley asked nervously.

"I don't think so. But I've never actually seen crack in person so don't really know what it looks like."

"Do not send me crack through the mail! I swear to God if you get me arrested, I'll kill you!"

"It's not crack!" Terrell said emphatically. "At least I don't think it is. Besides, I won't put it into the mail, I'll have it hand delivered if it will make you feel better."

"Alright," Wesley stated, "You owe me. If I get into trouble, you have to represent me for free."

"That's fair, thanks."

"Shouldn't you give this stuff to the police anyway?"

"I can't. I wouldn't be able to use it as evidence at this point. But if I didn't take it earlier, it would have been lost in the shuffle. I'm not even sure it has anything to do with the case. I'm just curious about it."

"Alright, send it to me and I'll see what I can find out about it."

"What's it going to cost me?"

"I'll let you know later," Wesley said slyly. "The kind of work you need is complicated and difficult. Not just anyone can do it," Wesley bragged. "It might cost a little, it might cost a lot, but it's definitely going to cost you."

"You're all heart," said Terrell.

"I know."

CHAPTER 8

Terrell smiled as he tied the belt around his robe. He was tired, but he had managed to finish what he thought was a pretty good research memorandum on pretrial publicity. It was only three in the morning and Mr. Bragg wasn't expected to arrive until at least nine. That gave him nearly six sweet hours of sleep. He had taken a hot shower and was wiping the water out of his ears when he realized that he was very hungry.

He'd spent the entire evening working in the cramped office adjoining his bedroom. He found it depressing that he was able to complete so much work in a place that was supposed to be a vacation site. With all the activity of the day, he had neglected to eat dinner. His stomach was now loudly reminding him of that fact. He made his way to the kitchen, hoping that one of the office runners had been told to stock the pantry.

Before he got to the kitchen, Terrell heard soft music drifting in from the parlor. He peeked inside to see if someone had left a radio playing and was surprised to see Jennifer. She sat with her back to the door, playing a tune on the piano that rested against the far wall. She looked like she should have been in a college dorm in her pajamas and bright red socks.

"Hey," Terrell called.

"Oh, I'm sorry," she said, startled. "I didn't wake you up, did I?"

"Nah, I wasn't sleeping," Terrell answered. "I just got finished working on some things for your case." Associates were instructed to constantly remind clients that they were working on their cases. It was the only way to justify the firm's outrageous fees.

"This place is nice. Is this your house?" she asked. She spun around on the piano bench and hugged her knees into her chest. It was the same position she took in the interrogation room and it made her look small and vulnerable.

"No," Terrell laughed. "It's a little bit out of my price range. This place belongs to the firm. This is actually the first time I've ever been here. But since you're stuck here, the partners thought I should be stuck here too. So here I am, at your service." Terrell bowed dramatically.

"Sorry," she said apologetically.

"For what?" he smiled. "I can think of worse things than having to share a house with international singing sensation Jennifer Weston. My friends are going to be very jealous. I can feel them hating me already." He hoped to lighten the mood with his comments, and Jennifer gave him an amused smirk.

"I didn't know you could really play the piano," he added. "I always figured that you were acting in your videos."

"You watch my videos?" she asked.

"Who doesn't?" Terrell answered.

"I don't know," she said. "Most of the lawyers I know don't listen to my music. I'm too young and too pop."

"I don't go home and watch the countdown everyday," he said. "But every once in a while I try see what's going on in the real world. I need to know what's hot on the street."

"What street are you talking about?" She laughed. For the moment, Terrell forget that he was hungry and tired.

"Why are you laughing?" he asked with mock consternation. "Don't let the suit and tie fool you, I represent the hood." He stood with his arms folded and legs apart, leaning against the dining room wall. This prompted more laughter from Jennifer.

"That's very gangster, but you should stick with the suits," she chuckled.

"So you say," Terrell retorted. "That sounded pretty good, how long have you been playing?"

"Four lessons a week, every week, for the last twelve years," she answered. "My dad says real musicians have to be able to read and play real music."

"What were you playing just now?" he asked.

"Nothing really," she said as her fingers flew across the keys. She recreated the soft tune he'd heard moments earlier. "It's just a practice melody I use to stretch out my fingers. I couldn't sleep, so I thought I'd come down here and play for awhile."

"You're not tired?" Terrell asked.

"I'm afraid to go to sleep," she answered quickly. "Got any requests?"

"No," Terrell answered. "I know music is probably the last thing you want to do right now."

"I like to play," she said. "It's the only thing that I've been able to do to take my mind off… well, off everything."

"Oh, then it doesn't matter."

She nodded and began playing her hit single, "Wherever". She played the music at a much slower tempo than the radio version. She began singing in a sorrowful voice and Terrell noticed some subtle nuances in the music that he hadn't ever noticed. Even though she sang softly, her voice was strong and beautiful. She transformed the club hit into a powerful ballad, and Terrell found himself hanging on her every melodic note. She held out the last note and finished the song with a piano flourish.

"Wow. That was fantastic! I really liked it slowed down that way," Terrell gushed. Suddenly, he ceased being Terrell Banks, attorney at law and became Terrell Banks, befuddled fan. "I've never heard anyone sing like that before. It was beautiful." He knew he was rambling, but he couldn't stop. "I mean, I'm sure you hear that all the time, but it was great."

"Thank you," she said. "This is the way I wrote it, but AMI told me to make it faster so it could be radio friendly."

"They're idiots. That was much better than the radio version. Not that I don't like that one, because I do," he hastily added. "It's just that I like it better that way."

"I'm glad you like it." Despite Jennifer's upbeat attitude, Terrell could feel her anxiousness. He knew that Mr. Bragg had stationed him in the house to gain her confidence and he figured that now was a good time to get started.

"What's the matter?" Terrell asked, before realizing the absurdity of his question. "I mean, other than being accused of murdering your boyfriend and stuck here in this house with a idiot like me."

She was quiet for a full minute. Terrell was beginning to think that he should just go make his sandwich and leave. She looked carefully at him as if to determine if he were trustworthy. Finally, she spoke.

"I know you already answered this when we were at the courthouse, but do you really believe that I didn't do it? I mean I know that you're my lawyer and you believe what ever I tell you to."

"Actually," Terrell corrected. "I don't get paid to believe or disbelieve, only to defend you. Honestly, I don't know what to think. They arrested you at the scene. You were covered in blood and he was lying in the bed. That's usually enough evidence to convince me. But sitting here with you, it's hard for me to believe that you could possibly do anything like that. Something is missing. I feel like I'm trying to put together a puzzle without knowing what it looks like. I guess that's the long way of saying, no, I don't believe that you did this awful thing."

"Do you know what scares me the most?" she asked.

Terrell shook his head.

"I have no idea what happened. I can't even tell you for sure that I didn't do it. I don't remember. There's a chunk of time from yesterday that is completely blank. What if I went crazy and killed him and blocked it out of my mind? Or what if I have one of those multiple personalities like in the movies? What if my other personality killed him or something? What if I wake up tomorrow and I've stabbed someone else?" Terrell could see that she wasn't fabricating any of this. She was terrified.

"Do you honestly think that's what happened?"

"No, but…"

"Do you have any history of blackouts?" Terrell asked seriously.

"Not that I know of."

"Then I don't think that's what happened. We'll have a doctor examine you to make sure. I don't think you'd all of a sudden start having blackouts and become a homicidal maniac. It has to be something else, I just don't know what yet. Trust me, we'll figure it out eventually."

Jennifer sat still, absorbing his words. She looked as if there was something else that she wanted to say, so Terrell waited for her.

"Do you know who Opal Rogers is?" she asked.

"Uh-huh, she's one of the other girls in Fantasy, right?"

"I've known her since we were little kids," said Jennifer. "We've been taking singing lessons together since we were five."

"You two are tight," Terrell agreed.

"It's more than that," she explained. "We were like sisters. She lived at my house when we were starting the group. I know that everyone wants to make up stories about how we fought and how the group was breaking up, but it wasn't like that."

Terrell nodded his head. Fantasy was the R&B trio of Jennifer Weston, Opal Rogers and Tamera Blount. They were only 16 when their debut album was released. They steadily gained popularity, capitalizing on poppy singles and crossover audience appeal. Their last album spent fourteen weeks atop the charts on its way to over nine million copies sold. Although people loved them as a group, it was clear that Jennifer was the shining star. Now that Jennifer had released her solo album and was touring with her high profile boyfriend Optimus, there was rampant speculation that Fantasy was finished.

"We had our fights about stuff," she continued, "but sisters fight sometimes."

Terrell nodded in understanding.

"I'd been trying to call her all day, but she wouldn't speak to me. Her assistant kept saying that's she was busy and that she'd call me back. After fifteen calls, she finally answers the phone. Do you know what she said to me?"

It was a rhetorical question, but Terrell shook his head no anyway.

"As soon as she got on the phone, she told me that she didn't have anything to say to me and that she hoped that I burned in hell for what I did to Felix. I guess I knew that some people were going to think the worst," Jennifer continued. "But I didn't think it would be her. I've known her forever. I can't believe that she thinks that I could ever do something like that. She wouldn't even listen to me. She just told me not to call back and hung up on me."

Terrell didn't know what to say. The betrayal of her friend had profoundly affected Jennifer. Since he didn't have any words of comfort, he decided to shift her focus to something else.

"Do you have a charm with your initials on it?"

"I did," she replied, caught off guard by his seemingly random question. "I don't know what happened to it." She fingered her thin necklace. It goes on here, but I haven't seen it since they arrested me. I think one of the policemen must have stolen it."

"Hold on a minute," Terrell said as he ran back to his room to retrieve the charm. He walked back to the parlor and dropped it into Jennifer's hand.

"Is this it?" he asked hopefully.

"Yes, where did you find it?" she asked.

"I found it next to one of the couches at Millennium," Terrell offered. "You told me that you remembered going there after the show last night, right?"

"Vaguely," she answered. "I think we were there, but I don't remember anything about it."

"Do you drink?" he asked.

"Sometimes," she answered. "But never a lot. Photographers would love to get pictures of me stumbling around drunk. But I'll have a Martini or some champagne every once in awhile."

"Did you have anything last night?" Terrell asked hopefully.

"I don't know. Since we were at Millennium, they probably brought me something, but I don't remember drinking. Why?"

"I'm just trying to get some background on last night," Terrell said. He didn't want to let her in on his hunch just yet.

"Felix gave me this for my birthday last year. He loved for me to wear this gaudy thing."

"I like my girlfriend Alicia to wear big, gaudy jewelry that I bought her." Terrell replied. "Big jewelry means that I like her a lot."

"Nice, classy jewelry means you like her a lot. Big, gaudy jewelry means that you don't know what you're doing in a jewelry store."

"Thanks for the advice, I'll try to remember that next time I buy her a gift."

"How long have you two been dating," she asked.

"About three years."

"Do you live together?"

"Oh no," Terrell answered quickly. "There will be no shacking up for me. We're not even living in the same city right now. She's on an internship in Spain. I haven't seen her for a couple of months."

"Distance relationships are hard," she said. "When are you going to see her?"

"I don't know," Terrell replied. "I was supposed to go this weekend, but... well, you know."

"I'm sorry," she apologized.

"Don't be, it's not your fault," Terrell comforted. However, he thought to himself that it would be her fault if she actually did it. He pushed the thought from his mind.

"Jenny! Are you alright?" a booming voice said from the doorway. Terrell saw the bodyguard from the front door standing behind him. The white crust on the edge of his lip revealed that he'd been sleeping on the job.

"I'm fine Luther," she answered. "I was just playing some things on the piano and Terrell decided to join me."

"You should get some rest," Luther said as he looked at Terrell mistrustfully. "It's been a long day."

"Sure," she said. "I guess I should go to bed. G'night Terrell." She eased past Luther who lingered in the doorway glaring at Terrell. Terrell smirked and waved before he walked into the kitchen to make his sandwich.

CHAPTER 9

Terrell's emergency jaunt to Miami had become a month of imprisonment in the house. Terrell spent eighteen-hour days working in the house's cramped office. Karen Rojas dropped the gauntlet early in an effort to let them know that she was not intimidated. Terrell guessed that every assistant state attorney in Miami was working on this case because he received a new motion almost every day. They fought for three days over limiting pre-trial publicity. When the firm won, they fought for another three days about exactly what pre-trial publicity meant.

Despite the court's rulings, grisly details of the murder kept surfacing in the tabloids as well as the mainstream news outlets. Mr. Bragg was convinced the leaks were coming from the State. It was clear to them that Karen's intent was to poison any possible jury pool that they could find.

Each and every one of these hearings meant that Terrell had to spend countless hours researching and writing. Mr. Bragg had been right about his staying on the property with Jennifer. He was working so much that he barely knew she was there.

Terrell tried not to think too much about it because he had worries of his own. The constant demands of Mr. Bragg were taking their toll on his relationship with Alicia. He was always right in the middle of something important when she called. She constantly complained about his lack of attention. Even when they did speak, he was so tired that he was apt to doze off while she was talking.

Felix Caldwell, known to millions of fans as Optimus, was laid to rest on a cold afternoon in Brooklyn, New York. The funeral attendees were a who's who list of the most important and influential people in the music industry. Fans lined the streets along the processional route, throwing white roses as the casket passed. One person notably absence from the funeral was his girlfriend and rumored fiancée, Jennifer Weston. Her bond prevented her from leaving Miami, but even if it hadn't, Mr. Foster never would have allowed her to attend. Optimus' mother had already been making the rounds on the talk show circuit. She told anyone that would listen about her firm belief that Jennifer should receive the death penalty for what she had done to her son. A son that in her own words "had never done anything to hurt anyone."

AMI received bags full of hate mail and death threats to Jennifer from Optimus' fans everyday. Much like Terrell, Jennifer was also a prisoner of the house. She had been excused from singing the national anthem during the NBA All-Star Weekend and her endorsement offers had all but vanished. Mr. Bragg worried that the downturn in positive publicity would hurt her chances with potential jurors. They needed something easy and positive for her and the Music Awards were just the thing.

Prior to being charged with murder, Jennifer Weston had received six nominations for her album Lovesick, including Album of the Year, Record of the Year, Best Female Pop Vocal Performance, Best R&B Female Vocal Performance, Best R&B Song and Best Contemporary R&B Album. Furthermore, the circumstances of the Music Awards were tailor made for her. The ceremony was being held in the James L. Knight center in downtown Miami. The firm didn't even have to go through the trouble of getting the court's permission for Jennifer to attend. There would be tons of press, but it would be controlled and she could pick and choose her interviewers. Additionally, Jennifer stood a very good chance of winning multiple awards. Her album sales seemed unaffected by the case against her. If anything, sales had even risen slightly since her arrest.

As usual, Mr. Foster thought it was a horrible idea. He wanted her to accept any awards she won by video. That way, they could control her every word and gesture. He was certain that if the media got a chance at her, she would say or do something to hurt the case. Mr. Bragg disagreed and thought she would look guilty if she remained locked in the house until the trial. They spent days bickering over the proper course of action until a compromise was reached. Terrell would go with her and act as a sort of chaperone. He was responsible for guiding her away from tough questions and ensuring that nothing went awry. Mr. Foster made it clear that he doubted Terrell's ability to control the situation, but he eventually acquiesced.

Terrell tried to look at his reflection in the window of the black limousine so that he could straighten his bowtie. It was crooked and nothing he did seemed to help. He'd wanted to rent the kind of plain black tuxedo that came with a perfect pre-tied bow. However, Jennifer's wardrobe coordinator was adamant that everyone traveling with the entourage had to wear complementing attire. So, Terrell was stuck wearing a brand new tuxedo with the black and gold bow tie. It didn't help his mood that he had to pay for the suit out of his own pocket.

Joining Jennifer and him on the excursion was her album's producer Eddie Pace, Brian Dunn, the vice-president of urban music at AMI and Jennifer's bodyguard Luther. They rode in silence save for Terrell's drumming his fingers on the armrest.

"Will you stop doing that?" Luther shouted. "You're going to make Jennifer nervous."

Sharing close quarters had really made Terrell despise Luther. During the few free moments when Terrell wasn't working in the office, Luther followed him around the house. He watched him as if he was some kind of rapist, just waiting for the opportunity to attack Jennifer. Terrell tried to ignore him, but it was getting harder and harder to do.

"You remember whose safe, right?" Terrell asked Jennifer. He stopped drumming his fingers just in case it did make her nervous, but he refused to acknowledge Luther.

"Yes," she answered. They had drilled Jennifer all week with questions and how she should answer them. She'd been a good sport, but Terrell could hear the frustration in her voice. "Henry Lawrence from The Times will be somewhere on the left. He's the only one that's getting an interview. Then I'm going to walk to photo area for a few pictures and then we'll go inside. I'm to avoid making eye contact with any other reporter and I'm supposed to ignore any questions not asked by Mr. Lawrence."

"Just making sure," said Terrell apologetically. AMI made a deal with Henry Lawrence for an exclusive interview as long as he submitted his questions to them in advance. The answers to the questions had been meticulously crafted by the firm and then memorized by Jennifer. They were arriving late to the award show by design. She only had enough time to talk to him.

The limousine stopped at the curb and an unseen usher opened the door to help Jennifer out of the car. She was stunning in her Grecian inspired pale green dress. It had a plunging neckline that stopped just above her navel. The golden medallions comprising her belt clicked together when she moved and the high split of the dress displayed her toned legs. She wore her hair up because the image consultant said that showcasing her face would make her more attractive and honest to potential jurors. She smiled and waved at the flashbulbs of the paparazzi while the rest of her entourage climbed out of the car.

"Henry Lawrence, The Times," one of the reporters shouted, "You're nominated for six Grammy's, how many do you think you'll win?"

Jennifer stepped closer to the reporter before answering the question with the pat response of being happy to be nominated. Before she could answer the next question, Terrell saw something that made him nervous. Directly behind Jennifer were two tall men with picket signs. The words 'Jennifer Weston: Singer, Actress, Murderer' were written in dripping, blood red letters. Directly below the phrase was a computer-generated photo of Jennifer singing in a dress soaked with blood.

"Luther!" Terrell exclaimed in a harsh whisper. He pointed to the sign carriers and Luther pushed his way through the crowd to get to them. Terrell saw TV cameras honing in on Jennifer and worried that the two protesters would be in all the shots. He acted quickly and sidled up to Jennifer, taking her arm in his. She flinched as their arms came into contact, but continued speaking smoothly as if she had expected him to be there. He deftly maneuvered her slightly to her left, and used his body to block the view of the protesters.

"And who is this handsome gentleman?" the reporter asked in a curious tone. Terrell cringed. They told him to keep a low profile. Mr. Bragg was adamant that he didn't want the public to think that Jennifer had a lawyer coaching her answers.

"Terrell Banks," he replied without offering further explanation.

Sensing that he was treading on thin ice, Mr. Lawrence dropped it and returned to the scripted portion of the interview.

"There is a lot of controversy surrounding the murder of Optimus and your subsequent arrest," Mr. Lawrence asked somberly, "Can you tell us anything about that?"

"It's an ongoing case, and as you know, I'm under court order not to talk about it," she answered. Judge Keller had made it very clear that he wouldn't tolerate any more breaches of his gag order. "I only ask that everyone be patient. Have faith as I do that when the truth comes out I will be cleared of these horrible charges." It was the kind of non-committal answer that tested well with the people they polled. It denied everything in general, but it didn't contest any easily proven facts. Jennifer excused herself from the interview and led Terrell further up the carpet towards the photo area. The rest of the entourage fell in behind them as the flashbulbs from the photographers popped rapidly to capture her approach.

"How was that?" she whispered. He was amazed at how she could whisper through her smile without moving her lips.

"Fantastic," he answered.

"What's this all about?" she asked, gesturing to their intertwined arms.

"There was some people behind you that I didn't want in the photos," Terrell answered. "I couldn't think of a good way to move them out of the way, so I just stood in front of them."

"Oh. Are you going to stand with me to take pictures too?"

"No, I don't think I have the figure for it," he joked. "I'll leave that kind of thing up to you."

They paused for a moment while teen pop sensation Skylar Green posed for the shots that would undoubtedly find their way into middle school lockers across the country in the next few days. This was the first time since he'd met Jennifer that she seemed happy. He knew that she was beautiful when he met her, but tonight she was spectacular.

"Stop looking at my boobs," she whispered as she poked him in the ribs with her elbow. "The picture will be every tabloid by tomorrow."

"What, I wasn't," Terrell's eked before realizing that his eyes had lingered a moment too long. Her dress showed a lot.

"Sorry," he said in a sheepish voice.

"It's okay," she whispered. "Up until now I wasn't sure you were actually a human. I thought you were some kind of working all the time, never sleeping robot."

"No," he answered. "I was just wondering how you keep things from, you know, falling out."

"Tape," she winked. "Lots and lots of tape."

***

Terrell rested his chin on his fist as he listened to a rock band he'd never heard of perform. Only the volume of the performance kept him awake. Jennifer, Edward Pace and Brian Dunn sat in front of him while Luther sat on his left. Watching awards shows on television hadn't prepared him for how boring they were in person. The jokes were less funny, the performances were stale and the commercial breaks seemed to last forever.

With only three awards left to present, it was clear that Jennifer had been snubbed. Her shoulders sagged in disappointment when the winners of the Best Female Pop Vocal Performance, Best R&B Song and Best Contemporary R&B Album were revealed without her name being called. Terrell was wondering how much work he'd be able to squeeze in that evening when he heard something that he didn't expect.

Marion Henshaw was a very popular country singer and self admitted redneck. She proudly wore her cowboy boots with her evening gown and sang songs about boys with big trucks. For some reason, the selection committee thought that she would be the perfect person to present the award for Best R&B Female Vocal Performance.

"And the winner is," Marion said in a twangy voice, "... well I'll be damned. Jennifer Weston, Lovesick." Jennifer's song 'Wherever' began playing over the loudspeakers accompanied by nervous applause from the audience.

Terrell wanted to remain seated while she accepted her award, but Luther pushed him roughly from his chair and into the isle. He followed the crew up on stage, but stood off to the side as Marion passed the Award to Jennifer.

"Thank-you," Jennifer spoke with a cracked voice into the microphone. Terrell looked up and saw a teleprompter atop the camera informing Jennifer that she had exactly 19 seconds to finish her acceptance speech. Mr. Bragg and Terrell had spent two days writing the speech she would give in the event that she won in one of the categories. Terrell got worried when he saw that she was not reaching for it.

"Thank-you for supporting me," she said in an unsure voice. "There are so many people that helped..." she trailed off. "So much went into the album and I... I don't want to forget anyone and... This means so much to me." She was shaking by this point, and on the brink of an emotional breakdown. Terrell didn't know if it was the joy or grief or anger, but whatever it was, it was too much for her to handle all at once. Tears streamed down her face and she paused in a futile attempt to compose herself.

"I'm sorry," she said as she turned away from the podium. Brian Dunn AMI threw his arm around her in support as the ushers escorted them from the stage area.

As they left the stage, Terrell heard a smattering of boos and catcalls from a group in the front row. The lights pointed at the stage were blinding, so he couldn't quite see who they were.

Brian Dunn gave Jennifer a reassuring hug backstage as she composed herself. Terrell saw Luther surveying the room and he did the same. Several entertainment reporters stood waiting rabidly for their chance at Jennifer. He had no desire to push his way through that gauntlet.

"Is there any way we can get her out of here and bypass the press?" Terrell asked Luther softly.

"No," he answered. "I scoped escape routes yesterday, this is the only way." He pointed to a particularly thick knot of reporters blocking what appeared to be the exit.

"Can't she just do one?" Brian Dunn interrupted. "A win is always followed by a sales spike for the album. We need to do some kind of promotion while we're here."

"I don't think so," Terrell answered. Mr. Bragg had been very specific about limiting the press' access to Jennifer.

"Just one," he said. "I see Marcus Washington over there next to the couches. He's a friend of mine. This will work. Trust me. Jennifer can do a quick interview with him and then we'll get out of here."

"I think it's a bad idea," Terrell started, but Brian had already grabbed Jennifer's hand and was pulling her toward Marcus.

"Stop worrying," Brian said over his shoulder. "She's a big girl, I think she can handle it."

Brian rushed Jennifer past the throng of questioners to a man sitting comfortably on a couch in a tee shirt that read Street Signz Magazine. He wore oversized jeans, sneakers and a huge diamond pendant around his neck. He was the only reporter not clamoring to speak with Jennifer.

"J-Dub," he said as she approached, "It's been a long time. I guess when you blow up, you forget all the little people."

Jennifer offered a weak smile and sat on the small seat opposite Marcus. Terrell and Luther followed her.

"So, how does it feel to win?" It was a soft question, and one that they had spent time prepping her answer. Terrell thought that maybe she could get out of the interview in one piece.

"Good," Jennifer answered. "I put a lot of my heart into this album and I hope that my music touches people the way music touches me." Terrell looked up at the large television screen mounted on the wall. It had a live feed from the stage so that the reporters could see what was happening. They were announcing the winner of the best Rap Album.

"And the winner is," Skylar paused for dramatic effect, "Optimus, The Invasion."

The thunderous applause from the crowd could be felt even back stage. Terrell watched the screen as Optimus' entourage, known as the Armada, filed onstage to accept the award in the place of their fallen leader. They had been the ones in the front row jeering Jennifer. It was immediately obvious to anyone watching the telecast that the vast majority of the Armada was drunk, high or both. They screamed praises of Optimus into the microphone without taking turns, making the entire speech a garbled mess. They finally exited the stage, throwing up hand symbols and shouting unintelligibly. They were heading backstage and a rock fell into the pit of Terrell's stomach.

"Now that the soft stuff is out of the way," Marcus said as his gaze fell from the screen back to Jennifer, "I can ask about what everyone really wants to know. You killed Optimus, didn't you?"

"Ahh…" Jennifer said taken aback by his bluntness. "As I already told you, I can't talk about…"

"Don't give me that," Marcus said dismissively. "It's a simple question. Either you stabbed him to death or you didn't. Why don't you just tell us your side of the story?"

"I didn't… I don't…" Jennifer stammered.

"This interview is over," Terrell said as he quickly stepped between them. "I thought you said that this guy was okay," Terrell turned to accuse Brian Dunn, but he was no longer there.

"We need to get out of here," Terrell said to Jennifer, but it was too late. The Armada had made their way to the backstage area and one of them had spotted her. Terrell had been to enough nightclubs to know when trouble was about to start.

"Whassup, bitch!" one of the men in a baseball jersey shouted as he pointed in their direction.

"I got something for that right here." He grabbed his crotch with both hands and made a lewd motion.

"This is just perfect," Terrell mumbled as he frantically began looking around for a security guard or a policeman that could help.

"Hey man," Terrell said to them. "This isn't necessary. Why are you trying to start something?"

Another one of them responded with unintelligible expletives as he threw a bottle. The bottle shattered at Jennifer's feet, spraying champagne everywhere. Marcus leapt out of the way and took off running in the opposite direction.

"I called the car!" Luther shouted. "I'll hold them here. Go now!" He ran towards the Armada, but it didn't look promising. Terrell counted twelve of them. Terrell glanced around and saw that Eddie Pace, the producer had disappeared too.

"Figures," he mumbled as he and Jennifer ran towards the door marked emergency exit. Unfortunately, though Jennifer was accustomed to walking in four-inch heels, she wasn't as good running in them. She had only taken a few steps before her left heel broke, spilling her onto the floor. Terrell helped her to her feet and took a cautious look over his shoulder. Luther was trying to block their way with his massive bulk, but he couldn't to hold them for long. Most of the reporters backstage took note of the conflict and decided that backstage wasn't the safest place to be.

Terrell threw open the exit door for Jennifer and pushed her through it. As he tried to follow, he felt a strong arm grab his jacket collar and violently spin him around. He vaguely recognized the face of the man from one of his CD covers when he felt a heavy fist land squarely on his chin. His teeth snapped shut with a loud click. The harsh, metallic taste in his mouth let him know instantly that he had bitten his tongue. He fell backward against the exit door, slamming it shut.

At least Jennifer got out, he thought to himself before another heavy fist smashed into his nose. Pain erupted from his face and his head snapped back hard against the metal exit door. He was stunned and stars danced in front of his eyes. He saw the man rearing back to kick him, and he knew that if he went to the ground, he might not get up again. Terrell gathered himself just enough to prevent his legs from buckling. Then he rushed forward, driving his shoulder into the man's midsection. They fell backwards and the corner of a table jabbed deeply into the side of Terrell's attacker. The man gasped in pain before crumbling to the ground.

Terrell leapt to his feet and fumbled at the door, finally pulling it back open. He darted into the dark alleyway and saw Jennifer standing a few feet away.

"Are you alright?" she asked, concerned.

"Keep going!" he shouted. He could feel a warm liquid flowing over his lips, and he was suddenly unable to breathe through his nose. As he ran down the alley with Jennifer, small droplets of blood splashed onto his crisp white shirt. The limo was idling at the far end of the alley, only a few yards away. As he yanked on the car's door handle, Terrell heard the door to the auditorium being slammed open. To his horror, he saw two men spill out into the alley and neither was Luther. One was the guy that had bloodied his nose and the other was the man wearing the baseball jersey. Each man was holding a black pistol. Terrell shoved Jennifer into the backseat and dove in behind her.

"Drive!" he shouted as the first shots rang out. They ducked down in the seat and he could hear the bullets punch into the car's metal frame. Then, the rear window shattered, spraying glass everywhere as the black limo screeched off into the night.

CHAPTER 10

"Do you speak English?" Mr. Foster shouted as he slung the newspaper at Terrell. The paper struck him squarely in the chest and fell to the table.

"Yes sir. I do." Terrell didn't bother to look at the headline, he really didn't need to see it to know what it said.

"So you understood us when we told you to keep a low profile?"

It hadn't been a good morning. Terrell had spent the last six hours at the emergency room having his broken nose set. The doctor told him he'd also bitten through the side of his tongue. His tuxedo shirt was stained brown with dried blood. His mouth ached, his nose was swollen and dark bruises had formed under his eyes. At the moment, Mr. Foster's ranting was the least of his worries.

"We gave you one simple job. We gave you one easy thing to handle on your own and you botched it. I don't think it could have gone any worse if you tried," Mr. Foster yelled.

The story of the fracas backstage was being reported on every channel. Terrell watched the first reports from the back of the limo as it drove him to the hospital.

"Terrell, look at this," Mr. Bragg took the newspaper and spread it flat on the table. "This is exactly the kind of thing we sent you there to prevent. I sincerely hope that you have a good explanation for how you let this happen."

The headline in the Herald read in 20-point font, 'Troubled Songstress Involved In Backstage Brawl At Music Awards.' Directly below the headline was a fuzzy security camera image of Luther rushing towards Optimus' entourage. Terrell and Jennifer could clearly be seen in the background. The caption read, 'Members of accused murderer Jennifer Weston's entourage attack men backstage.'

"That's some pretty slanted journalism," Terrell muttered. "She wasn't involved in anything except for running away from Optimus' goons. Those guys came backstage looking for trouble and the next thing I knew, someone was punching me in the face. We didn't have anything to do with it."

"Why were you even back there?" Mr. Foster asked suspiciously.

"When you win," Terrell explained, "You can't just walk back down to your seat, so we had to go backstage. She was supposed to walk around the back hallway and re-enter the auditorium from the front. But, she got sidetracked by an interview with some dude from Bricks Magazine and…"

"Some dude?" Mr. Foster asked incredulously. "What do you mean she went to do an interview with some dude? We specifically told you not to let her speak to anyone that wasn't on our safe list."

"I know that," Terrell responded. "That's what I told them, but that Dunn guy from AMI wouldn't listen. He said that he knew the guy and he dragged her over there."

"Now that's odd," Mr. Bragg said. "We just spoke with Mr. Dunn. He says that the interview was your idea and that he was against it. He told us that the entire debacle was a direct result of your decisions. Furthermore, he wants us to remove you from the case."

"I'm inclined to agree with him," Mr. Foster added. "Stupidity on this level cannot be overlooked."

"Are you serious?" Terrell responded. "That slimy sack of filth is saying this is somehow my fault?"

"No, not somehow your fault," Mr. Bragg corrected, "He says it's all your fault. He also claims that you ran out and left him there to fend for himself."

"That's true," Terrell responded. "I did leave him there, because I didn't know where that coward ran off to. He let Jennifer get ambushed by that hack reporter and then he disappeared as soon as things went south. So yes, I did leave him there and I hope something very bad happened to him."

"Listen," Mr. Bragg said. "That slimy sack of filth, as you call him, hired us on Ms. Weston's behalf. We can't just ignore what he says."

"I'm not asking you to ignore it," Terrell replied. "I'm just telling you that it's not true. With all due respect sir, Jennifer Weston is our client, not him. All he cared about last night was getting his product back in the spotlight."

"Regardless," Mr. Foster accused, "You still should have found a way to prevent this from happening."

"What would you have had me do?" Terrell asked. "If I had tried to stop him, it would have created more of a scene than the interview did."

"So I guess we're to believe that you're blameless in all of this," Mr. Foster said sarcastically.

"No," Terrell answered. "It was not my fault, but it was my responsibility. I should have led her out of there as soon those goons started making their way back stage. I should have realized that it was going to be a bad situation earlier. Because of my mistake, I have a broken nose, I nearly bit my tongue off, and someone shot at me. I'm sorry things didn't go as you expected them too, but that's the best I could do under the circumstances."

"Well," Mr. Bragg said thoughtfully, "I suppose there really wasn't much you could have done to stop what happened. And Brian Dunn is a slimeball."

"What did you do after you left the auditorium?" Mr. Foster asked.

"We came straight back here. Jennifer wasn't hurt but my nose was bleeding pretty bad." He hoped to strike a compassionate nerve, but they didn't seem to care about his pain. "I had the limo driver take me to the ER to get it checked out."

Mr. Bragg mulled this over before asking, "Did anyone follow you to the hospital?"

"I don't think so," Terrell replied. "But I wasn't watching carefully." The press activity outside the walls had calmed down significantly over the past few weeks. Most of the reporters realized that they wouldn't be able to get a glimpse of Jennifer while she was in the house.

"Still, we're not happy about this," Mr. Bragg continued as he scanned down through the newspaper article. "This kind of thing makes her look like some kind of street hooligan. I suppose you have an explanation for this too." He pointed to a smaller photo within the text of the article. It was a photo taken with Terrell and Jennifer standing side by side. The picture clearly showed their arms intertwined. It was captioned, 'Jennifer Weston with her attorney Terrell Banks.'

"Actually I do," Terrell began. "There were these guys…"

"Save it," Mr. Foster interrupted. "I'm sure whatever excuse you come up with will be quite interesting and will absolve you from all blame. The fact remains that we told you to stay out of the pictures. Whatever you had to do, you should have done it without standing next to the client. The picture makes you look like her new boyfriend or something."

"Sorry," Terrell apologized.

"You should be," Mr. Foster responded. "When we give you directions, we expect those directions to be followed without deviation. We didn't build this firm by letting hotheaded young lawyers do whatever fool thought crossed their minds." The lecture continued for another thirty minutes. Terrell had become accustomed to being on the receiving end of these little tirades and had become quite adept at ignoring the sound of Mr. Foster's voice.

"Before I go to the police station, I wanted to know how I should handle the report about the shooting." He asked after he'd spent the requisite time looking remorseful.

"Why would you be going to the police station to make a report?" Mr. Foster asked.

"Well," Terrell said, making no effort to mask the sarcasm in his voice. "Last time I checked, shooting at people is a crime. And there is the matter of this," he pointed at the splint covering the bridge of his nose. "I can think of about 20 different charges for those guys."

"No one shot at you," Mr. Foster said flatly. "And no one beat you up. You fell in the alleyway when you and Jennifer were leaving and broke your nose."

"What?" Terrell said in disbelief. "I don't think you understand. I saw who shot at me and I certainly remember someone breaking my nose. What do you mean it didn't happen?"

"Think about it Terrell," Mr. Bragg explained. "What happens if our trial strategy turns out to be blaming one of these gang members for the murder?"

Terrell wasn't certain that any of them were actually gang members, but he remained quiet.

"If we report this, it will look like you have some kind of grudge against them because of this incident. Our credibility would be ruined."

"And that's only if we managed to make it to trial," Mr. Foster added. "Karen would love nothing better than to disqualify us from representing Ms. Weston. If you go to the police, you will give her all the ammunition she needs to argue that we have a genuine conflict of interest. I have no intention of allowing Judge Keller to remove us as counsel. So, as I said, no one shot at you."

Terrell was livid. He knew that Mr. Foster and Mr. Bragg could talk all they wanted to about conflicts of interest and loss of credibility, but he knew better. What they were afraid of was losing the huge fee that this case was generating for the firm.

"What if they come and ask me about it?" Terrell asked. "I can't lie."

"They won't ask," Mr. Bragg assured. "No one else saw a shooting."

"What about the car? The back window has been shot to pieces."

"No it hasn't," Mr. Foster said calmly. Terrell turned his head and looked through the window at the driveway. The glass had already been replaced, and there was a truck from a auto body shop repairing the bullet holes as they spoke.

"What about the driver? He was there too."

"He didn't see any shooting either, and neither did Ms. Weston," Mr. Foster answered. Terrell didn't bother asking any more questions. He was certain that the two of them had tied up all the loose ends.

"How long are you going to look like that?" Mr. Foster asked, pointing at his face.

"I can take the brace off anytime I want, it's just for protection. The doctor told me the swelling won't go down for a about a week though."

"Stay inside until it does. We don't want anyone getting any pictures of you looking like that."

They dismissed Terrell and started arguing about how to best spin the incident to their advantage. Terrell was glad for the break. He was exhausted, and this was his chance to grab a couple hours of sleep before they figured out something else for him to do. He walked down to his room and began stripping off the remnants of his tuxedo. He pulled his new cell phone out of the jacket pocket and saw that the message light was flashing. He had turned the phone off when he went inside for the awards. He flipped open the screen and saw that he had missed seven calls from Mr. Bragg, two from Alicia and one from Wesley. He decided to call Wesley first.

"What do you want?" Wesley answered after a couple of rings.

"I don't know, I'm calling you back," Terrell responded.

"Oh yeah," he said cheerily. "I saw you on TV last night. What are you, some kind of music producer now?"

"It's a long story," Terrell said.

"I heard there was a little scrap backstage," Wesley probed.

"Not really," Terrell said noncommittally. "It's blown way out of proportion." The thing he hated most about working on this case was the way that people tried to worm information out of him. "Do you have something for me?"

"Yeah, your analysis is done."

"It's about time. You told me it would only take a week."

"I know, but I had some other stuff to do. It was a little trickier than I thought. Are you sick or something? You sound funny."

"I've got a stuffy nose," Terrell lied. "Just tell me what was in the cup," he said again.

"Okay. I found what most people would expect to find in a glass found in a nightclub. There was a concentration of alcohol, citric acid, sucrose, fructose and several very complex compounds that I determined to be herb and berry derivatives." Wesley was good at his job and he seemed pleased with his results.

"So, it was some kind of poison?" Terrell asked.

"I don't think so. Based on the concentrations I found, I would guess that it was lemon juice, vermouth and gin. Those three things mixed together make martini's."

"Oh," Terrell said dejected. "Is that all?"

"I wouldn't say that was all," Wesley said slyly. "There was something else in the mix, but it had degraded. So I turned my attention to the little speck on the stirrer." He paused to build tension.

"And?" Terrell asked impatiently.

"It turned out to be Flunitrazepam."

"Flu what?"

"Flunitrazepam, it's a benzodiazepine."

"English words only please," Terrell said.

"The layman, such as yourself," Wesley chided, "may know Flunitrazepam by its more common moniker, Rohypnol." Wesley's tone indicated that he expected this term to have some meaning for Terrell, but it did not.

"I still don't know what you're talking about," Terrell answered.

"Boy, they don't teach you lawyers anything about the real world," Wesley complained. "The date rape drug? Does that ring any bells?" Wesley slipped into the condescending tone that he used with his students. "Rohypnol, or Roofies as it's commonly known, is a very potent tranquilizer. It's similar in nature to Diazepam."

"English, English, I told you to speak English!" Terrell complained.

"Sorry," Wesley sighed. "I'll talk slower. It's like Valium except it's a whole lot stronger. The drug produces a strong sedative effect. It starts by causing muscle relaxation and a slowing of psychomotor responses. Sedation occurs 20-30 minutes after administration and lasts for a few hours."

"So it makes you pass out?" Terrell questioned.

"Not exactly," Wesley answered. "That's what makes it so useful to would be date rapists. If I gave you some Flunitrazepam, you would appear to be very drunk. You might have slurred speech or the inability to walk, that kind of thing. Most people would just think you were smashed."

"Anything else?"

"It often produces amnesia. That's why it's so common in date rapes. Most people don't remember what happened to them after they take it."

"How do you know so much about it?" Terrell asked.

"I don't," Wesley confessed. "I had one of my students research it for extra credit. I'm reading all this off his report."

"You didn't tell him where it came from did you?" Terrell asked alarmed.

"Of course I didn't. What am I, an idiot?" he replied crossly. "I just told him to find out what Flunitrazepam did for 20 extra credit points."

"Sorry," Terrell apologized. "I didn't mean to make it sound like that. Thanks, I appreciate the help."

"Any time," he responded. "I noticed something else too. This sample is kinda strange."

"How so?"

"Typically, stock chemical compounds like Flunitrazepam have the same dosage ratios. Two samples of the same drug should be identical. There might be small fluctuations between batches, but variation in this sample versus its common dosage is statistically significant."

"What does that mean?" Terrell asked.

"I'm not a pathologist, but I'd guess this was made for a specific person of a particular gender, height and weight. Whoever made this would have put their target down for a very specific amount of time using this."

"Really?" Terrell asked.

"Yeah," Wesley replied. "It's not all that different than what anesthesiologists do when they prep people for surgery." Terrell's mind raced with possibilities.

"Now it's your turn," Wesley said.

"My turn to what?"

"To answer questions, and I've got one for you. Have you been holding out on me?"

"What do you mean," Terrell asked, confused. "Holding out on what?"

"You know what I mean," he answered. "I saw you and your girl on the red carpet."

"What are you getting at?" Terrell asked suspiciously.

"You're hooking up with her, aren't you?"

"No," Terrell sighed. Wesley always thought the worst.

"Don't lie to me," Wesley prodded. "I would do it. No one would blame you for it."

"It's not like that and it's never going to be like that."

"Whatever, I saw you on TV."

"TV has a slant," Terrell answered.

"I'm sure it does, but most people only dream about an opportunity like this. Shacked up with a beautiful celebrity? You'd be a fool not to at least be trying."

"I'm really not interested."

"So you say."

"I'm not."

"Okay then, have you told Alicia that she's living there with you?"

"Ahh… No, it hasn't really come up in conversation."

"Is that a fact?" Wesley chided. "I wonder why would you neglect to mention that?"

"I didn't neglect to mention it, it just hasn't come up yet. I was going to say something the next time I talked to her."

"Sure you were," Wesley said smugly.

"Nothing's going to happen," Terrell answered.

"That's the same thing you said about Alicia before you two hooked up."

"It's not the same thing. I love Alicia."

"Love doesn't have anything to do with this. Celebrities are like free passes when it comes to cheating. I don't even see how Alicia could be mad at you. Hell, if you had a kid with her, she'd have to pay you child support. You and Alicia would be on easy street for the rest of your life. Don't think of it as cheating, think of it as an investment."

Terrell heard a knock on his bedroom door. He walked over, expecting Mr. Bragg to be there ready to give him another assignment. He was surprised when he opened the door and saw Jennifer.

"Hi," she said meekly. "I just wanted to make sure you were okay."

"I gotta go," Terrell said into the phone.

"Why?" Wesley asked. "Who is that? It's her isn't it? I knew it! I knew it! Put her on the phone!"

"Thank you sir, but I'm not interested in saving 40% on my phone bill right now," Terrell said calmly.

"What are you talking about?" Wesley shouted. "Don't do me like this, let me talk to her!"

"You have a good day too sir," Terrell smiled. "Good-bye." He ended the call and tossed the phone on his unmade bed.

She surveyed the damage to his face and cringed.

"I'm sorry about this," she said. "It's all my fault."

"Don't be silly," Terrell comforted. "I'll be alright, I get into fights all the time."

"You do?"

"Well, I have ever since I got this case anyway," he smiled, even though doing so made his nose ache. "I'm sure I'll get used to it." Terrell looked over and caught a glimpse of his face in the dresser mirror. The dark circles around his eyes were even blacker than before.

"Wow," he said aloud. "Trust me, it looks worse than it is."

She nodded, seemingly reassured by his comments.

"How's Luther?"

"He's got a broken hand and a separated shoulder," she answered. Luther had arrived in the emergency room only minutes after Terrell.

"I told him to take some time off," she continued, "but he won't leave."

"I know the feeling," Terrell smiled. "Let me ask you something, you told me that sometimes you drink martinis."

"Yeah, sometimes. Why?"

"When I found your charm, it was near an overturned martini glass. I had some people analyze what was in it. I think maybe you were drugged, and that's why you don't remember anything."

"How do you know that it was my glass?" she asked.

"I don't. At least, I don't in any way that I could prove in court. However, it would explain why you don't remember what happened after you went to the club. What I really need to find is someone that was there with you. We have to find someone that can tell us what happened that night. Can you think of anybody at all?"

"Most of the people that were with us were there with Felix. I don't think any of them will want to help me."

"There has to be someone that would talk to us."

"Well, maybe," Jennifer said thoughtfully. "If anybody would help, it might be Clarence."

"Who's Clarence?" Terrell asked. The name was familiar, but he couldn't place it.

"He's Felix's road manager. They've been friends since they were kids."

"Why do you think he would talk to us?"

"He's been calling me."

"Since when?"

"Since all this started. I ignored his messages at first because I thought he was just going to say something nasty like everyone else. But he left me another message last night. He apologized for what happened at the awards show and asked how I was doing."

"How well do you know him?" Terrell asked.

"Pretty well. He was always around with Felix," she answered, "He didn't talk much to me. He just kind of hung around in the background."

"Do you think he would try to burn you?" Terrell asked. Jennifer had received several calls from distant relatives and acquaintances fishing for information that they could sell to the tabloids.

"I don't think so. He sounded like he really cared. I was going to ask if was okay to talk to him."

"Yes," Terrell replied thoughtfully. "I think that talking to him might be a really good idea."

CHAPTER 11

Terrell learned many things about Clarence Ferguson prior to meeting him. He knew that Clarence was a chubby man with a small puffy Afro and skin pockmarked by childhood acne. He knew Clarence and Optimus grew up together in the McCovey housing project in Brooklyn. He knew that Clarence had no discernable talent of his own, so he'd kept himself busy as Optimus' road manager. He knew that Clarence had a raspy smoker's voice. He also knew that Clarence was never at home between the hours of nine at night and six in the morning. Further, he knew that Clarence called Jennifer at least three times a week. He continued to call despite the fact that he was never successful in reaching her. Terrell knew all these things because every phone message that Clarence made to Jennifer had been recorded and saved for review. Terrell had listened to the awkward tapes ad nauseam for over week.

After painfully analyzing every word, statement and pause in the messages, they decided that Clarence was someone the firm could use. Consequentially, Mr. Bragg sent Joe and Terrell to New York City to pick Clarence's brain for any useful information. As Terrell sat in Clarence's small apartment, he couldn't help feeling a little bit phony. Terrell wore a white polo shirt from Optimus' clothing line, jeans and white sneakers. He wore these things instead of a suit, not because he wanted to, but because Mr. Bragg thought that it would make Clarence more comfortable with his appearance.

Terrell thought it was trite and flatly refused when they asked him to wear a rented diamond necklace for the meeting. The swelling in his nose had subsided and the dark circles had disappeared from around his eyes. His nose was still extremely sore, but he wasn't going out in public with the brace. It was embarrassing.

Cold rain pelted the window of the apartment, making a constant rapping sound. Joe had remained in the car and Terrell had been making small talk on the couch for about twenty minutes. He thought that it was time to move the conversation into a more productive mode.

"You want anything to sip on?" Clarence asked. He poured a dark liquid into his cup from a crystal decanter. "I got that fire over here."

"Nah, I'm alright," Terrell answered. He glanced at his watch and saw that it was only a quarter past noon. "I just wondered if you could tell me anything about what happened at the club before Optimus and Jennifer left. You were there, weren't you?"

"Yeah, I was there," Clarence answered as he took a sip of his drink. "You sure you don't want anything?" He looked like a person that hadn't ever turned down a drink himself.

"Yeah, I'm sure," Terrell answered. "When I leave here, I've got a few other people to interview about that night." It was a lie, but was important to make Clarence think he wasn't their only source of information. He would likely be more truthful if he thought they could check up on his answers.

"So what are you, like a detective or something?"

"No, I told you, I'm one of Jennifer's lawyers."

"Yeah, I know what you said, but you look like you're the same age as me. I thought you had to be old to be a lawyer."

"Not really."

"You must be one of them smarty-art dudes then?"

"I do alright for myself," Terrell answered.

"Yeah, you are one of those smarty-art dudes. I can tell by the way that you talk. You say all the letters in the words."

Terrell couldn't help but wonder what kind of people Clarence hung around if pronouncing all the letters in words meant that you were smart.

"You know," Clarence continued, "I'm pretty smart, do you think I could be a lawyer too?"

"Sure, I don't see why not." He tried to force the conversation back to Jennifer. "When did you arrive at the club?"

"What club?"

"Millennium." Terrell pulled a legal pad out of his briefcase to take notes.

"I don't know," Clarence answered. "It was after the show, so I'm guessing it was somewhere around midnight, maybe one. You know what man? I've been looking at you since you got here. Where do I know you from man?"

Terrell was surprised the Clarence remembered his face. He met Clarence at the same time he met Optimus.

"You must have me mistaken for someone else," Terrell responded. "I was on television a couple of weeks ago during Jennifer's arraignment. You probably remember me from that."

"Maybe," he answered.

"Did you ride to the club with Optimus and Jennifer?" Terrell asked.

"Yeah, I drove the truck. I always drive when it's the two of them. They ride in the back where the tint is darkest."

"Who told you to go to Millennium?" Terrell questioned.

"I don't remember, probably O."

"Why did you have to drive, was Optimus drunk?"

"I dunno, maybe. But that's not why I drove. O didn't have a driver's license."

"Anybody else ride with you?"

"No, that was their alone time. J always complained that she never got to talk to him without fifty-eleven people around. So whenever possible, they rode alone."

"You're the road manager, right?" Terrell asked.

"Yeah."

"You didn't make vehicle arrangements for anyone else except Optimus and Jennifer?"

"For who? Those Armada dudes? Hell no. They get to ride on the tour bus from city to city. In between that, they're on their own."

"Anybody else meet you there?"

"Not really," Clarence answered. "I mean, except for a couple of hos."

"Prostitutes?" Terrell questioned.

"Not real hos, if that's what you're asking. At least, I don't think they were. I guess I should say groupies. The squad never travels anywhere with out a nice stable of them."

"You know any of their names?"

"I wasn't trying to find out their names," Clarence smiled. "I like it better when I don't know. Usually they're waiting for us when we get there. I think the club takes care of it."

"How many girls are you talking about?" Terrell asked.

"I don't know, 10 or 15 maybe."

"What about Opal Rodgers? Were she there?"

Clarence laughed as if Terrell had said something ridiculous. "Nah man, she's way too good to hang with grimy dudes like us. Besides, Opal hates Jennifer."

"What do you mean she hates her?" Terrell asked. "Jennifer says that they're close."

"That's because J can be stupid sometimes."

"Really?"

"Not stupid, but... J doesn't live in the real world. Money changes things between people. That's all I'm saying. Keep your friends close and all that, know what I mean?"

"Why?"

"You can't tell with broads. They hate because they can."

"What does she have to hate?" Terrell asked. "Fantasy is one of the biggest groups ever."

"Maybe so, but J's the star. J's the one that gets all the magazine covers. J's the one that gets the movie deals. J's the one that they always want to interview. Hell, Opal knows that J could replace her with any chick in a short skirt and no one would even notice."

"And you're telling me that Jennifer is clueless about Opal feeling this way?" Terrell asked.

"Am I speaking Chinese? Check it, you know Opal put out a solo album last year right?"

"No, I didn't know that," Terrell answered.

"Exactly. No one knew about it because it was garbage. I don't think it sold fifty copies."

"That's not Jennifer's fault," Terrell said.

"I know that, but she doesn't. Jealousy makes you stupid. Opal's album wouldn't have even come out if J didn't go to the label and strong-arm them into releasing it. I guess that just let Opal know that she wasn't as big a star as she thought she was."

Terrell made a quick notation on his legal pad to explore the relationship between Opal and Jennifer.

"Do you think Opal would do something like this to get back at Jennifer?"

"Do something like what?"

"Kill Optimus."

"Are you smoking crack? Why would she do that? No J means no Fantasy and no Fantasy means no cash in her pocket. Besides, everybody knows J did it."

"Why do you say that?" Terrell asked, suddenly worried. Clarence had been the only person thus far that they thought might speak on Jennifer's behalf.

"Because," he paused, "I mean, well, everybody knows how it was between her and O."

"I don't know how it was," Terrell answered.

Clarence squirmed uncomfortably in his seat.

"Look man, if you know something about what happened, you need to tell me. That's the only way I'm going to be able to help Jennifer."

Clarence finished his drink before getting up and pouring another.

"I'm not going to say that O deserved it, because he was my man," Clarence said. "I mean, I'd like to help J, I really would. But she didn't have to do him like that. I heard she stabbed him like 50 times and then cut his throat. That's cold-blooded."

"Why would you think that he deserved it?"

"I don't think he deserved it."

"That's not what you said," Terrell retorted. "What you said was that you weren't going to say he deserved it. What was it? Did he hit her?"

"Look man, it ain't as simple as all that. You wouldn't understand."

"Try me."

"Fine. If you're asking me if he ever hit her, then yeah, he hit her. But, I've seen her hit him way more times than him hitting her."

"What?"

"I like J, I do. She was good for O, be she has all you guys fooled. She ain't delicate like you think she is."

Clarence drained the rest of his drink before continuing, "I'm not testifying to any of this. It's just between you and me, right?"

"Sure," Terrell lied. If the information was good enough, he was certain that the firm would be able to exert enough pressure to make him to take the stand.

"O was my man and I wouldn't normally put him on blast like this, but I understand why J acted like she did."

"What do you mean?"

"It was a lot of little things, but you have to understand their relationship. They were usually good, but when they weren't, they were real bad. They were always together, like cops and donuts. Remember how I was telling you about all the groupies?"

"Yeah," Terrell answered as he jotted down notes.

"J loved O, don't even get that twisted, but he was a man. Every once in awhile, a groupie would catch is eye."

Terrell nodded.

"That's just how it is on the road." Clarence paused momentarily as he thought. "You know what I'm talking about. You're making good paper doing your lawyer thing I bet. You know how easy it is."

"So he had other girls?" Terrell asked.

"Nah," Clarence smiled. "If he thought they were catching feelings for him, he was out. It was strictly hit it and quit it."

"All the women he met on the road were like that?" Terrell asked.

"I won't say all of them were like that. It's just that, nice girls don't push their way up to the front of the line, know what I mean? It didn't even matter if J was with him, these scandalous women would make a play for him anyway."

"Right there in front of her?" Terrell asked.

"Pretty much. He wasn't going to do anything if she was around, but he liked the attention."

"But if she wasn't there," Terrell added.

"No wife? Anything could happen in a night."

"And Jennifer knew about it?" Terrell had difficulty believing that the Jennifer he met would put up with something like that.

"She had to know. I mean, everybody knew."

"Did she ever say anything to you about it?"

"She didn't have to say anything," he answered.

"Why not?"

"I feel like I'm snitchin'," Clarence confessed. "O did her dirty, but still, she shouldn't have stabbed him like that."

"I don't know that she stabbed him," Terrell said.

"Yeah, whatever," Clarence said. "You don't know her like I do. Check this out. Last year we were out partying after a Knicks game. J called and said she would meet us afterward. It was like the only time they didn't ride together. Anyway, we were all going to some club in Manhattan. I forget which one."

Terrell scribbled furiously as he tried to keep the details straight.

"We get to the club and I walk inside, but J is already there. O is supposed to be right behind us, but he never makes it inside. J waits with me for a couple of minutes and then she goes back outside to find out where he went. They both came back in a little while later. Both of them are all scuffed up. Her elbow is bleeding and she's walking funny. O's cheek is all red and his lip is busted open. They get inside and pretend like nothing happened for the rest of the night."

"What happened?"

"My man tells me a few day later that he has this little freak in the car with him. That's why he didn't want J to come. He was in there getting it and J opened the door."

"Jennifer and the girl fought," Terrell said.

"No fool, she fought him. O said he got out of the car and J bowed up on him like a man. He said J got him twice in the grill, closed fist, like she wasn't playing."

"Really?"

"O said he had to give her a couple of shots to stomach and the ribs just to get her to stop."

Terrell stared at him.

"Hey, you asked."

"I know," Terrell said. "I'm just surprised. They just went at it in the parking lot?"

"That time it was the parking lot," Clarence answered. "It didn't really matter where though. Parking lot, apartment, club VIP room, every few months it was the same thing. She'd catch him cheating, they would fight and then they'd be back together like it never happened. They were on some real Ike and Tina mess."

"Whoa."

"Yeah, that night was the worst though. They came inside and everyone could see she was still mad and he was smiling about the whole thing. I'll never forget it. She looked at him and said that if he ever embarrassed her like that again, she'd kill him. I never thought she'd really do it."

"How many people heard her say that?"

"Six or seven I guess. I took her home. O just laughed at her while we walked out. I think I heard him say something like, 'she's mad now, but tonight, she'll love me again'. He didn't seem too worried about it, so neither was I."

Terrell cursed under his breath. Things just continued to get worse. In addition to providing a motive for murder, Clarence had also been kind enough to point out that Jennifer could be physically violent and had threatened to kill Optimus.

"Did something like that happen in Miami?" Terrell asked, praying that it had not.

"I don't know, I wasn't watching them all night. I guess it could have, but I didn't see it. I was concentrating on other things. There was plenty of scattered tail all around that place."

"Did you leave with them?"

"No, I hooked up with this light skinned broad that night. I took her back to the hotel."

"The same one where Jennifer and Optimus stayed?"

"Yeah, they had a suite on the same floor as me, but I think they left the club before I did."

"Did you hear anything strange later on?"

"Well," Clarence smiled, "I wouldn't say strange."

"From their room," Terrell clarified. "Did you hear anything strange coming out of their room?"

"I vaguely remember hearing someone shouting, but I couldn't tell you what room that was coming out of. Maybe they were fighting. I don't know. I was drunk by then."

"Do you have any idea how I could get in touch with the girl?" Terrell asked.

"Who? The chick I was with?" Clarence chuckled. "I told

you, I don't take names. It was Crystal or Chrissy or something like that. I haven't seen her since then."

Terrell sighed. The information that Clarence was providing hurt far more than it helped. Jealous rage was always an easy way for prosecutors to create a motive.

"Do you know anyone else that might have a reason to hurt Optimus?" Terrell asked.

"No. I told you J did it."

"For someone who seems so certain that she did it, you're pretty eager to help."

"I've always liked J. I think she killed O, but I also think he probably did something to make her do it. The whole situation is messed up."

"What about the rest of Optimus' crew? You think they might want to talk to me about what happened?" Terrell asked.

"Those dudes? Nah, I'd stay away from them if I were you. They protected O like he was a lotto ticket. I guess in their eyes he was. Those dudes are crazy. Did you know those fools were busting shots backstage at the Music Awards?"

Terrell had seen it up close and personal, but he shook his head anyway.

"Well, they will put slugs in J's chest if they see her anywhere. She screwed up their whole game."

"What do you mean?"

"All of those dudes gravy-trained off of O's leftovers. If O went to the mall and bought shoes, they all got shoes. If O got lap dances at the strip club, they all got lap dances. If O got a bag of hydro, they all got bags of hydro. All that's over now. Those dudes are going back to the street and they know it. They'd like nothing better than to pop J on their way back to the gutter."

"That's just great," Terrell muttered to himself.

"Sorry I couldn't be more help," Clarence said.

"It's alright," Terrell answered. He paused for a moment before continuing. "You said that you went to the club with Optimus and Jennifer, but you didn't see them leave."

"That's right."

"How'd you get back to the hotel?"

"A cab. Me and the shorty took cab back to my room."

"What time did you end up leaving?"

"I don't know, maybe four or five. The club was starting to empty. I didn't see them around, so I figured that they had already left."

"Thanks man," Terrell said as he rose from the couch. "I appreciate you taking the time to talk to me about this."

"No problem," Clarence answered. "Hey, tell J to give me a call alright?"

Terrell nodded affirmatively as he moved toward the exit. He opened the door, stepped outside, and was shocked to see Joe resting against the wall in the cramped hallway. Terrell closed the door behind him.

"What are you doing up here?" he asked Joe curiously. "I thought you were going to wait in the car?"

"I needed to hear what that guy had to say," Joe answered. He reached up and removed a small device attached to the back of his ear. It was linked to a small tape recorder on his belt.

"How could you possibly hear what we said all the way out here?"

"Penetrating microphone," Joe answered as he held up his hand. Terrell saw a small circular microphone taped to Joe's palm. "The walls in this place are thin enough for me to hear everything that you said."

"What'd you think?" Terrell asked. Joe shrugged as they walked to the rental car through the rain.

"Come on, tell me," Terrell said as he got into the passenger seat. "You might have picked up on something that I missed."

"I'm certain that I did pick up on something you missed," he said in a superior tone.

Terrell folded his arms and scowled out the window, thinking to himself that Joe was a jackass.

"Do you think he told you anything useful?" Joe said suddenly.

"Ahh… No, not really," Terrell answered. "Most of the stuff he said hurt our case.

"And you don't think that's useful?"

"I didn't until now," Terrell replied.

"You should ask yourself why someone that's been friends with the victim since childhood be so eager to talk to the defense lawyer?"

"Maybe he likes Jennifer?"

"I'm sure he does, but that's not the point."

"I did seem kind of weird that he volunteered so much information about Optimus and Jennifer's private relationship. I didn't even have to prod him much."

"I agree. He sounded rehearsed to me. He's hiding something."

"Something like what?"

"I don't know yet, but I'm sure I'll get to the bottom of it."

CHAPTER 12

The plane touched down in Miami just after five in the afternoon, but Terrell knew that his evening's work was just beginning. Terrell didn't recognize any of the streets they traveled on, but since Joe always drove a different route to the firm's house, him didn't think too much about it. Then Joe entered in a run down section of North Miami. Terrell saw a small sign that read, 'Hope House – A Community of Second Chances' marking a cracked cement driveway just off the main road. The building itself was down the short path, nestled in between a run down strip mall and an abandoned auto dealership.

Terrell wondered why Joe made this detour, but he had long since given up trying to figure out Joe's motivations. The Hope House had freshly painted white walls and a well manicured front yard. It was strangely out of place among its dilapidated surroundings. A shirtless middle-aged man in khaki pants busied himself in a flowerbed. Joe parked the car behind an old truck.

"Is this going to take a long time?" Terrell asked. "Mr. Bragg and Mr. Foster are waiting for our report back at the house."

"It will take as long as it takes," Joe said brusquely as he opened his door.

"Well, if you're not going to be long, I'd just as soon stay in the car. I'll go over my notes."

"Get out and come with me," Joe commanded. Terrell thought about refusing but his hand instinctively went up to his chest. It could have been his imagination, but he still remembered the wind rushing out of his lungs every time he thought about the last time he challenged Joe. They walked up to the man working in the flowerbed and Joe tapped him on the shoulder. The man turned his head and his eyes went wide in shock. He looked familiar, but Terrell couldn't place his face. The man gasped and tried to stand up too quickly. He tripped over his own feet and sprawled backward into the fresh dirt.

"Why do you keep messing with me man?" he asked. "I'm not bothering anybody."

"Because I can. Now get up." Joe replied.

"But I swear I haven't done anything!" the man exclaimed as he brushed the soil from his pants. It suddenly dawned on Terrell that this was the homeless man they encountered outside of Club Millennium. His sunken eyes had filled out and he had shaved his scraggly beard. A healthy glow had returned to his scrubbed face and he looked much better than the last time Terrell saw him.

"I'm just here to check on you Henry," Joe said. His tone was quiet, yet menacing. "How's it going for you?"

"Ah… okay I guess," Henry replied. "The guy here, Mr. Benjamin is real nice. He helped me out and got me off the street."

"Are you working?" Joe asked.

"A little," Henry answered. "They have us doing landscaping most days. If there's not much work, we do projects around the house here."

"Clean?"

"And sober since I got here," Henry answered confidently.

Joe glared at Henry, quickly melting Henry's façade.

"Alright, alright. Me and this other guy Willie snuck a couple of beers last week. We finished early, but I swear we did a good job. And we didn't get drunk. We just had a couple apiece."

"You wouldn't be lying to me, would you?" Joe questioned. "You know how I hate it when you lie."

"No sir, I wouldn't lie to you sir," Henry said quickly.

"Excellent," Joe said. "I'd hate for our reunion to become unpleasant."

"No sir," Henry added. "You won't have any trouble out of me sir."

"Good. I have a question for you Henry. Take a look at this photo and tell me if you've seen this man before." Joe pulled a small snapshot out of his jacket pocket and shoved under Henry's nose. Terrell glanced at it and saw that it was a picture of Clarence.

Henry's brow furrowed in concentration as he stared at the picture.

"Yeah," he said thoughtfully. "I have seen this fella before."

"Where?" Terrell interrupted.

"Outside the bar. This was the other guy I told you about. This is the fat guy that helped carry that drunk gal to the car."

"Are you certain?" Joe asked calmly. "You weren't high or anything were you?"

"No I wasn't," Henry answered indignantly. "I don't get high, I just drink."

"Fine," Joe replied, "Then were you drunk?"

"No, I was sober. I hadn't found any bottles yet."

"And you're sure that this is the guy?" Terrell asked.

"Yeah."

"How can you be sure?" Joe asked in a patronizing tone. "Your brain is probably Swiss cheese by now."

"I'm not crazy!" Henry said angrily. "And I'm not a retard either! This is the guy!"

"Okay, okay, take it easy," Joe said as he stepped closer to Henry. "I just wanted to be sure."

"I know this is the guy," Henry said as his anger subsided.

"Because I remember all the scars on his face. My kid brother had bad acne when he was a kid and his face is like this too. That's what I thought when I saw him."

"Did he get in the car with the other two?" Joe asked.

"Yeah, they tossed the girl in the back seat and then left."

"All three of them together?" Terrell stressed.

"Yeah. I think this one was driving."

"But you still don't remember what kind of car it was?" Terrell asked.

"No. It was dark and I wasn't really looking."

"You were looking," Joe interrupted. "You just weren't paying attention to the car. What did you see?"

Henry looked sheepish, but admitted, "I was watching her. She had a short skirt on and they weren't being careful when they put her in the back seat. I don't want you guys to think I'm some kind of perv, but it's not like a guy like me sees that everyday."

"At least he's being honest," Terrell shrugged.

"Okay Henry," Joe said in his most friendly voice. "Stay out of trouble. I'll be watching." Joe turned to leave without saying goodbye.

"Hey!" Henry called after him. "You're not going to tell Mr. Benjamin about the beer are you? They might kick me out and I really need this."

"You probably should have thought about that before you decided to sneak some beer like a couple of teenagers. I don't know what I'm going to do, keep your nose clean."

Terrell followed Joe back to the car.

"How did you know he was here?" Terrell asked as Joe began backing the car out of the driveway.

"Don't be stupid," Joe answered callously. "I put him here. I know Roger Benjamin. He runs this halfway house so I stashed Henry here."

"That's a very decent thing for you to have done," Terrell said surprised. "It seems kinda out of your character. I figured you'd just keep beating on him whenever you needed to talk to him."

"I am not interested in his personal welfare, if that's what you're saying," Joe responded. "And I certainly would smash his face in if I thought it'd be helpful to my investigation. But how else can I keep track of a bum? Roger tells me where he is, what he's doing and keeps him clean so that I can use him. Your firm pays for him to be here."

"Oh," Terrell replied. "Now that seems more in line with something you'd do. Too bad he's such an unreliable witness."

"He's not as bad as you think. He suffers from depression. He started self-medicating with alcohol a couple of years ago. Like all bums, he lost his job, his family, all that. I'll make sure he's sober enough if he has to take the stand."

"How do you know so much about him?"

"It's my job to know everything," Joe replied.

"Do you think he really saw Clarence outside, or was he just making it up to please us?"

"I don't have any doubt that he saw Clarence."

"But why would Clarence lie about it?"

"Don't know," Joe answered. "Could be a lot of reasons. Maybe he doesn't want to be a witness out of loyalty to his friend. Or, maybe he was too drunk to remember what he did. Or, most likely, he's the one that slipped the drugs in Ms. Weston's drink."

Terrell's eyes widened in shock. He hadn't told anyone about the results of the test that Wesley did for him.

"How did you know about that?" he demanded.

"I already told you, they pay me to know everything." Joe's superior tone was increasingly frustrating for Terrell.

"I'm serious, how did you find out about that?"

"When I asked you what you found at the club, I knew you weren't telling the truth, so I put a bug in your phone. I listened to your friend give you the lab results. It was very easy."

"You're not supposed to set up phone taps without my knowledge!" Terrell screamed. His pulse quickened and he felt a hot burst of sweat break out over his body.

"You not supposed to remove evidence from a crime scene." Joe said calmly. "But you did it anyway. So I guess we're both bad boys."

"Stop patronizing me! I'm sick and tired of you and your wild cowboy act. I hope you know it's a federal offense to unlawfully wiretap a phone."

"Why don't you turn me in then," Joe said calmly. "I'll be sure to inform the bar about your hiding exculpatory evidence from your client and your bosses. Then I'll let the sheriff's department know you're tampering with crime scenes. I'll be off probation long before you get out of prison."

"I didn't hide anything. I told Jennifer about it. I just haven't figured out how we can use it without some other proof. I wasn't... I mean I was going to tell Mr. Bragg and Mr. Foster as soon as I had a good theory put together."

"I'm sure you were," Joe answered. "Just as soon as you figured out a way to make it look like you cracked the case open all by yourself. It still looks bad. I can make it look worse."

Terrell crossed his arms and stared out the window.

"Look, I respect what you did. You had a hunch and you played it. It's the same thing I would do in that situation."

"That still doesn't give you the right to listen to my phone calls."

"It gives me the right to do whatever I damn well please. I'll do whatever's necessary to get the result I want. If you want me out of your business, then don't make it necessary for me to get in it. Understand?"

Terrell steamed silently.

"Stop pouting," Joe said. "It's unbecoming for a man. Don't worry; I only used what I needed. Trust me, I'm not interested in your conversations with your girlfriend."

"You taped that too!" Terrell exclaimed.

"I taped everything."

"Give me those tapes! I want them right now." Terrell had

never felt so violated in his life. He shuddered as he imagined Joe listening to his intimate conversations with Alicia.

"No. I don't think I'll be doing that. It's always a good idea to keep embarrassing information, you never know when you might need it."

"Give them back or I'll…"

"You'll what?" Joe barked. "You'll get really mad? I'll give you a little bit of advice. Don't make empty threats. You will ruin your credibility. So sit back and shut up."

Just then, Terrell's cell phone began ringing. He was sure that it was Mr. Foster calling to complain about their tardiness. When he glanced at the screen he was surprised to see Alicia's name."

"Hello," Terrell said, anger still clinging to his words.

"Hi babe," she said cheerfully. "What are you doing?"

Terrell scowled at Joe while he wondered whether some machine was recording this call too.

"Nothing much," he said curtly. "I just flew back from New York. I'm in the car on the way back to the house."

"Your house?" she asked hopefully.

"No," he said flatly. "The firm's house in Miami."

"What were you doing up in New York?"

"I had to interview a witness. What do you want?"

"What do I want?" she asked. "Since when did you start thinking that you could talk to me like that?"

"Sorry," Terrell sighed. "That's not how I meant to say it."

"You better be sorry," Alicia said. "I didn't wake up this early just to fight with you."

"I know, sorry. It's been a long day."

"I had a long day too. You'd know that if you ever bothered to call me."

Terrell imagined that he could hear the soft whine of recording equipment.

"Well, as you can hear, I'm still alive," he said in an exasperated voice.

"I don't know what crawled up your butt, but you should pull it out before I reach through this phone and smack you."

"Okay, okay," Terrell replied. "I'm sorry. It hasn't been a good day."

"Really? Well maybe I can fix that. Guess what?" she asked.

"What?"

"I'm coming to see you!" she shouted in the phone. "I can get a flight to Miami next weekend. I'll get there Friday and leave on Monday."

"You can? Is this really a good time for you to come? I know that you've got a lot to do over there."

"You know, I expected to hear more happiness in your voice," she answered.

"I am happy," Terrell stressed. "I just thought that…"

"I'm only missing two days. What are they going to do, fire me? I'm between projects right now anyway. I'll be back before they even know I'm gone."

"Where are you going to stay" Terrell asked.

"Where am I going to stay?" she asked rhetorically. "Duh, with you."

"Yeah, but you can't," Terrell explained. He still hadn't gotten around to telling Alicia that Jennifer was staying in the house too. "Mr. Foster would have a conniption if he caught you there."

"Alright," she said nonplussed. "I'll just get a hotel room. Maybe we could stay at that place we were in last time. You know the one with the Jacuzzi on the balcony?"

"I remember," he answered. The thought was very tempting.

"I miss snuggling up next to you when I fall asleep. I can't wait to do that," she said.

"Ahh…" Terrell said, "I don't know if I can stay over. I told you they want me to stay at the house."

"But if you don't stay," she purred, "how am I going to…"

"Look, I can't really talk right now," Terrell interrupted. He had no desire to let Joe capture any more private conversations.

"We've got some motions coming up and that means Mr. Foster will have me working a lot."

"Are you trying to tell me that if I fly all the way over there, you're not going to spend any time with me?"

"No, I'm just saying that I'll have to juggle around some things. A lot of times, stuff comes up suddenly and I have to deal with it. Like this trip to New York, I didn't know I was going until yesterday."

"So are you telling me not to come?" she asked.

"No, I'm not saying that. It's just… Look, I gotta go. I've got a meeting with the partners in a minute and we're almost at the house."

"What's the matter?" Alicia asked.

"Nothing," Terrell answered. "I'll just have to call you back."

"Are you sure? You're acting kinda weird."

"I know," he answered quietly, trying to mask his voice from Joe. "It's just… You know what? If they want to fire me for spending some long overdue quality time with my woman, then screw them. We're going to spend the whole weekend together. I'm not working at all."

"I'll believe that when I see it."

"I'm serious. I'm not even going to bring my Blackberry."

"Wow. Are you sure?" she asked. "I don't want you to get in trouble."

"Yeah, I'm sure. I can't wait to see you."

"Okay, Will you have time to pick me up from the airport?"

"Probably not," Terrell laughed, "but I will anyway. I'll have to call you back tonight." Preferably from a non-tapped phone Terrell thought to himself.

"Okay," she replied. "I love you Terrell."

"I love you too," he answered quietly, hoping that Joe didn't hear. Terrell pressed the end button on his phone and smiled. Mr. Bragg did everything in his power to keep Terrell too busy to think about Alicia, but he missed her anyway. At least he'd had the forethought to bring the ring to Miami.

CHAPTER 13

"What is he doing here?" asked Brian Dunn as soon as Terrell and Joe walked inside the conference room. "I thought that I had made it very clear that he was not to be anywhere near this case or Ms. Weston! He almost got her killed for Christ sake!"

"I almost got her killed?" Terrell responded. He hadn't seen Brian since the fiasco at the music awards. "You almost got all of us killed! Have you forgotten who thought that it'd be a great idea to have her do the interview with that idiot? If you had just listened to me none of that would have ever happened!"

The condo's dining room had been transformed into a makeshift conference area. It was refitted with a couple of computer terminals and a wall screen but the huge oak dining table remained. Its bulk was the only thing that kept Terrell from leaping across the table and throttling Brian.

"I'm not the one that disappeared when those goons came backstage. Where the hell did you disappear to anyway? Terrell continued.

"Are you trying to imply that somehow I'm to blame for that mess?" Brian asked.

"Gold star for you," Terrell answered. It was not a good business practice to belittle a client, but Terrell couldn't resist.

"Sit down Terrell," Mr. Bragg calmly interjected. "And be quiet. Brian, I have been practicing law for more than thirty years. And at the risk of sounding pompous, I am a master of a myriad of legal conventions. I am the best trial strategist your money could ever hope to buy. The only advice I will listen to as to who will be a part of my team is my own. I have decided that Mr. Banks will remain on this case. We've looked into the incident, and as far as we can tell, it was a bad set of circumstances and not anyone's fault."

"The hell it isn't," Brian answered as his face became flushed with anger. "That interview was all his idea!" He pointed at Terrell. "I was against it from the start because I knew it'd be trouble. Our artists never talk to that rag. For him to suggest that I was in any way involved with that decision is patently ridiculous. I can't believe his unprofessionalism in trying duck his responsibility to Ms. Weston. It borders on malpractice."

"What!" Terrell shouted in disbelief. "You've got to be kidding me!"

"Earnest, if you think he can help with the case, I'll defer to your judgment. However, at the very least, I think he owes me an apology. To even imply that I would ever put Ms. Weston in the path of harm is careless and negligent and I can't believe that your firm would tolerate half-baked accusations like these from some still wet behind the ears nig…"

Terrell was leaping from his seat before Brian finished the word. A red haze of rage enveloped him and all he could see was using his fists to pound Brian Dunn into the cherry hardwood floor. Luckily, before he could even rise from his seat, a strong hand fell upon his left shoulder and pressed him firmly back into the chair. Joe stood over him, shaking his head from side to side and mouthing the words, "Not worth it."

"That is enough!" Mr. Bragg said abruptly, his usually calm demeanor tossed aside. "I do not care whose fault it was. It's irrelevant. While you are our client and we work on your behalf, I will not tolerate that kind of name-calling. Mr. Banks works for me, so whatever you call him, you call me. It would behoove you to choose your words more carefully in the future."

"New lawyer," Brian quickly backpedaled. "You misunderstand, I was going to say new lawyer."

"Sure you were," Terrell muttered.

"We at AMI records are fully committed to diversity. Not only among our artists, but on our corporate level as well," Brian said as he slid into full damage control mode. "We have executives and vice-presidents representing a wide range of cultures and ethnic backgrounds. We value our differences and I would never say anything to betray those ideals. Frankly, that kind of thing has no place in our company."

"Good," Mr. Bragg responded. "I'm glad that's the company philosophy. It would be rather unfortunate if our firm were to find a civil-rights suit that had anything to do with AMI. That would be costly to everyone and would damage what I feel is a good and productive relationship between AMI and Bragg & Shuttlesworth." Mr. Bragg made his thinly veiled threat while wearing the nicest of expressions.

"Now, I don't tell you how to handle your artists and I don't take kindly to you telling me how to discipline my associates." Mr. Bragg explained. "Terrell is very important to Ms. Weston's defense team. He's spent a lot of long hours on this case and his working knowledge of the law is on par with anyone's. He's going to remain a part of this defense team. Since you're not going anywhere either, it might be a good idea for the two of you to put aside your differences and concentrate on how we can help Ms. Weston. Wouldn't both of you agree?" The tone in which Mr. Bragg said this told Terrell that he expected this to be the last outburst from either of them.

"Yes sir," Terrell said.

"Fine," Brian said. "No hard feelings?" he extended his hand across the table.

Terrell quickly manufactured a cough and covered his mouth. He made sure a fine mist of spittle coated his hand before he reached out and shook Brian's hand. It was a juvenile thing to do, but it made him feel better.

"I'm not going to waste any more of my energy on that issue, do I make myself clear?"

"Yes sir," answered Terrell.

"Good. What did you find out from our friend Clarence?" Mr. Bragg asked.

"Well…" Terrell started.

"Nothing useful," Joe interrupted.

"Nothing at all?" Mr. Foster asked. "We sent you all the way to New York and he didn't have anything to say?"

"He told us that…" Terrell started to answer, but Joe interrupted him again.

"He said lots," Joe continued. "None of it was helpful. He told us that he was with Ms. Weston that night and that he remembers her being at that nightclub, but he didn't see her leave or who she left with."

"Did he see Ms. Weston or Mr. Caldwell get into a fight or argument with anyone?" It was still odd for Terrell to hear Optimus referred to as Mr. Caldwell.

"No," Joe answered. "Clarence was far too interested in pursuing his own pleasures to watch what other people were doing."

Terrell wondered why Joe wasn't saying anything about their conversation with Henry the bum. Seeing Clarence carry Jennifer from the club seemed to be a very important detail, but Joe wasn't mentioning it.

"Can we at least put him on the list of potential character witnesses?"

"I wouldn't," Joe answered. "He comes across as very sleazy. Besides, he has convictions on his record for marijuana distribution and gun possession. I don't think we'll be able to use him at all."

"I was hoping that we'd get something out of him," Mr. Bragg said.

"I'm still checking out a few other leads," Joe explained. "Nothing concrete, but you'll know something as soon as I do." Joe didn't wait to be dismissed. He simply turned around walked out.

"What about you Terrell? Did you pick up anything useful from this guy?" Mr. Foster asked. Terrell briefly thought about telling them about their conversation with Henry, but decided against it. Joe must have had a reason not to say anything.

"No," Terrell answered. "I agree with Joe. Clarence the second slimiest guy I've ever met," Terrell paused and purposefully looked at Brian. "I think we'll be much better off just leaving him out of it."

"Alright then," Mr. Bragg said. "Brian was just telling us about an ancillary civil matter that he'd like us to handle for him. You were saying something about the catalogue?"

"Yes," Brian answered, still perturbed that Terrell remained in the room. "But I thought Mr. Banks was only involved in the criminal matter."

"He is," Mr. Bragg answered, "But it would make sense to send him back to Tampa to help the civil team get familiarized with the facts. He needs to hear this too."

"Fine," Brian started grudgingly. "As you may or may not be aware, Optimus has quite an extensive catalog of unreleased music. Our sound engineers estimate that he has about eight hours of raw vocals in the recording vault."

Terrell shifted in his seat, wondering where the conversation was going.

"Through careful editing," Brian continued, "that translates into about ten albums."

"Wow," Terrell said. "That's a lot of music."

"Yes, it is," Brian echoed.

"Tell him why that's important," Mr. Foster added.

"Optimus has released four albums to date for AMI records.

His average sales are just under 5.1 million per album. Since his death, we've seen an unprecedented sales spike. We estimate that his last album will sell around seven million units by year's end."

"It sounds like he is making you a lot of money. How's it related Jennifer's case." Terrell said.

"Yes, he is, but let me finish," Brian said in a perturbed voice. "Optimus' future album sales will be hurt by his inability to promote the songs through videos and touring. Still, our accountants think that the entire catalog has a value upwards of $50 million dollars."

"And you're worried that someone will make a claim on the catalog." Terrell concluded.

"Perhaps, but that's not our primary concern. Optimus' mother suffers from liver disease and is in rapidly declining health. We do not anticipate her surviving until the end of the probate proceedings. She is Optimus' only surviving relative. He never knew his father and he has no brothers, sisters, or children."

"Okay. So what's the complication?" Terrell asked.

"It's a long story," Brian answered. "It's not one single complication so much as it is a series of compounding problems. You may want to take some notes."

"Terrell grabbed a pen and began scribbling on a legal pad.

"About six years ago, AMI signed Optimus to a five album deal," Brian sighed. "Optimus met certain contractual goals for the first four albums, triggering an artist option."

"What kind of option?" Terrell asked.

"Well, he was selling better than five million albums a pop. He had an out clause at twenty million albums sold. Do the math."

"Are things like that common?" Terrell asked.

"I wouldn't say that they are unusual. It was seemed important to him when he signed. Optimus had a good street buzz going before we signed him. He eschewed a lot of advance money for the ability to retain more on the back end of the contract. He practically paid for the publishing and promotion of the first album all on his own. He represented very little risk for AMI, so we were happy to give him that concession. We didn't think that there was any chance in hell that he'd hit his sales goals."

"But he did. Okay, so what? He sold a lot of records, how does that affect Jennifer?"

"I'm getting to that. The important thing is that at the time of his death, Optimus had not opted out of his contract. In fact, we were very close to re-signing him to a deal that would've made both us very happy."

Brian looked first to Mr. Bragg and then to Mr. Foster as if he still wasn't quite sure he could trust Terrell.

"But," Mr. Bragg questioned.

"But his new contract wasn't signed yet. Because of his untimely death, it never will be.

"Okay," Terrell interjected. "There's something here that no one is telling me. Why is it important whether or not a dead guy has a record deal?"

"If Optimus decided to opt out, he would get to take his catalog of music with him. That would include publishing, royalties, merchandising and everything else."

"So I guess you want us to make sure AMI gets to retain the rights to that?" Terrell asked.

"Yes, but that isn't the complication," Brian answered. "Mr. Bragg and Mr. Foster assure me that AMI should win on this issue in court. There's a rumor. We don't know for sure if it's true, but it could be problematic on several different levels. As I told you, Optimus doesn't have any living relatives, but he may have a will floating around somewhere."

"And this is bad because?"

"We have reason to believe that he would have left his interest in his music catalog to Ms. Weston."

"I thought you just said that Optimus hadn't exercised his option and that you still owned everything."

"We're confident that we do," Brian said adamantly. "But, a willed heir to his interest would have the ability to make things difficult for us. Even though Mr. Bragg and Mr. Foster assure me that AMI would ultimately win, the fight would be long and protracted. It could be years before we reach a resolution. By that time, the catalog will have lost a significant portion of its value."

"If this information gets out," Mr. Bragg said, "it will have a profound effect on our criminal case."

Terrell nodded in agreement. Jennifer Weston was as close to poverty as she was to the next galaxy. Still, a 50 million-dollar windfall established a motive for anyone to kill.

"You said maybe he has a will floating around somewhere. Does that mean no one has seen it?" Terrell asked.

"We're not sure about that," Brian answered. "Ms. Weston hasn't mentioned it, but I think she could be hiding it from us. It's unlikely that Optimus would have made the decision to give her controlling interest in his estate without telling her."

"Well then why don't we just ask her?" Terrell asked.

"Not a good idea," Mr. Foster answered firmly. "Plausible deniability. Let's assume she doesn't know. If we ask her, then she will know. And if Karen learns about it, she won't be able to deny it when she takes the stand. It's much better if we just keep her in the dark."

"That was my thought as well," Mr. Bragg responded. "And if she does know about it…" he trailed off.

"If she does what?" Terrell asked.

"Well Terrell," Mr. Bragg answered, "we can't totally discount the possibility that she's guilty. If the evidence keeps mounting, we have to think about the possibility of her entering a plea."

"What? Is that Brian's idea, telling us to consider the possibility that she's guilty?" Terrell knew that Mr. Bragg and Mr. Foster did not have all the information he did, but it didn't matter. He had never heard the partners discussing the possibility that they might lose at trial. It wasn't an option.

"Don't be stupid," Brian responded. "She's the biggest act we have right now. We've set up a 35-city tour to go along with the release of her new album. We've got lots of money invested in her and we won't see a dime of it in return if she's behind bars."

"Exactly," Mr. Foster chimed in. "But we can't ignore the facts. "She was found at the scene of the murder, covered in his blood. She can't explain how she got there or what happened. Maybe he was cheating on her or beating the snot out of her on a regular basis. Then on top of all that, she stands to make a fortune on his death."

"So you can see the kind of difficulty this puts us in Terrell," Mr. Bragg explained. "The prosecution has a compelling case. I am not interested in a guilty plea, but I'm not too keen on losing at trial either."

"So what exactly are we supposed to be doing about this?" Terrell asked.

"Damage control," answered Mr. Bragg. "If we can figure out a way to shift control of the money back to AMI and keep all of this quiet, then the jury doesn't have to hear about Jennifer's 50 million dollar motive."

"I hear what you're saying," Terrell answered. "But... If she didn't do anything wrong, shifting the money back to AMI will cheat her out of a lot of cash."

"No, no, no," Brian chimed in. "We're not trying to cheat her out of anything. We believe that catalog belongs to us anyway. All we're doing is providing her with a better defense. I assure you that once this criminal matter is disposed of, AMI will take good care of Ms. Weston."

"I bet you will," Terrell said under his breath.

"Once you have a little more experience you'll learn to look at the big picture," Mr. Foster lectured. "The only thing of importance to you should be keeping Ms. Weston out of prison. Her finances should come second to her freedom."

"I understand that sir," Terrell answered. He knew from the tone of Mr. Foster's voice that he should drop the subject, but he couldn't. "But this seems like a clear conflict of interest. How can we represent Jennifer's interests on these criminal charges and at the same time, represent AMI's interest in retaining control of the music catalog?"

Brian exchanged a worried look with Mr. Bragg and Mr. Foster, but Mr. Foster waved him off.

"Mr. Banks, you are an associate at Bragg and Shuttlesworth, are you not?" Mr. Foster asked.

"I am," Terrell answered.

"You are also member of the Florida Bar, correct?"

"Yes sir," Terrell answered.

"Then I assume you are familiar with the Florida Code of Professional Conduct."

"Again, yes."

"Are you familiar with the section of the code that deals with subordinate attorneys and their responsibilities when confronted with requests from their senior partners?"

"I am."

"Would you tell us those responsibilities?"

"Yes," Terrell sighed. "An associate or subordinate attorney may not be sanctioned for conduct he believes to be unethical if that conduct is at the direction of a senior or managing partner so long as the subordinate is acting out of genuine fear of reprisal."

"Very good," Mr. Foster said in a cold voice. "I've never been particularly impressed by you Banks. Earnest seems to think you're pretty smart. Prove him right, what am I going to say next?"

"I'd imagine that you're going to tell me to do as I'm told and leave worrying about the ethical considerations to you and Mr. Bragg." He paused momentarily before continuing. "Then I would guess that you'll say that I should remember to shut my know-it-all mouth because you've forgotten more law than I'll ever know."

"Excellent," Mr. Foster smiled. "Maybe you do have a future at the firm after all."

"Fine," Terrell said, giving up. He knew that since AMI was footing the legal bills, Mr. Foster would jump through any hoops necessary to keep the money flowing into the firm. It wouldn't be the first time they had asked him to skirt some ethical rules. "So what do you need me to do?"

"Go back to Tampa and meet with Doug. You know him, he's in corporate litigation." Mr. Bragg answered. "Bring him up to speed about everything that's going on down here. Then, the two of you are going to need to fly out to Los Angeles to retrieve some documents from AMI."

"All right, I'll take care of it."

"Terrell," Mr. Bragg grabbed his arm before he could rise from the table. "Make sure Doug understands the importance of this assignment. Help him remain focused."

"Yes sir, I will," Terrell sighed. Keeping Doug focused was the firm's code for making sure he didn't slip off the wagon before he'd finished his task. Doug Paul was an unkempt, three-time divorcee with a monstrous cocaine problem. He spent at least six weeks a year in one detox center or another. But despite that, he was without a doubt one of the sharpest attorneys at the firm. If there were a way for AMI to keep Optimus' catalog, he'd find it. And if he couldn't find a way, he'd invent one.

"When do you want me to go?"

"Immediately," Mr. Bragg answered. "Drive one of the cars in the garage."

"And how long should this take?"

"I expect you back in a week, Brenda can handle your travel itinerary."

Terrell left the conference room thinking that he'd come to hate living inside of inside a suitcase. There was no way he was going to see Alicia this weekend either.

CHAPTER 14

The firm employed a service to keep the house pristine for any visitors. Since the house was usually empty, their normal duties consisted of light dusting and spot cleaning. The service was ill prepared to serve as full time maid service for an outfit like Jennifer Weston and her entourage. In the short time that Terrell shared space with them, he noticed most of her handlers had the nasty habit of leaving trash wherever it fell. Now, the cleaners had to work overtime just to keep the house from degenerating into a complete sty.

Consequentially, the housekeepers had fallen behind in some of their more mundane duties. Terrell's room had fallen into that category and was the first thing that they began to neglect. As he entered his room, he noticed that it had a sour smell. He realized the cause of the odor when he caught sight of his overflowing trashcan. They were supposed to empty it twice a week. He plopped down on the unmade bed and sighed. He was tired, he had a long drive ahead of him and he needed to call Alicia and tell her to cancel her flight. It was not something he looked forward to doing.

He unzipped his travel bag and tried tossing his dirty clothes into the hamper. It was overflowing just like the trashcan. He went over to the dresser to get a few pairs of boxer shorts and cursed when he realized that the entire drawer was empty.

"Perfect," he mumbled to himself. He found that he was also out of socks, so he rummaged through the hamper until he found two pair that smelled slightly less pungent than the others. He didn't get genuinely angry until he found out that he was out of clean undershirts.

He stormed out of his room toward the housekeeper's closet carrying the stuffed hamper under his arm. He knew that the housekeepers changed Jennifer's linens every day, so there had to be a washing machine somewhere. He also intended to leave the staff a not so friendly reminder that his room needed occasional cleaning too. He opened the door to the housekeeper's closet. It was full of brooms, mops and cleaning supplies, but there was no washing machine. He supposed that there might be one out in the pool house. As he stepped back out into the hallway and turned the corner into the foyer, he was nearly decapitated by a gigantic keyboard that two movers were bringing inside.

The shaggy haired mover greeted him with an apologetic nod before plopping the keyboard down on the floor in the midst of other sound apparatus. Terrell saw mixing boards, microphones, rolls of sound dampening foam and cables of assorted lengths stacked in the center of the foyer. Luther was holding the front door open while two other men carried equipment inside the house.

"What's all of this?" Terrell asked curiously.

"They're setting up a temporary studio for J so she can work here." Terrell's performance at the music awards had earned him a grudging respect from the bodyguard.

"Where?" Terrell asked warily. He prayed that they weren't going to convert his bedroom.

"In that back bedroom," Luther pointed in the direction away from Terrell's bedroom.

"Oh," Terrell responded, relieved. He realized that he hadn't seen Jennifer since he'd returned from New York. "Where is she?"

Luther didn't answer. Instead he just raised his eyebrows and glanced at her room to let Terrell know that she was upstairs. Terrell nodded in understanding. He sat the hamper down and made his way up the winding stairs to her bedroom. He knocked gently on the door to the master suite. Much to his surprise, his soft raps caused the unlatched door to swing open.

"Jennifer," he said as he stuck his head into the narrow crack between the door and the jamb, "you in here?" He peered around the room, but didn't see her anywhere. A star of Jennifer Weston's magnitude commanded the best in accommodations and the master suite of the firm's resort home didn't disappoint. The room had a sunken parlor about ten feet in front of the bed. In the middle of the parlor was a whirlpool set flush with the floor. It fooled the eye so that it was unclear where the plush carpeting stopped and the whirlpool began.

"Jennifer," Terrell called out again as he walked into the room. He peered past the bed and through the open bathroom door. The gold and marble bathroom conveyed a sense of power and luxury. It was a perfect match for the firm's image.

"It's me, Terrell," he said as he searched the room. He was sure that she was in there somewhere. For all intensive purposes, she'd been a prisoner in that room for months. The only time she had been allowed to leave was the ill-fated trip to the music awards. After that, she was effectively on house arrest.

A French door led out onto a balcony. The door was ajar. Terrell stepped out on the balcony, but he still didn't see her. He guessed that she must be downstairs in the kitchen or something when he heard a scratching sound coming from somewhere above him. There was a small, waist high ledge built into the wall. It looked as if it was designed to hold potted plants, but it was empty. He swung his leg onto the ledge and pulled himself up, resting on his knees. Then he balanced himself, grabbed the edge and pulled himself onto the roof.

"There you are," he said. Jennifer was sitting on a couple of large pillows and looking into a photo album. There were pens and several pads of paper strewn around her. She looked up, surprised to see him.

"What are you doing up here?" he asked.

"I told myself that I was coming up here to write some new songs," she answered as she closed the book on her lap. "But I don't really feel like it."

Terrell carefully walked toward her. The Spanish-style roof was angled. Terrell worried that if one of the clay tiles slipped out, that section of the roof would go pouring down into the back yard. He carefully sat down beside her on an empty pillow.

"You know," he said, "There's probably a hundred thousand dollars worth of chairs in this house. You don't have to sit on a pillow on the roof."

"I can't use the ones inside," she answered. "At least not while those guys are here building the studio. Brian says that he doesn't want them trying to take pictures of me while they're here."

"Why would they do that?"

"Are you kidding?" she asked, amused. "When I was just Jennifer Weston, popstar, the tabloids paid a thousand dollars for a shot of me eating a taco. Now that I'm Jennifer Weston, alleged murder, I bet they could get ten times that."

"Really?" Terrell asked.

"Yeah. Anytime someone new is walking around the house, I have to hide."

"Brian makes you hide on the roof?"

"No, he doesn't make me. I like it up here. It reminds me of home."

"So your parents made you sleep on the roof?" Terrell joked. "I've heard about crazy stage parents, but that's insane."

"No," she smiled. "When I was a little girl I used to climb up onto our roof and sit. It was the only place that I could think."

"Quiet?" Terrell asked.

"No, not really. We lived close to the railroad tracks. Trains were coming and going all the time. When I heard them leaving I always wondered where the train was going and who was on it. I always used to dream about hopping on one of the trains and riding until it took me somewhere else."

"What stopped you?" Terrell asked.

"I dunno," she said wistfully. "Sometimes I wish that I had."

"But then you might not be a big star."

"It's not all it's cracked up to be."

"I'm sure it's not," Terrell said sarcastically. "Who would want the love of the masses and ridiculous riches? I'm sure it's terrible."

"It's hard to explain. You've got a girlfriend right?"

"Yeah," Terrell answered, remembering that he was supposed to call her. He made a mental note to do it after he talked to Jennifer.

"Have you ever taken her out to dinner? You know, just the two of you?"

"Yeah, plenty of times."

"I've never done that. If I go out to a restaurant with somebody, it's all over the front page of the Hollywood Celebrity the next day. Twenty people ask for my autograph and then I don't get to eat my food because someone will take pictures of me shoveling it into my mouth. The next thing you know, they'll be reporting that I've got bulimia."

"I guess," Terrell said. "But isn't that a part of being famous?"

"Depends," she replied. "Is working 90 hours a week and never having personal time a part of being a lawyer?"

"Touché," Terrell responded.

"Don't get me wrong, I love my life. Nothing feels as good as having thousands people singing your song along with you. I'm just saying it would be nice to be able to go to the Waffle Hut without spending an hour on my makeup and having to take two bodyguards and publicist along with me."

"Sometimes the golden handcuffs can chafe," Terrell said.

"What?"

"The golden handcuffs. It's a theory about wealth."

"What does it mean?"

"It's simple really," Terrell answered. "What's the first thing you did when you got your record deal?"

"I bought a new house for my parents."

"Thought so," Terrell answered. "The first thing I did when Bragg & Shuttlesworth gave me my signing bonus was to buy way more house than I needed. Then what?"

"I bought a new car. I was only 15 and I couldn't even drive it yet."

"I bought a new car too," Terrell smiled. "It cost almost as much as undergrad. Let me guess, then you went out and bought expensive clothes and jewelry and a whole lot of other stuff you probably didn't need, right?"

"Yeah."

"Everyone that gets money for the first time does the exact same thing. Before you even know if you like being what you are, you mortgage your life to it. Then a couple of months pass and you realize that you hate your job, but you can't quit. You have to keep paying for the house and the car and boat and the clothes and all the other garbage that you never even have time to enjoy. The things that you own end up owning you. The next thing you know, you're trapped in a set of golden handcuffs."

"Is that where you are right now?" Jennifer asked. "Trapped in your golden handcuffs?"

"No more than you are," Terrell answered. "I guess that is the price we pay for being so beautiful and talented."

Jennifer chuckled and looked out over the canal. There was very little boat traffic, just a couple of small schooners drifting aimlessly through the channel.

"What's that?" Terrell asked casually and pointed to her lap.

"Photo album of me," Jennifer answered. "My mom made it."

"Mind if I take a look?"

"No, go ahead."

Jennifer slid the album across to Terrell and opened it. The photos weren't in any sort of order, chronological or otherwise. It was as if Jennifer's life was a series of random moments juxtaposed against one another. The first page was a collage of her singing, the next, pictures of a childhood dance recital. Several photos of her and Optimus together followed that. The pictures on that page weren't glued down like the other photos. Terrell suspected that she'd been looking at those when he interrupted.

"Is that you," he asked as he pointed to a picture of a chubby newborn on the next page.

"Yup, that's me. Eight pounds and two ounces of baby girl."

"You were huge."

"I'm still huge. Since I'm cooped up in this house all day, I haven't been able to run as much as I like. My thighs are disgusting."

"Oh please, you're not much more than eight pounds and two ounces now." Terrell could see her thighs. Huge and disgusting weren't the adjectives he would have used to describe them.

"Hurumph."

Terrell flipped through a couple more pages and saw Jennifer's transformation from bouncy cherub to skinny little girl.

"Your mom didn't miss much," Terrell mused. "I don't think my mother has any pictures of me between the ages of two and sixteen."

"You should see all the pictures that didn't make it into the photo album. She's got shoeboxes full of them at home."

"That's sweet. She loves her daughter."

Terrell flipped through several more pages before he found something truly special.

"Well, well, well, what do we have here?" Terrell asked. He looked down at picture of a very awkward 13-year-old Jennifer in a horrible seafoam formal dress with huge puffy shoulders. The caption next to the picture read Warrenburg Middle School Sweetheart's Social. The little girl in the photo was a caricature of the Jennifer he knew. She smiled with adult teeth that were too large for her adolescent head. Her arms were a little too short and her legs were a little too long. She had on clumpy red lipstick and dark blue eyeshadow that she'd apparently applied with a paint roller.

"Oh my God!" Jennifer exclaimed, "I can't believe that she put that in there!" Jennifer tried to cover up the photo with her hand, but Terrell was too quick. Before she could get to it, he snatched it from the album.

"I don't remember seeing this in the little booklet that comes in your CD," he laughed as he held the picture in his outstretched arm.

"Give that back," she begged as she reached for the photo. "That wasn't supposed to be in there."

"Oh no," Terrell laughed. "I think it was. Tell me, did you have makeup artists back then to? Because I have to say that the job they did for this was fantastic."

"Stop laughing at me." Jennifer said, as she pulled on Terrell's arm in a futile attempt to get him to release the photo. "My mom wouldn't let me wear makeup, so I had to borrow some from my friend. I put it on in the bathroom."

"You must have went to a really poor school if they didn't have lights and mirrors in the bathroom," Terrell joked.

"Very funny," she said as she tried to crawl over Terrell. "That's enough, now give that back so I can burn it."

"I don't think so," Terrell answered. He fended her off with his left arm and used his body to shield the picture from her. "If people can get thousands of bucks for regular pictures of you, I wonder what I could get for this? I could give up this stressful life and retire to the south of France if I sold this."

Jennifer said nothing, but intensified her struggles to make him release the picture.

"Besides, I think your fans deserve to see all of you," Terrell mused, "Singer, actress and awkward teenager."

Jennifer paid his words no attention. Instead, she formed a

claw with her fingers and dug into the handful of fat around Terrell's midsection.

"Ahhh!" Terrell screeched. He attempted to twist away from the searing pain, but only ended up making it worse as her grip tightened.

"Give it back," Jennifer said in a sweet voice.

"Never!" Terrell replied. He again tried to wrench away from her grip, but he lost his balance on the pillow and toppled onto the roof. Even this did not make Jennifer release her grip. Instead, she fell with him and landed on top of him. Her weight pinned him and he slid down the roof with her riding him like a surfboard. Terrell flailed his arms in a desperate attempt to slow their slide. Jennifer used the opportunity to grab hold of his other lovehandle.

"Aaauugh!" Terrell screamed in pain. "Let go! We're going to fall!"

"I'm not worried," she said calmly. "I'm sure you'll break my fall." Her face was only inches from his as she continued, "Now, my picture please."

"Okay, okay," Terrell surrendered, "here."

She released his side and took the horrible photo from his hand. She rolled off of him, and with the deftness of a cat, scampered back up the roof's slope. Terrell carefully crawled back to join her.

"Sheesh," Terrell said, rubbing at his sides, "That really hurt."

"I know," Jennifer smiled. "My mom used to do that to me."

"What on earth for?"

"To keep me skinny. She always said that it was hard enough to make it in the music business without the burden of being chunky. So if I ever looked fat to her, she'd walk by and grab my fat like that."

"On your sides?" Terrell asked.

"Stomach, thighs, whatever she thought looked too big."

"Ouch," Terrell said empathetically. "That's harsh."

"It worked," she answered and lifted up the bottom of her shirt. Terrell could see the definition of each muscle through her taught and toned skin. There wasn't an ounce of fat to be found anywhere.

"Wow, when this thing is over, I'm hiring you to be my personal trainer. If you were grabbing my fat like that I might actually have the motivation to do some sit-ups."

"Sit-ups only build muscle," she explained. "You need cardio if you want to loose fat."

"That's exactly what I'm talking about. I'm definitely hiring you when you get out of this."

"If," she said, sounding depressed. "Don't you mean if I get out of this?" She looked back out over the channel. Now, only a single boat bobbed up and down in the light current.

"Have a little faith," Terrell smiled. "Everything will turn out alright. You'll see."

"Don't lie," she replied. "I know how it looks. Everybody thinks I'm guilty. Everybody."

"I don't."

"Yeah, and I only had to pay you like, five million dollars to think that way."

"Look at me," Terrell answered. He gently placed his fingers on her chin and turned her face toward his. "I know you didn't do it. I defended a lot of guilty people in my life and I know how they act. You're different. I know that you didn't do this thing and pretty soon, I'm going to be able to prove it. Trust me."

He saw in her eyes that she wanted to believe him. She wanted to think that he really could make everything all right, but she was skeptical. To be honest, so was he.

"Besides," he continued, "You're not paying us five million dollars, AMI is."

"Sure they are," Jennifer gave a humorless laugh. "The first thing you learn in the music business is that the label doesn't pay for anything. They're fronting the money now, but I'm sure they'll send me the bill when it's all over."

"Oh, I didn't know."

"So," she said as she returned her gaze to the channel, "What are you working on now?"

"You know I went to talk to Clarence earlier today, right?"

"Yeah, in New York. Did he have anything useful to say?"

"No, he didn't really have anything useful to say. He told us that he saw you and Optimus at the club, but he didn't see you leave."

"So it was another dead end?"

"Not quite. I'm still working on a theory. Maybe it will help, but I need to check out a few other leads first."

"Leads here?"

"No, I've got to go back to Tampa."

"Why?"

"Well," Terrell stalled. He didn't want to explain that he was going there to take 50 million dollars from her. "I've got to do some boring contract stuff with Optimus' music catalog. I think AMI wants to do a greatest hits album or something."

"They might want to but they can't," she said.

"Why not?" Terrell asked, curious as to how much Jennifer knew.

"Because they don't own his master recordings anymore."

"If they don't, who does?" he asked, praying that she wasn't going to say that she did.

"I'm not sure exactly, but I'm know it's not AMI. Optimus got out of his deal with them about a week before he died. It was all he talked about."

"No," Terrell answered. "I don't think that's right. I know he had an option to get out, but he never did."

"Yes he did," Jennifer corrected. "I'm telling you, it was all he talked about. Everyday I would have to hear about how he was going to have so much more money because now he owned all the publishing rights to everything. He kept saying that he was going to end up owning AMI instead of the other way around."

"Are you sure about that?"

"Of course I'm sure. It's not like he came up with that scheme overnight. I think that's how he planned it from the beginning. He even had another deal set up with Southside Records."

"Who?"

"Southside. You know, it's out of Atlanta."

"How are you so sure? Were you there?"

"No, but I do remember that the last time we were in New York he left the house and told me that he was going over to see Brian about his contract. He came back an hour later and said that it was done and that he was going to Atlanta to see some guy about setting up a new deal with Southside."

"What guy?" Terrell asked.

"I don't know. I think his name was Stony or something like that."

"Did he meet this guy?"

"Maybe. I went from Philadelphia to DC and then here. Felix left DC before I did. I think he stopped in Atlanta before he… before he came here."

There was a depressing finality in her voice. A whirlwind had been ripping through Jennifer's life ever since Optimus was killed. As he looked at her profile while she stared out into the canal, Terrell finally figured out the reason she was up on the roof. She needed time alone to miss him. No matter what anyone else said, Terrell could see that Jennifer loved Optimus.

"I've gotta go," he said, rising from his cushion. "Don't spend too much time up here by yourself, okay."

She nodded, but didn't look at him.

"Hey," he added, "You know that if you need to talk about anything, there's people inside that care about you."

"Whatever," she said pessimistically. "People that care about how much money they can make off me. When are you coming back?"

"A week or two. I'll be back as soon as I have this catalog thing finished."

"Thanks."

"Thanks for what?" he asked.

"Everything. I know you're working really hard for me. I appreciate it."

"Everybody at the firm is working hard for you." He said truthfully. This case was the firm's biggest earner.

"Not like you. Everybody else comes and goes, but you're always here. In all the time we've been stuck in this house, I don't think I've ever seen you sleep. Sometimes I go downstairs late at night to get a snack and I can hear you in that back room working. I think this is the first break I've seen you take."

"Well, don't get too mushy," Terrell smiled. "You're going to get a bill for all that time."

"I know," she stood up and gave him a hug. "Thank you anyway."

"Don't thank me until we've won," he said as he hugged her back.

Terrell carefully walked down to the edge of the roof and climbed back down to the balcony. His mind swirled with unanswered questions, most notably about Brian Dunn and Optimus' contract. As he began to focus on how to solve that problem, he pushed all other thoughts out of his mind. That was why he forgot that he was supposed to call Alicia to tell her not to come to Miami. That was also the reason why he didn't notice that the little schooner had been drifting aimlessly in the exact same spot for the past ten minutes. And it was definitely the reason why he didn't notice the faint click-whirr, click-whirr noise the expensive telephoto camera made every time it took a picture.

CHAPTER 15

Terrell stole a glance at his watch as he shoved his way through the mob changing trains in the Atlanta airport's subway. His layover was only three-and-a-half hours. If he was going to make it back to the terminal for the flight back to Tampa, he was going to have to hustle.

He mouthed, "I'm sorry," to an old man that he knocked aside as he ran up the escalator leading to the cabstand. He had been holed up in Tampa for nearly a week with Doug pouring over the minutia of Optimus' contract. It was not the kind of work Terrell enjoyed and he was preoccupied with Jennifer's murder case.

Making matters worse was the fact that he hadn't been able to get a hold of Alicia. He'd tried to reach her at work but he always just missed her. There was always some complication. If she wasn't at lunch, she was in a meeting. If she hadn't stepped away from her desk, then it was siesta. He felt awful, but he had to break their weekend plans by leaving a message with her secretary. He knew that he'd never hear the end of it, but he figured that was a better alternative than standing her up at the airport.

Despite the distraction of his rapidly devolving love life, he remained calm and patient while he waited for his opportunity to investigate Jennifer's lead. His patience had finally been rewarded. Several documents pertinent to Optimus' contract were located in AMI's Los Angeles office. Terrell convinced Doug that he could locate what they needed and didn't require his help. Then, he searched every airline until he found a flight that included a sizeable stopover in Atlanta. A few phone calls later, and he had scheduled a meeting with Stephen "Stony" Williams, CEO of Southside records. He was proud of himself for being able to set up the meeting in such a clandestine manner. He stepped out of the airport onto the sidewalk and smiled as he hailed a taxi.

Almost immediately, a taxi waiting on the opposite curb dashed across the lanes and swooped in front of him. He grabbed the handle to the back door and opened, only to discover that he wasn't the cab's only passenger.

"What are you doing here?" Terrell asked, shocked. Joe sat on the rear seat and motioned for him to get inside the cab.

"I could ask you the same question," he answered, "but I already know why you're here. Now get in, we're on a tight schedule."

Terrell slid into the car and shut the door behind him. The cab driver took off immediately.

"I need you to take me to the corner of Peachtree and..." Terrell started.

"Don't bother," Joe interrupted, "he already knows where we're headed."

"How do you do that?" Terrell asked.

"Do what?" Joe asked flatly.

"How did you know where I'd be?" Since Terrell learned that Joe was monitoring all of his phone calls, he'd been very careful in making his plans. He hadn't made the reservations on his cell or from the firm's phone lines.

"When I found out you scheduled a flight with such a long layover," Joe answered, "I knew you were up to something, so

I did a little digging and figured the rest out myself. Your ideas may be half garbage, but they're also half good."

"Wow," Terrell answered. "Coming from you, that almost sounded like a compliment. What would you have done if I'd given you the slip by taking the Marta instead of a cab?"

"You're not that smart," Joe answered. "Besides, I would have caught up to you before your meeting with Mr. Williams."

It bugged Terrell that he couldn't give Joe the slip, but he figured that must be the reason that Bragg & Shuttlesworth kept him on retainer.

"Did you tell anyone else that I was coming here?" Terrell asked. Joe looked at him as if he'd asked whether or not B came after A in the alphabet.

"No, Terrell," he stated, "I only make a report when I have something to report. That won't be until after you've talked things over with Mr. Williams."

The cab slid seamlessly into the congested Atlanta traffic, but to his credit, the driver made excellent time through the swarm of daily commuters and it only took 25 minutes to reach the offices of Southside Records.

The building's façade wasn't impressive and Terrell had his doubts that he had the correct address. It was an old building with weathered bricks and blackened windows in a dilapidated industrial section of the city. The street was deserted and Terrell had serious reservations about getting out of the car.

"Hey mister," he asked the cabbie quizzically, "Are you sure this is it? I needed to go to Peachtree and 51st."

"This is it," Joe answered gruffly, "I checked it out this morning. Now get out, we'll be around to pick you up when you're done. Try to remember what he tells you, it could be important." Joe reached across Terrell and opened his door. Then he gave him a rough shove in the back that nearly sent him sprawling onto the street.

"Was that really necessary?" Terrell asked as he glared at Joe.

Joe said nothing. Instead he tossed Terrell's small briefcase at him and slammed the car door shut. The driver sped away immediately. Terrell slowly walked over to the building, taking special care to watch his environment from the corners of his eyes. As he neared the door, he saw the first hint that he was in the correct place. A small, modern looking keypad and speaker were mounted into the wall outside the front door. He looked above him and a small black globe hung from the eaves of the overhang. It was the kind of thing that typically housed security cameras. He pressed the green call button on the keypad.

"Yes?" a wary female voice answered from the tinny speaker.

"Ahh, hello?" Terrell said. "My name is Terrell Banks. I'm looking for Southside Records."

"What is your business sir?" the irritated voice answered.

"I'm here from the law firm Bragg & Shuttlesworth. I've got a meeting scheduled with Mr. Williams. He should be expecting me."

"One moment," the woman answered. Terrell stood on the stoop for a few seconds before hearing the click of the magnetic lock disengaging.

"Please come in," the voice instructed him. Terrell swung open the door and was surprised to see a very modern office. A pretty woman sat behind a large desk and several cushy chairs were arranged in the waiting area.

"Mr. Williams will be with you in just a couple of minutes. Please have a seat," the woman said before returning her attention to the magazine that she'd been reading. Terrell sat down and scanned the coffee table in front of him. He was surprised to see that all the magazines were current, a rarity in any waiting room. A bold headline caught his attention. When he picked it up, he realized that it was the current issue of Bricks magazine. It had a photo of Jennifer at the music awards and underneath in bright red print was the headline, "Jennifer Weston: Is Death Row the Next Stop for the Princess of R&B?"

"Ugh," Terrell mumbled under his breath while he thumbed through the magazine looking for the article. He was surprised to see that one of the interior photographs of Jennifer included him holding her arm at red carpet. It identified him as her companion, Terrell Banks of Florida's premier criminal defense firm, Bragg & Shuttlesworth. Most of the article rehashed Jennifer's history with Optimus, the charges she now faced and her win on award night. While the magazine didn't say anything about shots being fired backstage, it did make it seem as though Jennifer had encouraged the confrontation.

It read, "With confidence, Ms. Weston proudly proclaimed her innocence just as the remaining members of the Armada walked backstage carrying Optimus' posthumous award. Sparks erupted as members of the two entourages exchanged heated words and scuffled with security. Members of her elite security team whisked Ms. Weston out of the room, leaving the two crews to handle the beef. Industry insiders speculate that this feud will continue to escalate no matter the outcome of Ms. Weston's upcoming murder trial."

"Fantastic," Terrell muttered to himself. He tossed the magazine back onto the coffee table and waited. A few minutes later, Stony emerged.

"Mr. Banks," he said as he extended his palm.

"Thank you for your time, Mr. Williams," Terrell said as stood and shook his hand.

"No problem. Please, call me Stony, everybody does. Let's go to my office." Terrell followed Stony down the narrow corridor into the bowels of the building. He could see that the inside of the building had been completely renovated and modernized.

"You're probably wondering why I picked this neighborhood to build my studio," Stony said in a practiced voice that indicated to Terrell that he'd had to explain this before. "The advantage to building in the grimy part of town, other than the cheap mortgage, is the lack of noise. I'm pretty sure that this is the only place in Atlanta that doesn't have gridlock everyday. Passing cars can ruin a recording session."

They passed the windows of two state of the art studios as

they walked down hallway. Terrell could see busy technicians feverously adjusting knobs and sound controls while a skinny kid in a white tee shirt fired lyrics into the microphone in the recording booth.

"That's X-Static," Stony commented, following Terrell's glance. "The kid's got talent. His album will be out in two months. Should I reserve a copy for you?"

"Thanks, but no," Terrell answered. Stony opened the last door on the hallway and ushered Terrell inside with him.

"Now, what can I do for you?" Stony said, sliding into the plush leather chair behind his desk.

"I know you're a busy man, and I have a flight to catch, so I'm going to get right to the point. You know who I am and who I represent."

"Yeah," Stony replied. "You're J-Dub's lawyer. I saw you sitting next to her at the music awards. I was sitting three rows behind you." Stony reached out to a small wooden humidor that sat on the edge of his desk. "Mind if I smoke?" he asked.

"No, that's fine," Terrell answered.

"You want one?"

"No thanks."

"I don't usually smoke in here," he said as he clipped the end of a fat cigar with his razor. "But lawyers make me nervous. Every time I see one, I end up with less money in my pocket."

"It's nothing like that," Terrell assured him, conveniently forgetting the week he'd spent in Tampa ensuring that neither Stony, nor anyone else besides AMI would collect on Optimus' huge estate.

"Well, if you're not here to steal cash from me then I can't imagine how you think I could help her. We've never even met."

"That's fine," Terrell answered. "Because I'm only here to talk to you about your dealings with Optimus."

Stony sat back in his seat and took a long drag off his cigar. He held it in for a moment before blowing the thick, blue tinged smoke from his lips.

"Optimus was a terrific MC and a valuable leader in the hip-hop community. We all mourn his passing," he said warily as he inspected Terrell more closely. "But I'm sure you already knew that. I'm afraid there isn't much more that I can add, as I didn't really have any professional dealings with him."

"Really?" Terrell said calmly.

"Really," Stony reiterated. "Now, if you'll excuse me, I have a lot of work to do."

"I'll only be a minute," Terrell said. He didn't rise from his seat. "And I've come a long way to see you, so would you please humor me for a minute. Are you sure you haven't had any personal dealings with him?"

"How could I?" Stony replied. "He's the property of AMI records. If you didn't know, this is Southside Records. I run a small independent label. I would never dream of tampering with another company's product. It's unethical." Stony blew another mouthful of smoke across the table.

"I'm sure you wouldn't," Terrell said with false sincerity. "Still, I've heard a few things."

"We all hear things Mr. Banks," Stony said as he took another long drag from his cigar. "I hear that Jennifer Weston murdered her boyfriend. But just because I heard it doesn't mean that it actually happened, right?"

"That's my point exactly," Terrell retorted. "I heard something and now I'm trying to sort out the truth from the fiction. So I'd really appreciate it if you could shed some light on your deal with Optimus."

"Somebody must have given you some bad information," Stony chuckled softly. "I told you, I didn't even know Optimus, and I certainly didn't have any kind of dealings with him. As I said before, he was the property of AMI records. It would have been most unwise and very expensive for me to tamper with that relationship. Now if you'll excuse me."

Terrell smacked the palm of his hand down onto the heavy

desk making a tremendous clapping sound. He stood up, leaned across the desk and looked Stony squarely in the eye.

"If I were your attorney, I'd probably say that it is in your best business interest not to say anything about Optimus at all. If your company had tried to entice Optimus to sign with you while he was still under contract with AMI, then you might be liable for millions of dollars in tampering damages. Though you have a nice little establishment here, I seriously doubt that's something you could afford. So, if I were your attorney, I'd tell you to keep your mouth shut."

Terrell paused for effect. He hoped his gambit would work, because he didn't have any other ideas.

"But I'm not your attorney. I'm Jennifer Weston's attorney and right now I don't care about whatever tampering lawsuit you're afraid AMI might file against you. My only concern is preventing an innocent woman from spending the rest of her life in a cinderblock cell that's not quite wide enough to lie down in and not quite tall enough to stand. Nothing else matters to me. I'm not interested in divulging anything you say to me to AMI. So please, just tell me about your deal with Optimus."

Stony remained silent for a few moments, carefully measuring Terrell.

"I like you man," he finally said. "It's nice to see a lawyer that cares about his people," Stony replied. "In fact, if I ever need one, you're going to be the first one I call. Still, I really don't know anything about…"

"Do you really expect AMI not to destroy whatever little deal you and Optimus worked out together?" Terrell sighed "Let me let you in on a little secret, I just spent last week crawling through every line of their contract with Optimus to make sure that AMI is entitled to keep all of his money."

"Yeah but," Stony tried to interrupt.

"Big companies screw over little ones. It's a fact of life. To be honest, it's probably going to happen to you again in the future.

That isn't a fight you're going to win. All you can do is help Jennifer. Will you do that?"

Stoney thought for several moments before saying, "You really think that I know something, don't you?"

"If I didn't, I wouldn't be here." Terrell answered.

"Okay. May I speak in a hypothetical?" Stony asked.

"Yes, of course," Terrell said, "Hypothetically speaking what do you know? I'm on a tight schedule and you said that you were busy too so let's get this over with."

"Hypothetically speaking, let's say we did have a deal. I don't see how any of this is relevant to your case."

"That's okay," Terrell said. "I'm the only one that needs see how it's relevant. So what was this hypothetical deal exactly?"

"I'm guessing you know about the option clause in Optimus' contract with AMI?"

"I'm aware of it."

"I met Optimus at a basketball tournament in New York last year. I graduated with my business degree and I was trying to get this label off the ground. I was trying to make some connections to sign talent."

Terrell nodded and checked the wall clock out of the corner of his eye. He had plenty of time.

"Let's just say things didn't go right. I didn't have any money, so I had to sleep in my car. Trust me, a record producer that's sleeping in the back seat of a ten year old Honda doesn't inspire a lot of confidence in new musicians. I'm bathing with wetnaps in the subway bathroom. I couldn't get into the nightclubs to see anybody perform because my clothes weren't right. Nobody one would return my calls or let me into their office. After about a week of nothing but bad luck, some dude stole my wallet. I didn't even have money to buy gas to get home. I was screwed. I noticed the sign for the basketball tournament, and I saw that they were giving away free hotdogs and chips. I wasn't too proud to get some."

"Uh-huh," Terrell responded.

"So I'm sitting there in the bleachers trying to figure out my next move and this dude sits down next to me. He starts complaining to me about how they ran out of hotdogs. He's acting like he paid for them. He won't shut up and he's really starting to get on my nerves. So I told him that he didn't know the meaning of bad day. I tell him about my trip. By the end of it he's grinning like a lunatic. So I asked him what was so damn funny."

"Then the dude says, 'You are so damn funny. That whole story is hilarious. If it didn't happen to you, you'd be laughing too.' Then he asked me if I was serious about making it. I told him yeah. A little set back like that wasn't going to stop me. He said that he respected that and then he pulled the biggest wad of cash I've ever seen out of his pocket. He counts off five hundred bucks and hands it to me. Then he says, 'That should be enough to get you some food, a motel room and gas back to Atlanta. He told me to get the motel room first and hit the shower, because I stunk. Then I finally realize who it is. He asks me for my card, and I give it to him. Then he says that maybe he'll look me up when he's in Atlanta and he gets up to leave."

"And all that happened hypothetically?" Terrell asked flippantly.

"No. That actually happened. The next part happened hypothetically. About six months later I get a call out of the blue. It's Optimus. Apparently, he liked one of my mixtapes and he remembered me. I told him that I was still working on getting the label off the ground. Then he said that he had a proposition for me."

"And what was this hypothetical proposition?" Terrell asked.

Stony explained to Terrell his entire arrangement with Optimus. Though Optimus had the ability to opt out of his contract, he could only sign with another national label. He was prohibited from publishing his own material. That was why he needed Stony and Southside records. Optimus provided the investment capital Stony needed to acquire production services, warehousing facilities and distribution agreements. Stony then incorporated Southside and, in exchange for his investment, Optimus was given enough stock options to make him the majority shareholder in the company.

"That's ingenious," Terrell commented. "And I'm pretty sure that would have worked. When did you do all this? Hypothetically, of course."

"Well, there's the problem. I'd signed all the contracts, but he couldn't sign them until he'd exercised his option with AMI. He had the original copy with my signature, but I never got it back from him. Even after he died, I hoped it would show up one day in a express mail envelope. If she could have waited just one more day, I'd be set."

Terrell looked at him strangely.

"Look," Stony explained. "I know that sounds bad. But you have to understand; we were going to be business partners, not friends. I'll always appreciate what he did for me. But now you're sitting here telling me that I'm probably not going to see a dime from any of his music. And on top of that I'm stuck with a truckload of expenses that I got financing this studio. Expenses that I'm sure his estate isn't going to pay for. She kills him before he can sign the contracts and now I'm stuck trying to figure out a way to stay out of bankruptcy."

"I don't think she did it," Terrell said.

"What-the-hell-ever. Whether she did or didn't doesn't really matter to me. All I know is that at the end of the day, I've got a mountain of bills, no money and record label with no talent. Now, can I get back to work?" Stony tapped out his cigar in the dish and rose from his seat.

"Okay," Terrell responded as he also rose from his chair. "Just one more thing. You said that you had given him a copy with your signature, right?"

"Yeah."

"How did you get it to him?" Terrell asked.

"One of his guys came by the day before he got killed and got it. He said that O had to go to Miami and that he'd sign his part there and send it back to me."

"Do you remember who?" Terrell questioned.

"I can't remember the guy's name. I've seen him a couple of times before. He's kinda fat and he's always hanging around O. I think he's his do-boy or something."

"Clarence?"

"That could have been it. I really don't remember. Anyway, I gave it to him and I haven't seen it since."

Terrell followed Stony back down the hallway to the reception area. As he turned to walk out the front door, Stony called to him.

"Hey, if you get her off, tell her we're always looking for talent."

"I'll be sure to do that," Terrell said and walked out the door.

The moment Terrell set foot on the sidewalk, he saw the yellow cab make a right turn back onto the street. He only had to wait a couple of seconds before it pulled up beside him. He opened the door and got inside with Joe.

"You'll never guess what I just found out," Terrell said excitedly.

"I probably could," Joe said in his flat monotone. "Optimus really did have a deal set up with this guy. On top of that his friend and trusted confidant Clarence also knew of this deal and forgot to tell us. Then Optimus goes and gets himself killed, saving AMI untold millions of dollars."

"Alright," Terrell said. "That's just creepy. How in the world did you know that?"

"It's pretty easy to figure things out when you can listen in on people's conversations. All the sound dampening equipment in the building makes my penetrating mike useless so I had to rely on this." Joe reached over and pulled what appeared to be a square of cloth no larger than a fingernail off Terrell's back. "Transmitter."

Terrell thought back to the rough shove Joe had given him when he exited the car and figured that was when he must have planted the bug on him. At least he wouldn't have to waste time telling Joe what he learned.

"So, what's our next move?" Terrell asked.

"You're going back to Tampa to do what ever it is you lawyers do. I am going to pay our friend Clarence a visit."

Terrell shivered. He could only imagine what it meant to get an unannounced visit from Joe. He was sure that there was going to be pain involved. They rode back to airport at breakneck speed and Terrell arrived in time to catch his connection back to Tampa. He made his way through the security checkpoints and finally to his departure gate. A blonde woman with a superficially wide smile greeted him and scanned his boarding pass.

"Oh, Mr. Banks, we have a message for you," she said. She hurried over to the airline kiosk situated between the two gates and read over the computer screen.

"Mr. Banks," we've received notification that you are to report to Gate 41 for your flight. It's down at the end of this concourse."

"Why," Terrell asked. "Is it going to Tampa too?"

"I don't know," the attendant answered. "The message said that your law firm sent a private plane to pick you up here. Your bags have already been transferred and it's ready for takeoff upon your arrival."

"Oh," Terrell answered, puzzled. "Okay then. You said it's down at the end of this concourse?"

"That's right sir. Have a wonderful flight."

Terrell walked slowly down to the end of the concourse. It didn't make any sense for the firm to send the plane to pick him up when he already had a commercial flight to Tampa. Whatever the reason was, Terrell doubted that it was going to be good news for him.

CHAPTER 16

Terrell learned that he didn't like flying alone. It was too quiet. Upon boarding the plane, the pilot informed him that he would be returning to Miami instead of Tampa. He hadn't heard a word from the cockpit since. He leaned his head back against the headrest and closed his eyes.

His mind was too full of unanswered questions to fall asleep. He wondered why was Brian Dunn so certain that he had Optimus re-signed with AMI when Stony had nearly closed a deal to get him to leave? And if Clarence was the courier for the new contracts, why didn't anyone one else know about it? Nothing he could think of explained what happened after Optimus and Clarence carried Jennifer out of the nightclub. The most frustrating thing for Terrell was that he was certain all of these things fit together, but he couldn't see exactly how. If he couldn't see it, then he certainly couldn't prove it. If he couldn't prove it, then there was no way he was going to be able to break the case against Jennifer.

The plane taxied into one of the numerous private hangars at the airport and Terrell disembarked as soon as the wheels stopped rolling. He stepped down the ladder and was surprised to see a car waiting in the hangar for him. He thought it was odd, because the cars usually waited outside the building. One of the firm's runners was leaning on the passenger door. Terrell had seen him around the house several times but didn't know his name.

"Over here sir," the kid said as if Terrell wouldn't notice him. "They told me to drive you back to the house."

"Okay," Terrell answered. "I'm coming."

Terrell walked toward the car and suddenly, a man dressed in an old tweed coat sprung out from behind some boxes. Terrell tensed and clenched his fist, but then he saw that the man was carrying a small tape recorder in his hand.

"Mr. Banks!" the man shouted as he approached Terrell, "Earl Wickman from the National Star, do you have a comment about your relationship with Jennifer Weston?"

"I'm sorry," Terrell parroted his usual response. "I cannot comment on our client's criminal case. As I'm sure you know, the judge has issued a gag order." He'd repeated that phrase ad nauseam for the past few months.

"I'm not talking about the case," the reporter shot back. "I asked about you and Jennifer."

"What?" Terrell asked before he felt a strong hand on his back, pushing him into the car.

"Mr. Banks will not be answering any questions or be available for comment," the runner said as he slammed the car door shut. "So go crawl back under your rock."

"I'm just trying to help you," the reporter said to Terrell through the tinted glass. "Why don't you come on out of there and give your side of the story. I'm giving you a golden opportunity."

"Get lost," The kid said as he hopped behind the wheel.

"Fine," the reporter said. "It's your funeral."

The runner gunned the motor and screeched out of the hangar.

"What was he talking about?" Terrell asked as the car moved

into the flow of the airport traffic. "What's going on? Why did the plane bring me back here? What's the deal?"

"I don't know," the kid answered. "They told me to pick you up and not to let you talk to anyone before we got back to the house."

An uncomfortable silence fell over the car during the drive back to the house. Terrell was worried. By the time the car pulled into the driveway, he felt like there was a little mouse running around in his belly. His mind raced as he desperately tried to think of why Mr. Bragg and Mr. Foster would have to have a face to face to face meeting with him. He figured that he must be in some kind of trouble, but he had no idea what it could be. He hadn't screwed up on anything that he knew about. In fact, he had completed the contract assignment ahead of schedule. He probably could've squeezed more billing hours out of AMI for it, but that wasn't egregious enough to land him in hot water. Even his impromptu trip to Atlanta could easily be explained as necessary research.

Terrell hopped out of the car as soon as it stopped in front of the house. He figured that whatever the trouble was, it was better to get it out of the way. He bounded up the front stairs and opened the front door. There were several people milling about inside, none of them seemed eager to make eye contact with him. He spotted a familiar face sitting in the kitchen.

"Gil," Terrell greeted, "what are you doing here?" Gilbert McCallister worked down the hall from Terrell. He was a part of the firm's litigation team, but he hadn't been involved in Jennifer's case.

"Ahh, nothing," he said nervously. "Peter wanted me to go over a couple of things."

"Oh, okay, is he inside?" Terrell asked and pointed to the closed conference room door.

"Yeah," Gil answered. "Earnest is in there too. I think they're waiting for you."

"Well then, since I'm the guest of honor, I guess I'd better get in there." Terrell forced a smile and turned the knob on the heavy door. When he walked in, he noticed that Mr. Bragg and Mr. Foster were sitting at the table in front of a couple of magazines. The television was broadcasting one of the numerous celebrity news programs that permeated evening television. Brian Dunn sat in the corner, looking even more smug than normal. Since he got the feeling that he was in some kind of trouble, he thought that his best option was to go on the offensive.

"I'm glad you sent the plane for me," Terrell lied, "I think I'm on to something. I went to Atlanta and had a very productive meeting with…"

"Shut up Terrell," Mr. Bragg said in a very tired voice.

"Excuse me sir?" Terrell blinked dumbly.

"I said shut up," Mr. Bragg repeated. "Sit down and shut up.

Terrell did as he was told.

After a heavy sigh, Mr. Bragg continued, "How long has it been going on?"

"How long has what been going on sir?" Terrell asked. He was thoroughly confused.

"I can't believe this guy," Brian shouted. "What? Are you going to deny it now?"

"I'm pretty sure no on is talking to you," Terrell snapped.

"But we are talking to you," Mr. Foster added. "Now tell us. How long has this been going on? From the very beginning?"

"How long has what been going on?" Terrell asked, becoming agitated. "I have no idea what you're talking about."

Brain threw up his hands in disgust, but he didn't say anything.

"You don't know what we're talking about?" Mr. Foster questioned.

"No sir, I don't" Terrell answered.

"Fine, then let me spell it out for you. How long have you been sleeping with our client?"

"What!?"

"How. Long. Have. You. Been. Sleeping. With. Our. Client? That's the last time I'm going to ask you nicely."

"Sir, I don't know what this is all about," Terrell said, "but I assure you that I am not sleeping with anyone right now, especially our client. I would never do something like that and I have no idea where you would get that impression." He said this even though he had more than a slight inclination that the idea originated in the imagination of Brian Dunn. "I would not jeopardize our client, our firm…"

"Or your law license," Mr. Bragg interrupted.

"Or my law license," Terrell continued, "by instigating an improper relationship with one of our clients. It's just not something that I would do and…"

"Terrell," Mr. Bragg cut him short, "Before you persist in proclaiming your innocence, perhaps you should take a look at this." Mr. Bragg slid a magazine across the table to Terrell. It was already open to the incriminating page.

"That's an advance copy of the Hollywood Insider. It goes on sale nationwide tomorrow, but it's all over the internet and several other media sources are already running with the story."

Terrell blinked stupidly for a couple of moments, as if the pictures would magically transform into something less wrong. Tragically, they did not. The pictures were all from the night Terrell and Jennifer sat on the roof. They did not paint a flattering picture. The first was a snapshot of the two of them standing atop the roof and hugging. The next one in the sequence showed the two of them sitting close together on the pillows, his head obscuring hers. Though Terrell knew better, the picture seemed to show that they were about to kiss. The next picture was a shot of Jennifer holding up the bottom of her shirt to show off her abs. In the sequence, it looked as if she were removing her shirt. The final and most damning photograph was her lying on top of him when she was trying to get her picture back. However, they appeared to be in the throws of passion. Terrell's mouth opened and closed like a fish suffocating on a riverbank, but he couldn't make a coherent sound.

"Do I need to ask you again? Or do you suddenly remember what I'm talking about?" Mr. Foster said sarcastically.

"Mr. Bragg... Mr. Foster, I..." Terrell stammered. "See, these pictures... They aren't... I mean, I didn't... It's not like it looks..."

"Just stop it Terrell," Mr. Bragg said in a defeated voice. "I never thought I'd have to give you the talk about keeping it in your pants."

"You don't. Listen, Mr. Bragg," Terrell finally found his voice. "You have to believe me. I know how those pictures look, but I promise it didn't happen."

"So these are doctored photos then?" Mr. Foster said, venomous sarcasm dripping from his tongue. "Well then, that explains everything!"

"No," Terrell answered. "I'm not saying that. What I am saying is that these pictures are out of order and out of context. See, this first one. I hugged her when I was leaving and..."

"Un-freaking-believable," Brian shouted from the corner. "Even with pictures, this guy is still denying it. I for one am not going to sit here while he delivers a sordid play by play of his sexual escapades with Ms. Weston."

"Didn't I just tell you that nothing happened?" Terrell yelled.

"How could you?" Brian asked. "This poor young woman has had the man she loved tragically murdered while she slept next to him. She's facing spending the rest of her life in prison. You were supposed to be someone she could trust, and what do you do? You pounce on a vulnerable girl the first chance you get. You're despicable."

"I'm despicable?" Terrell shot back. He wanted nothing more than to leap across the table at Brian and choke the life out of him. "Look who's talking. I found out something very interesting while I was gone and I..."

"Shut up Terrell," Mr. Bragg interrupted.

"You have to hear this," Terrell continued. "There's something fishy going on with..."

"I said shut up!" Mr. Bragg finally lost his temper. "I don't want to hear it. What's more, I can't hear it. I can't listen to anything you say! Don't you understand? You're tainted. We've got to get you as far away from this case as possible."

"Why?" Terrell asked dumbfounded.

"Why, you ask?" Mr. Bragg snatched the remote from the table and pointed it at the television to increase the sound.

An anchor man with impossibly polished white teeth began saying, "Recapping our top entertainment story, Rumors of pop diva Jennifer Weston's torrid love affair with her defense lawyer were verified today when the following photographs were unearthed." The photos began circulating in sequence as the voice continued, "Mere months after allegedly stabbing her boyfriend, rap artist Optimus, Jennifer Weston can be seen here in intimate detail canoodling on a rooftop with her new lover. This man has been identified as Terrell Banks of the Florida law firm, Bragg and Shuttlesworth. Bragg and Shuttlesworth were hired early on in the case, though it is unclear at the moment whether the relationship between Weston and Banks played a part in the crime itself. The couple was first seen together at this year's Music Awards."

The station ran a five-second clip of Jennifer and Terrell walking together at the music awards. The station played it in slow motion to give it a sinister air. Mr. Bragg clicked the remote and the television snapped off.

"That's been running all evening," he sighed. "And not just on the entertainment channels. You got a fifteen second blurb on two national news reports."

"Yeah but..." Terrell started.

"But nothing!" Mr. Bragg shouted. "It wasn't enough for you to make our client look like a cold-blooded whore to every potential juror in this country. No, you had to make it look like you were involved with the crime itself. We have no credibility now, do you understand that?"

"But sir, I didn't do it and I have theory about…"

"Shut up!" Mr. Bragg shouted. Terrell had never seen him so angry. "Just shut up! If you say one more word, I swear to God, I'm going to throw you through that window. I don't want to hear anything else from you. Because of your stupidity, we've got to start over from scratch and come up with a defense that is totally separate from anything you've contaminated. Mr. Dunn has been gracious enough not to sue us and we've agreed to handle the remainder of the case at a greatly reduced rate.

"Fine," Terrell said, utterly defeated. The loss of fees from this case would cost the firm millions. Knowing Mr. Bragg, he'd take it out of Terrell's pay. "Now what?"

"I want you to go and get all of your things from the back room." Mr. Bragg spoke slowly to emphasize his point. "Then I want you to get out of here. Take one of the SUV's in the garage and drive back to Tampa. I better not hear that you were even in the same room as Jennifer Weston until this trial is over. After that, you two can wallow around on all the rooftops you want."

"But I didn't," Terrell started until a stern look from Mr. Bragg convinced him that it wasn't a battle he was going to win. "Yes sir," he muttered as he moved to the door.

"And don't think the state bar won't hear of this," Brian needled. "I'm no lawyer, but I think having sexual relations with your clients is something that they frown upon."

"Oh," Mr. Foster added, "And don't bother going in to work tomorrow. I don't think we're going have the need for your services for awhile. Consider yourself suspended from the firm until you hear differently."

"Fine," Terrell said as he exited the room. He tried his best to ignore the smug expression on Brian Dunn's face.

A suspension from Bragg and Shuttlesworth wasn't the way he planned on making time to see Alicia. Still, now would be as good a time as any to fly to Spain. Then a sickening realization hit him. If this was on the news and in the magazines, Alicia was bound to see it too.

Terrell raced down the hallway toward his room. As bad as things were, they would infinitely be worse if Alicia heard the rumors before he had a chance to talk to her. He dove across the bed and dialed her number hurriedly. The answering machine picked up on the sixth ring. Terrell hung up and dialed again. This time, she picked up the phone.

"Hello," she answered.

"Hey, it's me," Terrell said, trying to sound happy. "What's going on?"

"Nothing."

"Sorry I haven't talked to you, but things have been kinda crazy for me."

"I bet."

"Is something wrong?" Terrell asked. "You don't sound like yourself."

"No Terrell. What could possibly be wrong?"

"Nothing I guess."

"It's late Terrell," Alicia said. "Why did you call?"

"I missed you," Terrell said in his sweetest voice. It was true. He did miss her.

"You missed me," she said. Terrell thought he detected disbelief in her voice. "That's weird. Did you miss me last week?"

"Of course I did, what kind of question is that?"

"But you didn't call me then."

"I tried, but I couldn't ever catch up to you. I left you messages."

"Oh yeah, I forgot. I did get one of your messages." There was a pause and Terrell could hear the rustling of papers. "It says that you're too busy and that I should cancel my plane tickets because you won't have time to see me."

"That's not how I said it," Terrell protested.

"You used nicer words, but don't worry, I got the message."

"Alicia," Terrell sighed, "I didn't call to fight."

"Okay," she said, "Then don't fight."

Terrell took a deep breath and plunged forward. "Alicia, I just wanted to let you know that you might hear some stuff about me. I wanted you to hear it from me that none of it is true and…"

"Stop," Alicia interrupted. "Is this about the pictures of you and Jennifer Weston on the roof?"

"You've seen them?" Terrell asked, flabbergasted.

"Yes, I've seen them. I'm in Europe, not on the moon. We do have the internet."

"Oh, well then you can see for yourself that the pictures don't really show what they imply. It's so slanted that it's just ridiculous. They're printing lies and I think I might just sue them for libel."

"Let me guess," Alicia said, "Now you're going to tell me that you didn't do anything wrong."

"I didn't."

"Really? Let me ask you something. Where have you been staying all this time that you've been down in Miami?"

"I told you. I'm staying at the firm's vacation house."

"And where has she been living?"

"In a vacation house," he answered meekly.

"The same one you're staying in?" she asked.

"Well yeah, but it's a pretty big place. We're not in the same room or anything."

"So you weren't doing anything wrong, but you couldn't tell me that you were shacked up with her? I still wouldn't know if I hadn't seen pictures of it."

"It's not like that," Terrell answered, "We're not shacked up. This isn't any different than staying in the same hotel. Since it's such a high profile case, Mr. Bragg thought it would be a good idea to keep someone here with her all the time."

"And I bet you jumped all over that assignment, didn't you?"

"No, I didn't," Terrell said trying to maintain his calm. "In fact, I was against it but you can't say no to a senior partner."

"You could have, you just didn't want to."

"Alicia…"

"Don't Alicia me," she interrupted. "You haven't even bothered to include me on any of this. If it's as innocent as you say it is, then why didn't you tell me about it from the beginning?"

"I thought that… Well, I figured that you would get mad or something."

"I only get mad when I have a reason to get mad Terrell. I know that this case is a great opportunity for your career. I've always supported you, haven't I?"

"Yes," Terrell answered. "You have." He felt the same way that he felt when his mother lectured him about keeping his priorities in order.

"We live thousands of miles apart right now. And until today, I never would have thought that you would cheat on me."

"I didn't," Terrell exclaimed. "I'm sorry. I know I should have told you, but I swear nothing happened with her."

"You lie to me about living with this woman for months. Now that there's pictures of the two of you on a rooftop you expect me to trust you when you say that you didn't cheat."

"I didn't lie to you." Terrell explained. "I just didn't tell you about it. And I didn't have sex with her. It's not like that at all. She knows all about you, I bring you up all the time."

"Wait," Alicia said with a different kind of anger in her voice. "You tell her everything about me but you lie to me about her? That's supposed to make it better?"

"No," Terrell sighed, realizing his mistake.

"Well, at least I know now why you told me to cancel my trip to Miami. It would have messed up your little celebrity hook-up."

"Alicia, you know that's not true. All I'm asking for is a chance to explain."

Alicia remained quiet on the phone, giving Terrell the first indication that perhaps she was willing to listen. He was just about to start his explanation of how the pictures came to be when Jennifer burst into his room.

"Terrell," she panicked, "What is going on around here? Nobody will tell me…"

"Who is that!" Alicia's voice screeched over the phone as Terrell held up a finger over his lips telling Jennifer to be quiet.

"What?" Terrell asked. "I didn't hear anything."

"Are you with her right now?" Alicia's voice had reached an angry pitch that Terrell had never heard from her. "Has she been with you this whole time!?"

"No, she just came in," Terrell tried to explain.

"Oh, so she just stops by your bedroom whenever she feels like it?"

"No, see…" he stammered.

"You're a piece of crap Terrell. Don't bother calling me back." Terrell heard the click of the phone disconnecting before he could even ask her to wait.

"Dammit!" Terrell shouted as he threw his phone against the wall. It shattered into a million pieces and fell to the floor.

"Sorry," said Jennifer, sensing that she had done something wrong. "Who was that?"

"My girlfriend Alicia," Terrell said, utterly defeated. "Well, probably ex-girlfriend now. I don't want to talk about it. You've got to get out of here before I get into any more trouble."

"What do you mean? Why is everybody acting so weird all of a sudden?"

Terrell gave Jennifer an abridged version of his meeting with Mr. Foster and Mr. Bragg.

"So what?" she asked. "It's not true. Besides, those stupid tabloids have me dating somebody new every week. If I buy a cappuccino from a guy, they print that I'm about to have his baby."

"It's a little different when you're accused of sleeping with your lawyer," Terrell said as he scanned the hallway and closed his door. "Did anyone see you come down here?"

"No, why?"

"Because Mr. Bragg said he'd have me killed if he caught us together and I'm not ready to die yet."

"Don't worry, I'll just go down there and tell him that I want you to stay."

"Don't do that, it will just make things worse. He says I'm tainted and he's right. Perception is reality. If a juror thinks we're sleeping together, then we might as well be. The State's Attorney will crucify you with it. Trust me, if you're going to have a chance to win, I can't be anywhere near this case."

"But it's not true," she said. "I'll tell him that it's not true. It's my case, they have to listen to me."

"It won't do any good. I can't be here anymore."

"But you can't leave," her eyes widened in terror. "You're the only one that believes me. Once you're gone, they'll try and make me plead guilty to something that I didn't do. I know they will. That's all they talk about when you're gone. They keep telling me that I need to be realistic about this and think about the future. They keep telling me that if I plea, I could be out of prison by the time I'm fifty. Fifty, Terrell!" Terrell could see the panic in her eyes.

"Listen to me," he said, placing his palms on her shoulders. "No one is going to make you do anything. Mr. Bragg and Mr. Foster are much better lawyers than I am. I'm sure that they can to get you out of this."

Jennifer did not look convinced.

"Now, I have to go," Terrell continued. "But there is something that I need to tell you. I think that Felix did sign that contract with Southside Records. I think it may have something to do with his murder."

"What?" she asked.

"I'm not sure, but I do know that Brian and AMI aren't being honest." He thought carefully before proceeding, "Jennifer, I have to ask you something, and you have to tell me the truth."

"I always do," she replied.

"I know, but this is really important. Did Felix have a will?"

She thought for a moment before answering, "I honestly don't know. Is it important?"

"It could be. Brian seems to think that he left everything, including the rights to his music, to you. If that's true, then you have a huge motive to kill him."

"For money?" she asked incredulously. "That's the stupidest thing I've ever heard. Not to sound like a jerk, but I have plenty of money. I wouldn't need to kill anyone for it."

"Still," Terrell said, "Fifty million is a lot of money."

"Yeah," she replied. "That's why Brian had been so crazy trying to keep Felix signed. Losing him would have cost Brian a job. He's got more motive than I do."

"I hadn't looked at it like that," Terrell said. "Do you think maybe…"

"He killed Felix?" she finished. "No, he couldn't have. He wasn't even in Miami."

"Maybe not, but something's definitely not right with him. I doesn't matter anyway. I still don't know where to find those contracts, and without them, his motive is all speculation on our part. I'm out of time. When I'm gone, you've got to tell this to Joe. Do you know who he is?"

"He's the creepy guy with the bald head that always wears those black suits," Jennifer nodded slowly.

"Yeah, that's the one," Terrell said. "Tell him that he has to find that contract. Maybe we can tie Brian or AMI or whoever else into this."

"O…Okay," she said. "Why can't you tell him?"

"Mr. Bragg and Mr. Foster can't know that this idea came from me. I wasn't even supposed to tell you about the contract situation. Tell them that you just remembered it or something. Whatever you do, don't let them know that the lead came from me. Do you understand?"

"Yeah, but I still don't understand why you can't stay."

"Because I can't," Terrell sighed. "I just can't. You've got to get out of here. Don't let anyone see you come from my room. I have enough problems as it is."

"Where are you going?" she asked.

"Home, I guess. They told me to take that rented SUV and go back to Tampa."

"And you're just going to sit there while the put me on trial?"

"I don't want to," Terrell explained, "but it's not like I have much choice."

"I guess this is goodbye then," she said dejected.

"Not goodbye," Terrell smiled. "It's just a see you later. We'll hook up after you're acquitted. Sorry, that was a bad choice of words, but you know what I mean. Joe should be back in a day or two. He's creepy, but he's good. If anyone can find that contract, he can."

"Okay," she responded. She looked as if she wanted to give him a hug before she left, but she thought better of it. All she could muster was a weak wave as she walked out the door.

"Disgrace and disbarment," Terrell muttered. What a fantastic way to end his first high profile case.

CHAPTER 17

It did not take long for Terrell to gather his belongings from the house. He'd been living out of a suitcase for months and he'd become proficient at traveling on a moment's notice. He wouldn't miss the house. Part of him even looked forward to going home and getting some much needed rest. Maybe Bragg and Shuttlesworth would be even be gracious enough to let him collect a couple of paychecks before they fired him.

He carried his suitcases out into the hallway. There were two housekeepers standing just outside his door waiting on him.

"Oh," Terrell said, momentarily startled. "I'm leaving, so you don't have to worry about cleaning up in there now.

"We know," the older of the two asked. She didn't look happy to be there. "We're supposed to change the linens and vacuum for someone named Gil."

"I see," Terrell answered, thinking that the firm hadn't wasted any time replacing him. They'd probably have the nameplate removed from his office door within the hour. "Well, I'm finished, so go ahead."

He trudged toward the front door, noticing that everyone

refused to make eye contact with him. He saw Justin, one of the firm's many paralegals, stacking boxes onto a dolly.

"Mr. Banks," Justin said as soon as he approached. "Give me one minute, these are the last boxes. Mr. Bragg says that this is all the research you've done for the case. He asked me to tell you that you need to carry it back to Tampa with you, but you are not to take it into the office under any circumstances."

"Of course he did." Terrell said as he stared at the conference room door. He figured that Gil was in there at that moment trying to get up to speed on the case. Maybe he could tell Gil his suspicions later, but he knew better than to try to make the point now. He hoped Joe was able to get something out of Clarence.

Terrell followed Justin out to the garage, and watched as he stacked the boxes on the second row seat.

"There, that does it," Justin said as he crammed the last box inside the vehicle. "Good-bye, Mr. Banks."

Justin didn't wait for a reply before wheeling the dolly back toward the house.

The housekeeping staff had been kind enough to stack his laundry in a huge pile in the back and cover it with a blanket. "At least they finally got around to washing my stuff," Terrell muttered.

He threw his suitcases on the passenger seat and climbed behind the wheel. He drove through the throng of media that remained camped out in front of the gated community. The mirrored glass tint prevented anyone from seeing who was inside the car, but that didn't stop the paparazzi from trying to take pictures anyway. Terrell wished he knew which one of them snapped his picture with Jennifer. In his current mood, he would have liked nothing more than to run him over with the SUV.

***

As he drove north on Interstate 95, he could feel his eyes starting to droop. It was only 10:15, but he was exhausted. He realized that he hadn't had any dinner. He saw a sign for a burger place at the next exit and decided to stop. Terrell cut across three lanes of highway traffic and zoomed up the exit ramp. He needed to use the restroom as well, so he wheeled the big SUV into one of the brightly lit parking spaces in the front of the store. Terrell got out of the car and stretched. He was still wearing his shirt and tie. He thought he had a couple of t-shirts in his laundry and any one of those would be far more comfortable to wear for the rest of the drive.

He opened the rear door and stuck his hand into the pile under the blanket. It wasn't quite as soft as he expected.

"Ow!" yelped a voice. Terrell snatched the blanket and was astonished to see Jennifer, curled up into a ball and rubbing her forehead. "You hit me in the face."

"This is not happening," Terrell said, shaking his head. "I'm obviously hallucinating or something, because there is absolutely no way that you are hiding in my backseat."

"Don't be mad," Jennifer said with big, innocent eyes.

"What's there to be mad about?" Terrell asked. "Other than the fact that Mr. Foster is going to send Joe to strangle me?"

"I can explain," Jennifer started.

"No explanation needed," Terrell said as he shut the door. He walked around to the driver's side and slid in behind the wheel.

"What are you doing?" Jennifer asked when Terrell turned the key and started the car.

"I'm about to get on I-95 South so I can take you back to Miami." Terrell said in his most polite voice. "If I'm extremely lucky, they will let me say goodbye to my parents before they drown me in the canal."

"You can't take me back!" she said.

"I most certainly can take you back, and I am taking you back," answered Terrell. "I told you that I couldn't be involved in this anymore. This is for your own good." He thought about his statement for a moment before adding, "Mine too."

"Just hear me out," she pleaded. "I only need five minutes,

then you can take me back if you still want to." He turned in his seat to look her in the eye.

"Whatever it is, I'm sure you could tell me on the way back to Miami," he suggested. "It will take us more than five minutes to get there."

"Please?" she begged.

"Fine," he acquiesced. He got back out of the car, walked around to the back and opened the door. "They can't kill me twice, so I guess it really doesn't matter. What do you need?"

"I listened to what you said earlier."

"Could've fooled me."

"I really did. Anyway, I left your room and I walked down to the conference room where Brian and those other lawyers were. I went inside and demanded that they put you back on the case."

"You didn't," Terrell groaned.

"I did. Why shouldn't I? It's my case."

"Yeah, it's your case, but with the pictures and all... Now they're sure something happened between us." He shook his head in disbelief. "I told you not to do that."

"I know what you said, but they're being stupid. Those pictures don't show anything."

Terrell held his face in both hands. "And how did they take your demands?"

"They totally ignored me!" she answered. "Mr. Bragg and Mr. Foster just kept talking to the new guy like I wasn't even there. Then, Brian puts his arm around me and walks me out of the room. He starts going into how he's so sorry that you took advantage of me when I was vulnerable. He told me that he was going to see to it that you never saw another courtroom unless you were in a blue jumpsuit and chains."

"That's fantastic." Terrell sighed. "I thought he just wanted me disbarred. It's good to know that he wants me incarcerated too."

"Then he says," she slipped into an imitation of Brian's voice,

"He was just using you to make himself famous. He's probably already writing a tell-all book about your relationship."

"That sounds like something he'd accuse me of."

"Then he said that I should leave all the decisions to the people he was paying to represent me. Then he went back inside and locked the door."

"Is that it?" Terrell asked. "You sneaked out of the house to tell me that Brian is a hard-headed bastard? Sorry to take the wind out of your sails, but I already knew that."

"No, that's not it," she responded. "Don't you get it? They don't listen to me. They're not interested in anything I have to say. I might as well be a statue in that place. The only person giving me the time of day is Brian, and he might have had something to do with it. How do you expect me to convince them to do anything? And even if I could, how exactly could I explain it to them without saying that the idea came from you?"

"I don't know," Terrell admitted. "But you have to."

"I can't. I've only seen that Joe guy like three times and I'm sure he's not going to listen to anything I have to say either."

"Okay, okay, I get it," Terrell said. "But sneaking out like this won't make them listen to you either."

"If you listen," she answered, "they won't have to."

"What is that supposed to mean?"

"I was walking back up to my room, thinking about what you said, and I got an idea."

"Uh-oh," Terrell said. "I don't like the sound of this. What ever this idea is, find a way to get it to Joe. He can give you more help than I can."

"Just listen," she said. "You remember when you said that Felix already had signed a new contract, right?"

"Yeah," Terrell nodded cautiously.

"Well, he must have gotten it after we left New York, because he would have mentioned it to me. And it he couldn't have had it with him in Miami, or they would have found it in the hotel room."

"Okay, what's your point?"

"I think I know where we can find it."

"Really? We?"

"Yeah, we. Felix and I have a couple of apartments scattered around the country. He leases them under a fake name and sometimes we would go to one of them when we wanted to get away from everybody. I don't think anyone else knows that he has them."

"Okay. I'm curious. Where are these places?"

"LA, Dallas, Chicago and Atlanta."

"And you think that he might have stashed the contract in the Atlanta apartment?"

"It has to be there," she replied, her eyes ablaze with hope. "If he had the contract like you say he did, there is no where else it could be."

"But you don't know for sure," Terrell said.

"No, but it couldn't hurt to see if it's there."

"It will hurt a lot when Joe's punching me in the face," Terrell replied.

"Nothing bad will happen. See, I even brought this." Jennifer pulled a silver key from her pocket and smiled mischievously. "All you have to do is drive. We'll find the contract and I'll call Luther to pick me up from the apartment. They'll never even know you had anything to do with it."

"No," Terrell tried to make excuses, "It's still a bad idea. They're probably already out looking for you. We'd never even make it to Atlanta."

"We will make it if we hurry. They don't even know I'm gone yet."

"Oh please," Terrell said. "You've been gone an hour and a half already. Someone is bound to notice that you're not there."

"I doubt it," she smiled.

"Come to think of it, how did you get out in the first place?" Terrell asked.

"The same way I snuck out of the house when I was fifteen," she replied. "The roof."

"The roof?"

"Yeah, it was easy. After I remembered the apartment, I told Luther that I was going upstairs and that I didn't want anyone to bother me."

"Yeah, but I'm sure he's been up there to check on you since you left."

"No he hasn't," she replied confidently. "I fired my last bodyguard for waking me up after I told him not to let anyone bother me."

"You?" Terrell asked. "But you always seemed so nice."

"What can I say," she shrugged. "I'm entitled to one diva moment every once in awhile, right? Anyway, since that happened, my staff does exactly as I say. Especially if I say that I don't want to be bothered."

"What if someone peeks in the room?"

"They'd think I was up on the roof. Everyone knows I go up there. That's how they got the pictures, remember?"

"How could I forget?" Terrell sighed.

"Anyway, after I told him, I just walked across the roof to the far side of the house. Then, I jumped down into the back yard and waited for you in the garage. I saw you coming in with that guy and so I hid in the backseat under that blanket."

"I can't believe you," Terrell shook his head. "Did it ever occur to you that this was a bad idea?"

"I didn't think it all the way through. I was going to say something, but I didn't want to scare you. And then I guess I fell asleep," she added.

Terrell stared at her with a disgusted look on his face.

"I'm sorry. I get sleepy on car trips."

"Is that it?" Terrell asked.

"Yeah that's it."

"Alright. I've listened to you. Now I'm going to turn this truck around and take you back to the house. Then you're going to tell Joe what you told me and he will go find our missing contract."

"No!" she shouted. "Just keep driving. This will work, I swear! They'll never know you were involved. Come on, please."

Terrell could see the first tears welling in her eyes. He knew that she was right. Mr. Bragg wouldn't listen to her because he would know it was Terrell's idea. Brian wouldn't care because finding that document would cost his company quite a bit of money. Terrell had made a lot of bad decisions during this case, and he knew that he was about to make another.

"Alright, I'll take you," he said.

"Yes!" she jumped out of the car and hugged him.

"Wait!" he said as he looked around the parking lot. "We can't let anyone see you."

"Oh, sorry." She hid behind the open door.

"I'll take you and help you look for this thing, but that's it. You're going to call them to come and pick you up, whether we find anything or not."

"Okay," she agreed.

"And then you can't talk to me anymore, okay?"

"Okay," she smiled as she started to climb into the front seat.

"Stay in the back," Terrell instructed.

"Why?"

"The tint is darker in the back. They'll be looking for a man and woman traveling together. We'll be less obvious if people can't see you."

"That makes sense," she said as she scrunched down in the seat. "Do you think they're going to put out some kind of APB out on us?"

"I doubt it," Terrell answered. "Right now, people are running wild with a story that we're having some kind of affair. The firm's not going to encourage that by telling them that we've run away together. Besides, they're limited as to what they can say. You're not supposed to leave Miami, remember?"

"Oh yeah, I forgot about that."

"They can't very well admit that their client has violated bond. They're going to want to do this as quietly as possible, so they'll probably send Joe to find us. And trust me, he will find us. I just hope it's after we get to Atlanta. Do you have any cash?"

"No," she said, "I left in a hurry. All I have besides that key is my cell phone."

"Take the battery out," Terrell said curtly.

"Why?" she asked as she began removing the case.

"Even when the phone's off it emits a signal to nearby cell towers. They can use that signal to track us."

"How do you know that?" she asked.

"We used that technique to follow a guy in a very nasty divorce case. You'd be surprised how easy it is to keep tabs on someone." He reached into his own pocket and pulled out a few bills.

"How much do you have?" she asked.

"Eight dollars," he answered. The SUV's gas gauge was already on the south side of the halfway mark. "That isn't going to come close to getting us to Atlanta." he said.

"You don't have your ATM card with you?"

"I do, but if I use it, they can track us." Terrell sat back in his seat and weighed his options. He didn't want to risk withdrawing cash. Joe would be on him before the machine spit out the bills. Besides, once they discovered that Jennifer was gone, it was quite likely that they'd find a way to freeze his account. He pulled a map out of the glove compartment.

"What are you looking for?" Jennifer asked.

"We have to get rid of this car," he answered. "They'll be looking for it. And it's a rental so they probably have some kind of tracking device in it." He quickly figured out his position and traced the back roads to Port St. Lucie. It wasn't far. They should be able to make it.

CHAPTER 18

Jennifer talked a lot when she was nervous, and she was nervous for the entire drive to Port St. Lucie. Luckily for Terrell, she didn't need him to participate in the conversation to keep talking. He listened while she told him details of her childhood. He enjoyed her stories of the embarrassing things that happened to her in middle school. He certainly could relate to being an awkward teenager. The mood was so casual that it was easy to forget that they were technically fugitives.

"…and even now," she chuckled, "I can't swim in an indoor pool."

"You know Jennifer," Terrell laughed. "You really are a regular person."

"I don't know how to take that. Am I supposed to be something else?"

"No," he answered quickly. "Well, actually, yes."

"Why?"

"I don't know. You're the biggest star in the world. I guess I expected you to have some kind of weird, crazy childhood, but you're just like everybody else I know. Well, except for the fact that you can sing."

"That's okay," she replied. "I thought only nerdy dorks grew up to be lawyers, so I guess we're even."

Terrell spotted the street sign marking Lorville Court. He slowed the vehicle turned into the cul-de-sac.

"Are you sure this is going to work?" she asked.

"I have no idea if it's going to work. I've never shown up on his doorstep in the middle of the night asking for a favor. Not since college anyway. But he is my friend, so this is the best shot we have." Terrell stopped the car in front of a taupe stucco house with dark blue trim.

"Okay, this is it. Stay out of sight until I give you the signal."

Jennifer nodded and Terrell hopped out of the car. He walked toward the door, making footprints on the dewy lawn. He heard a menacing bark and froze. A dark shape barreled down on him from behind the house. The big German Shepherd almost knocked him off his feet as he excitedly barked and licked at Terrell's face.

"Hey Beast," Terrell said to the dog. "I was worried that you weren't going to remember me." The porch light came on and Terrell saw a familiar silhouette standing in the doorway.

"Who is that?" Ricky asked.

"It's me! Get this dog off of me before he licks me to death!"

"What are you doing here?"

"I was going to ask you if I could come inside the house," Terrell answered. "Some guard dog you have here."

"Beast knows you're too soft to be a burglar." Ricky walked out and grabbed Beast by the collar to pull him off of Terrell.

"Either that or he's gotten lazy around here living the good life."

"You're one to talk about the good life. Come inside before you wake the baby. I'll put Beast in the back yard."

Ricky had been one of Terrell's closest friends since college. He married his long-time girlfriend Mya and Terrell had been a groomsman in the wedding. They had just had their first child, a little girl named Nadia.

"You don't visit, you don't write," Ricky whispered as he and Terrell entered the house. "Terrell Banks, lawyer to the stars, can't even find the time to return my phone calls."

"Yeah, sorry about that," Terrell apologized. "I've been kinda busy with…"

"Shhh!" Ricky whispered. "Keep your voice down. The baby just went back to sleep. Mya will not be happy if you wake her up."

It was dark inside the house. The only light came from two nightlights in the living room. Terrell could see the rise and fall of a small blanket in the playpen.

"What are you doing up anyway?" Terrell asked.

"Nadia wakes up every three hours and it's my turn for night duty. It's killing me. She won't go back to sleep unless you feed her, walk her around the living room and then put her in the playpen. That crib cost me a six hundred bucks and she won't even sleep in it."

"She's already got you wrapped around her little finger," Terrell said as he walked over to the couch to take a closer look. Nadia slept with her tiny little hands balled up into fists.

"She's beautiful man," Terrell smiled. "How old is she again?"

"Four months," Ricky answered. "Which you would know if you ever bothered to answer your messages. Last time I called, your cell number had been disconnected."

"I had to get it changed," Terrell answered. "You know, with this case and all, I've been getting a lot of crank phone calls."

"You changed your number and didn't give it to me?" Ricky said. "I thought we were boys!"

"Sorry." Terrell answered. "I've been really busy."

Ricky began staring at him with a devilish grin on his face.

"What?" Terrell asked.

"I know what's been keeping you so busy." Ricky said.

"Awwww man," Terrell replied. "What have you heard?"

"Everything," Ricky laughed. "It's been all over the TV since I got home. You do realize that hooking up with Jennifer Weston puts you on a whole different level, right?"

"Ricky," Terrell tried to interrupt.

"Most men can only dream about the places you've gone and the things that you've done."

"Ricky."

"I have to be content living vicariously through you. I'm proud that my expert coaching and knowledge of women has turned you into the ultimate player."

"It's not like that."

"You know, Mya won't even let me watch music videos because of her. That little dance she does with her hips, I didn't even think they could play things like that on TV."

"Ricky, listen. I'm sorry to tell you, but nothing happened."

"What?"

"Nothing happened. I'm telling you, it's not like it looks."

"What? I know what I saw. They have pictures of you on a rooftop. That gets you extra points for creativity."

"Whatever," Terrell said. "Think whatever you want."

"I plan to. I'm a happily married man, all I have are my thoughts."

"Jokes aside, I need a favor."

"What kind of favor?" Ricky asked.

"The big kind. Look, I need your help."

Ricky sized him up for a moment then asked, "You're serious, aren't you?"

"Yeah, I am."

"Just say the word and you got it. Just because you forgot your friends when you got a little taste of stardom doesn't mean we forgot you. It's not illegal is it?"

"No," Terrell answered. Then he thought for a moment and added "Not for you anyway."

"Okay, but you're going to tell me all the details about you and her when this is over, understand?"

"Sure," Terrell answered. "anything you want." He was too tired to argue about it. "Do you still have the El Dorado?" Terrell spotted two cars in Ricky's driveway, but he didn't see the El Dorado.

"Yeah, I still have it. It's in the garage." During college, Ricky drove around in a 1973 pearl white Cadillac El Dorado. Ricky loved that car but it had always been in terrible shape. He had kept it together mostly on prayers and duct tape.

"Is it still running?" Terrell asked hopefully.

"Is it running?" Ricky smiled. "Hold on a minute." He carefully picked up Nadia and walked toward the back of the house with her. He came back a few moments later and led Terrell out to the garage.

"I guess that answers my question," Terrell groaned when he got a look at the car. The dingy paint had been stripped, sanded and painted primer gray. The car was jacked up on stands and the front wheels and the hood had been removed. Oily car parts were scattered around the garage.

"I'm restoring it to factory specs. When I get finished, it's going to be nice."

"Dammit!" Terrell cursed. "I needed to borrow it."

"What's stopping you?" Ricky grinned. He walked over to the car, reached in the driver side and turned the key. Amazingly, the engine roared to life. "I rebuilt the block last month. The only reason it's up on jacks is because I need to change the shocks."

"How long will that take?" Terrell asked.

"An hour and a half maybe?"

"How far can it go?"

"It'll make it to California once I put the wheels back on."

"Great, I need to take it to Atlanta. I'll bring it back the day after tomorrow."

"What do you need my car for? You pulled up in a new SUV."

"I can't use it. It's a long story, but I need to stash that in your garage while I take your car."

"Did you steal it?" Ricky asked.

"No, I did not steal it," Terrell defended himself. "There are some people I'm trying to avoid. I need to lose them for a little while and hiding the SUV here was the best thing I could think of on short notice."

"Are you sure you're not getting me into anything illegal? I'm not trying going to jail. Mya would kill me."

"I'm positive. No one is going to jail. Now can I borrow the car or not?"

"I told you man, anything I can do, I will. But you're going to have to help me replace the shocks in the morning."

"How about tonight? I was hoping I could leave immediately."

"Sure, why not tonight?" Ricky grumbled. "It's not like I have to go to work or anything. Do you need anything else?"

"Now that you mention it," Terrell winced, "I was also hoping you could spot me a couple hundred bucks."

"You need me to spot you some cash?" Ricky asked. "You make like a million dollars a year! I thought you used twenties to light your cigars."

"That's real funny. I'll write you a check to cover it, but I need some cash and I can't go to the ATM."

"Why not? Are you trying to buy some crack or something?"

"I told you, it's a long story. I just need you to trust me. Do you have any cash?"

"Yeah, I think I do," Ricky said. "But you owe me big, and I expect to be compensated. I want football tickets to that luxury box your firm has at Tampa stadium. It better be tickets to a good game too."

"Fine, whatever you say," Terrell promised. He wasn't sure he or his guests would be welcome in the luxury box once he got fired. He'd figure that out later.

"Wait here." Ricky stepped back into the house, leaving Terrell alone in the garage. He was starting to believe that this crazy plan might actually work. Once they switched cars, it would be difficult for anyone to track them. Ricky returned a few minutes later with an odd look on his face. Terrell saw the reason for the look a moment later.

"Hello Mya," Terrell said cheerfully.

"Don't hello Mya me," she answered. "You are so pitiful. I saw you and your little girlfriend on the television."

"Yeah, about that…"

"I don't even want to hear it," shaking her head in disgust. "I'm so disappointed with you Terrell. I might assume that kind of foolishness from this one," she said, jerking her thumb at Ricky. "But I expected more from you."

"But you have to understand…" Terrell tried to interject.

"Ah-ah-ahh," she said holding her finger up. "No excuses. Does Alicia know?"

"Yes," Terrell answered.

"So what are you going to do?"

"I'm going to beg and grovel for forgiveness?"

"That's a start," she said. "Then what?"

"I'll tell her that I love her and hope that she can take me back even though I don't deserve it."

"That's a good boy. By the way, you should add some expensive presents to the begging. It helps, doesn't it Ricky?"

"Yeah baby," Ricky kissed her on the cheek. "That's right."

"You seem sorry enough, I guess you can stay. You two are lucky you didn't wake Nadia up while you were playing with that stupid car."

"Sorry," Terrell apologized. "I promise, we'll be quiet."

"You better be," she replied. She wasn't kidding. "It's good to see you Terrell. You should visit us again soon, but next time, come at a decent hour. You and Ricky aren't 19 anymore."

"I will," said Terrell.

"It's still your night if she wakes up again" she said, turning to Ricky. "I'm going back to bed." Mya kissed Ricky and left the garage.

"Sorry about that," Ricky apologized. "She heard me crank up the car."

"That was weird. She didn't even ask me why I was here."

"I told her that with everything that was going on with you, you needed a friend to talk to."

"That was quick thinking. She bought that?"

"Yeah man. Women are all about talking to their friends during a crisis."

"I'll never understand women."

"Me neither. It only gets worse after you get married. I've only got a hundred and forty bucks. Is that enough?"

"That will do. Thanks man, I really appreciate it."

"No problem. If there's nothing else, we should get started on replacing those shocks. I would like to get some sleep tonight."

"There is one more thing," Terrell said.

"Here it comes," Ricky lamented. "First you need to borrow my car to drive to Atlanta. Then you need me to loan you all the cash that I have. What is it now? Do you need my kidney too?"

"Not exactly," Terrell said, "I have to show you something and you can't tell anyone that you saw it." He rolled up the garage door and beckoned towards the SUV. Seeing his signal, Jennifer got out of the car.

"You dirty dog," Ricky said breathlessly. "She came with you? She's even better looking in person than she is on TV. Never mind what Mya said. I'm proud of you."

Terrell ignored him while Jennifer approached.

"Jennifer," Terrell said, "This is Ricky, a good friend of mine. He's been gracious enough to give us a little help getting to Atlanta."

"Thank-you, I really appreciate it," Jennifer said in a sweet voice.

"You're problem," Ricky answered, star-struck. "I mean, no welcome. I mean you're welcome, it's no problem."

"May I come in?" she asked.

"Oh yeah," Ricky answered, jolted from his stupor. "Sorry about that." Ricky led them both back inside the garage.

"I apologize for the mess, I wasn't expecting company," Ricky whispered.

"That's okay, you don't have to do anything special for…" Jennifer started.

Ricky quickly held up a finger over his lips.

"Ricky's got a newborn little girl that just went back to sleep," Terrell whispered.

"Aww!" Jennifer gushed. "Can I see her?"

"Maybe if she wakes up I'll go get her. I don't think my wife would like the idea of you being here."

"She's not a fan?" Jennifer asked.

"It's not that," Ricky said as he looked at Terrell. "I just don't think she'd like the idea of seeing the two of you here together."

"Oh," Jennifer said, understanding the implication. "She knows…"

"Alicia? Yeah. She does," Terrell answered.

"It's going to take me and Terrell a little while to get the car running." Ricky said. "Do you want something to drink or a snack or something?"

"You didn't offer me a snack." Terrell said. "I'm hurt."

"You're not a guest. Besides, you're getting a car and all my cash. You should be bringing food to me."

"Good point," Terrell conceded.

"I wouldn't normally ask, but I'd love something to eat. I haven't had anything all day."

"You're in luck," Ricky smiled. "I made spaghetti for dinner. There's plenty left over and not to brag, but it's fantastic."

"Mind if I have some?" Jennifer asked.

"Sure." Ricky ran back to the kitchen and emerged a few minutes later with a steaming bowl of noodles and sauce to give to Jennifer. Terrell and Ricky began the arduous task of installing new front shocks on the Cadillac.

Despite the circumstances, Terrell enjoyed the time he spent with Ricky. Working on the car took him back to college. When they were freshmen, Ricky had been the only one with a car and they had spent countless hours keeping it running. Jennifer sat quietly on Ricky's workbench and watched the two of them struggle and curse as they attempted to properly install the new parts. Luckily, the task didn't take as long as Terrell feared. As Ricky tightened the last nut holding the hood in place, Terrell stole a glance at his watch. It was just past 2:30 am.

"That's it," Ricky said with a sense of satisfaction. "She's not pretty, but she'll get you to Atlanta."

"Jennifer," Terrell said, "Pull the truck into the garage." He tossed her the keys while Ricky opened the garage door.

"I'll move the car out of the way," Terrell offered.

"No, don't start it up," Ricky stopped him. "I don't want to wake Mya up again. Put it in neutral and we'll roll it outside." The two of them pushed the car out of the garage and down the driveway. After they wheeled it a safe distance into the street, Jennifer parked the SUV inside the garage.

"Be careful," Ricky warned. "The odometer isn't hooked up and neither is the gas gauge, so I'd watch my speed and gas up every 250 miles or so. Are you sure you don't want to stay a little while and get some rest?"

"Nah, I'm good," Terrell said as Jennifer walked over to the car. "Besides, we really need to go. Thanks man, I owe you one."

"You owe me about ten actually and I plan on collecting."

"Don't worry, I'll get your tickets."

"I'll settle for nothing less than luxury box seats. I expect first class accommodations."

"Luxury box, I got it."

"It was nice meeting you," Jennifer said. "Thank you so much."

"No problem," Ricky said. "Hey, wait a minute." He sprinted back inside the house and returned a few moments later with a copy of Jennifer's CD and a pen. "Just in case I don't see you again, would you mind?"

"Not at all," she smiled as she took the CD. "To my good friend Ricky," she said the words aloud as she wrote, "I wouldn't have been able to do it without you."

"The guys at work are never going to believe this," Ricky said as she gave it back to him.

"Rick!" Terrell snapped.

"I know, I know," Ricky said. "I can't tell anyone you were here. It's all a big secret. I got it. I'll wait a couple of days and then I'll make up a story. You out?"

"Yeah, we're out," Terrell said as he and Jennifer got into the front seat of the Cadillac.

"Alright then. I expect my car to be back here the day after tomorrow with a full tank of gas. Good luck on your secret spy mission." Terrell and Jennifer waved and took off north into the night.

***

Clarence hated being awakened in the middle of the night by a ringing phone. It was a problem that he hadn't had to worry too much about since Optimus died, but that didn't do anything to improve his mood. He checked the caller ID and frowned.

"What do you want?" he barked into the receiver.

"She's gone," the raspy whisper replied.

"Who's gone?"

"Who the hell do you think? Jennifer you idiot! No body knows where she is."

"Don't call me an idiot."

"Don't act like an idiot and I won't call you one."

"Why are you telling me about it? You're supposed to be the one keeping an eye on her."

"Don't try to put this off on me. If you'd done your job at the music awards, we wouldn't even be in this mess."

"Whatever. So what if she ran away? That only makes her look guilty."

"I don't think she's running away. I think she's running to something."

"Something like what?"

"That prick lawyer is gone too. He's been poking around in Atlanta. I think he might know something."

"Are you sure?"

"No I'm not sure, but where else would they go? Is there anything there that could hurt us?"

"Maybe. I can guess where she'll take him."

"Well, if you know where they're going, then get down there and fix this."

"I have it under control, alright. I'll handle it."

"Handle it then, and do it permanently. Don't screw it up this time." Clarence heard the slam of the receiver being jammed back on the cradle before he hung up on his end. He rubbed his eyes and scratched the back of his head. He cursed himself for forgetting about the apartment. That had to be where it was.

He looked over to his left at the shape of the woman lying in bed next to him. She was beautiful, the kind of girl that Optimus always took away from him before his untimely demise. He gave the woman a rough shove to wake her up. He had a plane to catch.

CHAPTER 19

When they left Ricky's house, the night was so bright and clear that Terrell had hardly needed the headlights. Now, he activated the high beams in an effort to cut through the enveloping blackness. Terrell guided the Cadillac north on state road 91, desperately trying to avoid as much traffic as possible. Now he began to wonder if the scenic route had been such a good idea after all. As the hands of his watch creeped toward four, the lack of sleep began catching up with him.

Jennifer's breath was deep and steady. It wasn't quite a snore, but given time it might develop into one. Terrell could use the noise. The radio wasn't working, so Jennifer had promised to keep him company while he drove. She'd fallen asleep about twenty minutes into the drive. Terrell's eyes were getting very heavy. He was debating whether he should wake Jennifer when the first fat droplet of rain hit the windshield.

"Guess that explains why it got so dark all of a sudden," Terrell mumbled. A second and third droplet of rain fell on the windshield so Terrell turned on the wipers. Nothing happened. He switched the wipers on and off as several more droplets fell, but the wipers refused to move.

"It's okay," he hoped. "Maybe it won't rain very hard," At that moment, he saw a crack of lightning followed by the deep boom of thunder. The rain falling on the windshield picked up in intensity.

"Jennifer," Terrell said. She stirred in her seat, but did not wake.

"Jennifer," Terrell said again, this time a little louder. He reached across the seat and poked her in the side.

"Huh?" she awoke with a start.

"The windshield wipers don't work and it looks like it's about to rain pretty hard."

Jennifer blinked stupidly at him, still half-asleep.

"I won't be able to see," he explained. "If it keeps raining, I'm going to have to stop."

"You're going to stop right here on the side of the road?"

"I hope I won't have to. A primer gray car sitting on the side of the road will definitely get noticed by the highway patrol. They'll probably think it's abandoned." Terrell shook his head. "The last thing we need is some local cop recognizing you."

"You were all over the TV today too," she smiled. "Right now, you're just as famous as I am."

"I doubt that."

"How long was I sleeping?" she asked.

"About an hour, we're almost in St. Cloud. By the way, thanks a lot for keeping me company."

"Sorry," she said meekly. "I told you, I get sleepy on car trips."

"I see that," Terrell answered. "You've got something on your face." He jerked his thumb at a small trail of drool that had escaped her lips while she was sleeping. Jennifer wiped it off with the back of her hand.

"Gross," she said, rubbing her hand on her jeans. "That's really embarrassing. You've got to promise not to tell anyone."

"Why," he asked. "I think your adoring public would want to

know that the beautiful and talented Jennifer Weston drools in her sleep just like everyone else."

The rain began falling harder and it was very difficult for Terrell to see anything through the blurred windshield.

"I'm going to have to stop," Terrell said.

"Wait," Jennifer said. "I think I see some kind of sign up there."

Terrell squinted through the cascade of water falling down around them. He saw a neon sign about half mile ahead of them. He couldn't quite make out the words, but he was pretty sure that stopping there would generate less attention than parking on the shoulder. He slowed down to about twenty miles an hour and crept toward the sign.

"The Prince Motel," Terrell read the sign as he turned the car into the parking lot. "I'm sure these are some of Florida's finest accommodations."

"Yes they are," Jennifer giggled. "I've always refused to do shows in Florida unless I'm guaranteed a room here. Once you've stayed at a palace like this, nothing else compares."

In reality, the Prince was a seedy looking, one-story motel with brown painted cinderblock walls and faded orange doors. Only a couple of cars were parked in the gravely lot. He pulled the car into a space near the motel's dingy looking office and shut off the engine.

"Are we going in?" Jennifer asked.

"I don't know," Terrell yawned. "We could just sit here until the rain lets up enough to drive again. What do you think?"

"I think that you look sleepy and it's still a long way to Atlanta."

"You could drive for a little while."

"I don't think that would be a good idea."

"Why not?"

"I sorta don't have a driver's license," Jennifer admitted.

"You don't?" Terrell began laughing. "But you said you bought a brand new car when you got your first record deal."

"I did. I failed the driver's test three times when I was 16 and I never went back to get it."

Terrell laughed harder.

"Stop laughing! It's not like I need one. I don't think it's a big deal."

"I'm sorry," Terrell said between chuckles. "I just think it's funny that you have enough money to buy a fleet of Bentleys, but you can't drive. That's not ironic to you?"

"No. It isn't."

"Okay. Sorry." Terrell looked out the window at the downpour pelting the car. "It doesn't look like the rain is going to let up anytime soon." He yawned. "And since I'll be driving all the way to Atlanta, a couple hours of rest would do me some good. I'll be right back."

Although Terrell ran as fast as he could, he was soaked by the time he got to the motel's ratty office. A mountainous woman was sitting behind the faded yellow counter.

"Can I help yuh?" the woman said with a southern drawl between puffs from her cigarette. She was so massive, her bottom swallowed the bar stool on which she sat.

"Yeah, I need to get a room," Terrell answered.

The woman looked past Terrell to take a glance at the car. Jennifer's silhouette was visible in the passenger seat.

"It's nine dollars an hour," she stated. "Or thirty-five for the night plus a ten dollar deposit. Check-out's at noon. Cash only."

"I'll pay for the night," Terrell said pulling the small wad of cash from his pocket. She took the money and looked at him skeptically.

"Do you want some towels?" she said. "There three dollars extra."

"No, that's okay," Terrell answered. "I've got my own."

"Room 12," she said as she tossed him a set of tarnished keys. "It's down the side of the building." Terrell took the keys and rushed back out to the car, completely soaking the few spots on his clothes that hadn't been drenched the first time.

"The room's right down there," Terrell said as he got back into the car. He grabbed his bag from the back seat. "Alright, let's make a run for it."

They burst from the car simultaneously, Jennifer shrieked as the large cold raindrops pelted her. Since there was no overhang above the door, they had no protection from the rain while Terrell fumbled with the key. He finally got it open and they rushed inside the room.

The room was small and shabby, but it looked reasonably clean. Terrell breathed a sigh of relief that he didn't see any roaches or rats scurrying around.

"This ain't so bad," he said dropping his bag to the floor. Jennifer turned up her nose in polite disagreement, but didn't protest. There was a narrow bed against the wall.

"Crap," he said. "I forgot to ask for two beds. You take it, I'll sleep on the floor."

"Don't be silly," Jennifer said as she ran her fingers through her wet hair. "If you get anywhere near that disgusting floor, I'm not riding with you in the car. The bed's big enough to share. You stay on your side and I'll stay on mine."

He didn't agree with her appraisal of the bed size. It was hardly bigger than the bunk beds he and his brother had as kids. Still, he had no desire to put his face anywhere near the brown carpeting in the small room so he didn't argue the point.

"It's freezing in here," Jennifer said, switching off the air conditioning. The rain had completely soaked her. Her jeans were wet from the knee down and the red tee shirt she wore was dripping little pink droplets on the carpet. "I've got to dry my clothes. Do you have anything in there that I could wear?" She pointed to his bag.

"Let me see," Terrell answered. He rummaged around in his bag until he came across one of his blue button-up shirts. "That's all I got," he said as he tossed it to her.

"It will do," she said and took off for the bathroom. She

closed the door behind her, but immediately stuck her head back outside the door. "There aren't any towels," she complained.

"I know, those were extra. I wasn't too keen on using their towels anyway. I've got a few in my bag." He reached back in his bag and tossed her a towel and a small bar of soap.

"Thanks," she said as she quickly closed the door. He heard her turn on the faucet and begin to hum softly.

Terrell sat down on the edge of the bed and took notice of his own wet clothing. He stripped off his shirt and draped it over the room's dilapidated dresser. His pants were also sopping wet, so he laid them across the air conditioner and changed into a pair of basketball shorts. He wanted to check the news to see if Jennifer's disappearance had been reported but he couldn't. The television had a quarter slot installed over the on switch. The faded sticker on the set informed him that thirty minutes of television would cost fifty cents.

He waited for several minutes before Jennifer finally emerged from the bathroom. She wore only the dress shirt that he'd given her. She looked much better wearing it than he ever did. She had only bothered to fasten the middle three buttons. As she walked on the heels of her shoes toward the bed, the gaps in the shirt offered tantalizing glimpses of her skin.

"Hey, get up for a second," Jennifer said.

"Why?" Terrell asked.

"I don't know how you can stand to sit on that blanket. Even the good hotels don't wash them and I don't even want to think about what kind of freaky nastys are crawling around on this thing."

Terrell helped her pull the old blanket off the bed and was encouraged to see that, while the sheets were threadbare, they seemed clean. She tossed the pillows across the room.

"You don't use pillows?" Terrell asked curiously.

"Are you kidding?" she said, scrunching up her face. "I can tolerate sleeping on this bed, but I'm not putting my head on those things. They only wash the pillowcases, not the pillows. I bet there's all kinds of dried up drool on them," she shivered in disgust.

"You'd know all about that drool thing, wouldn't you?" Terrell joked.

"I told you that you can't ever say anything about that," she said. "I'd never hear the end of it from my mom." She flopped down on the bed, sitting half Indian-style with her other leg dangling down to the floor.

"My hair is going to be all frizzy in the morning," she complained as she leaned her head back and combed her fingers through the damp ends. She was complaining about something else, but Terrell didn't hear her. He was transfixed on the corner of his shirttail, which draped seductively over her right thigh. Jennifer had nice legs.

"I have to go brush my teeth," he said suddenly, breaking out of his trance. He grabbed his toothbrush and hurried into the bathroom. He splashed some cold water on his face to regain his composure. He looked up and saw her wet bra hanging over the shower curtain. Terrell wondered idly how much he could sell it for on the internet. He thought he might need to look into that once he lost his job and got disbarred. He brushed his teeth and went back out into the room, hoping that Jennifer had gotten under the sheets. She hadn't.

When he went back out, Jennifer sat on the bed, leaning against the headboard with her knees pulled up to her chest and her arms wrapped tightly around them. Terrell fixed his gaze on the floor and walked around to the other side of the bed.

"I know I don't have a license, but I'll help you drive some in the morning. If you want me to."

"No, I think I can handle it. I wouldn't be doing my job as your advocate if I let you get a driving without a license charge too."

"With my luck, that would happen. Do they have wake up calls here?" she asked.

"I doubt it," answered Terrell as he slid under the sheets,

taking extra care not to look at her. "The lobby didn't strike me as a wake up call kind of place. Don't worry. I'll wake up when the sunlight comes in through the window."

"Okay," she said. "Are you going to sleep now?"

"Yeah," he answered, turning his back to her. "As long as I get about three hours of sleep, I'll be fine to drive in the morning."

"I'm not sleepy," Jennifer said.

Why would she be, thought Terrell. She'd been asleep the entire time they were in the car. It was taking a tremendous amount of willpower for him to ignore her. Thanks to Ricky, he couldn't get the image of her wiggling her hips like she did in her music videos out of his mind.

"Can I turn off this lamp?" Terrell asked.

"Sure."

Terrell reached over and twisted the lamp's knob. The worn gear teeth clicked several times before the light finally switched off. The bright streetlights in the parking lot prevented the room from becoming completely dark.

"I hate hotels," Jennifer continued. "I've had to get used to it, because I've spent half of my life touring. But I've never liked them. It doesn't feel like home, you know?"

"I know what you mean," Terrell answered. He kept his back toward her. "I have to do a lot of traveling for the firm."

"You know what?" Jennifer asked. "I was just thinking that since you've been working on my case, you've learned everything there is to know about me."

"Not everything," Terrell replied. "I have no idea what your favorite color is."

"Green," she said without missing a beat. "There. Now you know everything about me, and I still don't know anything about you."

"There isn't much to say. My life's not nearly as interesting as yours," Terrell answered, turning over to face her. Her eyes instantly drew him in; they glimmered in the soft light. "What do you want to know?"

"Where are you from?" she asked curiously.

"Norfolk, Virginia. My parents are still there."

"Any brothers and sisters?"

"Just an older brother, he lives in Maryland."

"Are you guys close?" she asked.

"Yeah. He's a jackass, but we're still pretty close. You get pretty close to a person when you have to fight them everyday."

"That's the truth," she sighed.

"You've got brother too?" Terrell asked. Nothing he'd researched indicated that she had any siblings.

"No," she answered. "I was talking about Felix." Jennifer was looking past Terrell's face, lost in her own thoughts. Terrell debated himself as to whether he should ask her about that. His curiosity prevailed.

"Can I ask you something?" he asked cautiously.

"Sure," she replied.

"It's something that I've been meaning to talk to you about, but there never seemed to be a real good time," he explained.

"What is it?"

"It's about you and Op… about you and Felix. You know that I've been talking to other people about your relationship."

Terrell could see Jennifer nod in the dark.

"Well, I found out something that bothered me and I think it might be bad for our case. I really don't know an easy way to put this, so I'll just say it. Did Felix ever abuse you?"

Jennifer's shoulders sagged and a bit of her strength seemed to ebb from her body. Her back slid down the headboard until she was lying next to Terrell.

"What do you mean by abuse?" she asked in a tone that told Terrell she knew exactly what he meant.

"Did he cheat on you?" Terrell asked, backing away from his real question.

Her eyes closed and she sighed. Terrell couldn't tell if she was angry with him for asking or if the memory was difficult for her to think about.

"Our relationship has always been complicated," she finally answered. "I'm sure he did in the beginning. I never caught him, but it wasn't hard to tell. He was always on tour with his boys. There were always women around him. I would have to be a fool not to know."

"And you were okay with that?"

"No, I wouldn't say that. We weren't that serious at first. It was just one of those things that you read about in the tabloids. Everyone thought it was good for our images."

"So it wasn't real?" Terrell asked.

"I told you, it was complicated. At first, he used to say that our time together was our time to be together and our time apart was our time to be apart. Besides, it's not like I sat at home waiting for him."

"You dated other people too?"

"A couple," she answered. "You probably think I'm some kind of whore, but I went out and met other guys too."

"No, I don't. That sounds reasonable to me. Did things change?"

"Yeah, he changed. He wanted to be exclusive. I guess we started enjoying our time together much more that we enjoyed our time apart."

"And he cleaned up his act?"

"For the most part," she answered. "He was still a man though. No offense."

"None taken."

"Girls would stick their phone numbers or room keys in his pocket when they thought I wasn't looking. I remember one time in particular. We went to a game or something. I caught him in the car with some tramp and…"

"Clarence told me about that," Terrell interrupted, not needing to hear the details a second time. "Is that when you threatened him?"

"What?"

"Clarence said that you said you'd kill him when that

happened. He said that you fought him like a man and told him that if you ever caught him like that again you'd kill him."

"Clarence said that to you?" she asked.

"Yeah. He said that he remembered that specifically."

"That's not how it happened. I'd never do something like that, especially in public."

"He seemed pretty sure. He said that Felix was violent and that he thought that he was probably hitting you too."

Even in the darkness, Terrell could see the outrage on Jennifer's face. "That's just not true. Felix would never ever hit me. He would get mad. Sometimes he'd yell, sometimes he'd put holes in the wall, and sometimes he would even break things, but he never hit me. I overlooked a lot of his faults, but not that."

"So you're saying that he wasn't a violent guy?"

"No," she answered after a pause. "Not with me."

"But," Terrell added, feeling there was more to the story than she wanted to say.

"It's hard to explain. This will sound weird, but he really was two different people. To everybody else, he was Optimus. He was loud and thuggish and arrogant and everything else people expected from a rapper. But when it was just us, he was Felix. He was sweet and nice and smart."

Terrell nodded his head in understanding.

"Felix never had anything come to him easily. His dad died when he was a baby. His mom was always sick. I don't think anyone ever took care of him."

She paused for a moment, deep in thought before continuing, "The things that I loved about him were the things he never let anyone else see. He had a good soul. Life hadn't corrupted him the way it had his friends. Felix did things that I didn't like in order to hold their respect, but it wasn't really him. He was always able to keep the two parts of himself separate. He was Optimus at work and Felix at home. But near the end..." she trailed off.

"The line blurred?" Terrell prodded.

"A little," she answered. "That's a good way to put it. It was almost like he started to believe the things that he said on his albums. It was little stuff at first. For instance, he never used to curse around me. If his friends were doing it, he'd make them stop. Then all of a sudden it was like every other word out of his mouth was b-this and f-that. He used to smoke weed every one in awhile, but then he started doing it all the time. It was like he lost respect for everything."

"Even you?"

"No, not yet anyway."

"If he was doing all this, what made you stay?"

"I don't know," she sighed. "I guess I just hoped that things would eventually go back to the way they were when we first decided to be together. He made me feel special back then."

"How?" Terrell said across the six inch gap that separated their faces.

"I knew I was safe with him. I knew that he'd always protect me, no matter what. This probably sounds stupid, but he made me feel precious. Like I was the only thing in the world that he really cared about. For some reason I liked the fact that this hard guy was soft for me. Does that make sense?"

"That makes a lot of sense," Terrell answered. "You are precious. Felix and millions of other people agree."

"Yes," she whispered, a small smile tugging at her lips. Inexplicably, the gap separating their faces had shrunk to three inches. "It's kinda like how I feel I'm around you. My life is falling apart, but somehow, you make me feel like everything is going to be alright."

"No," Terrell muttered. The gap between their faces was now two inches and shrinking. "I'm just doing my job."

"No you're not," she said softly. "Mr. Bragg is doing his job. You're lying with me in a bad motel in Nowheresville, Florida just so we can drive to Atlanta to find some thing that might not even be there. That's doing more than your job."

"No it isn't," Terrell whispered unconvincingly. The space was now one inch and closing. Something in the back of his mind told Terrell to pull away, but he couldn't.

"Will you keep me safe?" she mouthed as their faces inched together.

"I will," Terrell said just before their lips slowly pressed against one another.

Jennifer's lips were warm and moist and they set off an excitement in Terrell that he hadn't felt in a long time. She kissed him eagerly, releasing a long bottled passion. He found himself kissing her back with equal excitement. He pulled her closer. It felt good. It felt very good.

He knew it was wrong, but he couldn't stop. Alicia had all but dumped him. Regardless of what happened in that motel room, he was very likely going to be disbarred anyway. Who would know?

He would know. If he did this, there was no going back. No matter how many men dreamed of being with Jennifer Weston, all Terrell ever dreamed of was being with Alicia. As long as there was still a chance to make things work with her, he knew that he had to stop.

"I can't do this," he said as he pulled away.

She leaned further into him, reconnecting the kiss and testing his will, but he stopped her.

"I'm sorry," he said as his eyes found hers in the darkness. "But I can't. It's not right."

"Why?" Jennifer looked at him, confusion and hurt on her face.

"It's not that I don't want to," Terrell explained "God knows that this is like my ultimate fantasy come true. But even though this is something that I really want, there is something I want even more. She's sitting in a little apartment four thousand miles away."

Jennifer looked at him and managed a weak smile. "You really love her don't you?"

"Yes. I do," Terrell answered. "She has my heart. The second after your jury comes back not guilty, I'm hopping on the first thing flying to Spain to give her the engagement ring I've been carrying with me."

"You carry it around with you?"

"It's in my bag right now. What kind of man would I be if I did this? Not the kind that deserves her," he reached over and stroked Jennifer's cheek, "and not the kind that would deserve you either. Both of you deserve better than that."

"You're a good guy Terrell," she smiled.

"Thanks," he replied. "Now that I have that off my chest, if she doesn't take me back, I can still call you right?"

"Get some sleep," Jennifer laughed.

"That wasn't a no," Terrell pointed out. "If I call you, you better not pretend that you don't know me."

"Get some sleep Terrell," she reiterated.

"Yeah," Terrell answered. "That's probably a good idea. Goodnight." He turned his back to her, hoping to curb any desires he might have during the night. She did the same, but the size of the bed made it impossible for their bodies not to touch.

"Jennifer," Terrell said after a couple of moments.

"Yes?"

"You're a great kisser."

"Thank you," she laughed. "You're not so bad yourself."

CHAPTER 20

For a fugitive, Terrell slept surprisingly well. He awoke slowly, lying still and letting consciousness creep up on him before opening his eyes. The first thing he noticed was that the room was entirely too bright to be seven o'clock in the morning.

"Damn," he mumbled, realizing that he'd overslept. Judging by the rays of bright sunshine that penetrated the room's dusty curtains, he'd missed his target by quite a bit. The next thing he noticed was far more troubling than oversleeping. He was alone in the bed.

"Jennifer?" he called out, hoping that she was in the bathroom. When he heard neither an answer, nor the sounds of the shower, he panicked. She wasn't in the room.

"Crap! Crap! Crap!" he repeated as he snatched his pants off the air conditioner. Where could she be? Did she ditch him? His foot got caught in the seam of his pants, causing him to lose his balance and fall to the floor.

"Ugh!" he grunted. Was she mad about last night, he wondered? Did she call someone to come and get her? He jumped up, grabbed a shirt and pulled it over his head. Where could she have gone?

Just as he finished tying his shoe, he heard someone insert a key into the front door.

"I'm paid up till' noon!" Terrell shouted, hoping to keep out the intruder. But as the door swung open, he was relieved to see Jennifer.

"Where did you go?" Terrell asked angrily. "You scared me to death!"

"I got breakfast." She held up two bags. "I was hungry and there is a little diner down the road. They had my favorite, pecan waffles. I brought you some too."

"Why didn't you wake me? I would have gotten it for you. You almost gave me a heart attack."

"You were tired," she answered. "And I knew you were going to drive most of the way today, so I figured you could use the extra couple of minutes of sleep." She wore the same button up shirt that he had given her the night before with a pair of sunglasses and a baseball cap.

"We can't afford to have some cashier calling the local radio station and telling them that you're in town."

"Relax," she smiled. "No one recognized me. The cashier was an old lady. And I made sure I pulled the hat down over my face."

Terrell shook his head. It was obvious that Jennifer was not accustomed to following directions. It wasn't necessarily a bad characteristic, but it was going to make their trip more difficult.

"Do you want yours or not?" she asked.

"Yeah, I want it." Terrell was starving too.

"I can't remember the last time I had these!" she said excitedly. "I never get to eat them."

"Why?" Terrell asked, pulling his food from the bag.

"Are you kidding? These things have a week's worth of carbs, fats and sugars," Jennifer answered as she spread butter and syrup over her waffles. "My trainer would freak out if she knew I was eating this."

"Poor baby."

"Don't start that with me," Jennifer said through a mouthful of food. "It sucks. I can buy anything in the world that I want except for food that tastes good. One time, my trainer tried to convince me that soy-honey pancakes were just as good as these. I almost punched her in the face for saying something that ignorant."

Terrell smiled at Jennifer as he devoured his breakfast.

"Heaven forbid I have a cheeseburger. I hear about it for days from her, then my mom, then the label, then my mom again, then Felix and finally, my mom again."

"Well, I'm glad that you see this time with me as an opportunity to let yourself go. It makes me feel real good about myself."

"Glad I could help," she said.

***

Despite Terrell's frequent pleas to hurry, Jennifer finished her breakfast at a leisurely pace. Then she took a twenty-minute shower. She was unfazed by his warnings that they'd be caught if she dawdled too long and she didn't take his threats to leave her behind seriously. They didn't leave the hotel until ten and after that, Jennifer needed frequent bathroom breaks. Terrell could feel his anger grow exponentially as he sat in the crawling traffic on I-85 just outside of Atlanta. It was after six o'clock and he was stuck in the thick of rush hour traffic.

"Terrell," Jennifer said.

"I'm not stopping again," Terrell snapped. "I told you not to drink that diet soda. We're almost there and there are way too many people around here that would recognize you. You're going to have to hold it or something."

"I don't have to go to the bathroom," she said, sounding like a quarrelsome five-year-old. "I was going to say that I think that the apartment's on the next exit."

"You think?" Terrell asked. "I thought you knew exactly where it was."

"I do," she answered defensively. "I told you I don't drive. I recognize this as the place where Felix got off the highway."

Terrell was in the carpool lane. He had to cross five lanes of traffic to get to the exit ramp.

"Wonderful," he grumbled. Just like everything else in the car, the turn signals didn't work. He tried to ease the land yacht into the right lane. Terrell swooped in front of a yellow sports car and offered an apologetic wave before moving further right. Luckily, since the traffic was slow, he found it relatively simple to move the car between the cracks in traffic. He exited the freeway and turned down a lightly wooded road.

"Turn here," she said as they came to a small driveway. A wrought iron gate blocked their way.

"Okay," Terrell said. "Now what?"

"Pull up to that box," Jennifer instructed. Terrell did as he was told and moved beside the small metal keypad near the gate.

"Hit the index button and scroll down to Ramona Stevens."

"Who is that?" Terrell asked.

"That's me," she smiled. "That's my alias when I'm incognito."

"Okay," Terrell said when he'd found the name. "Now what?"

"The code is 1-1-1-3-0-0."

Terrell quickly pressed the buttons and the gate rumbled to life. Terrell moved the car through the portal and into the complex. There were several large brick buildings. Terrell guessed that each one held four or five large apartments.

"We're in the Avalon building. It's in the back." He and Jennifer parked the car and walked up the short set of stairs leading to apartment C. Jennifer pulled the key out of her pocket and inserted it into the heavy deadbolt. The lock opened with a loud clack and she gently pushed it open.

"So, where would he put it?" Terrell asked as they walked

inside the dark apartment. The apartment had the dank smell of a place that hadn't been used in awhile.

"I'm not sure," she answered.

"Okay, where do you think he would put his important papers?"

"I never saw him with any important papers," she shrugged her shoulders.

"Alright, I guess this is going to take a while then. Where do you want to start?"

"In the kitchen. I'm hungry again." Jennifer walked through the living room and into the apartment's spacious kitchen. "You don't mind, do you?"

"Why would I mind?" Terrell said sarcastically. "It's not like there are people out there looking for us." He followed her into the kitchen and looked over her shoulder while she gazed into the nearly empty refrigerator.

"Eww," she said as she looked at a box of old Chinese takeout. There was so much mold growing on the remains of the Lo Mein that green fuzz had poked through the top of the box. She tossed the box over her shoulder and into the garbage. Then she spotted an energy bar in the door.

"I guess this will have to do," she said as she tore off the wrapper and began eating the granola and raisin.

"Good," Terrell said. "Can we get started now?"

They began their systematic search of the residence in the living room. Although Jennifer and Optimus didn't spend a lot of time in the apartment, they had managed to accumulate a lot of belongings. They turned over cushions and chairs and rifled through the end table drawers. They moved like a whirlwind through the kitchen, emptying drawers and scattering papers. They searched the closets, the bed, the desk and anywhere that they thought Optimus might have hidden important papers. They found nothing.

"It has to be here somewhere," Jennifer said, desperation in her voice. "Where could he have hidden it?"

"I don't know," Terrell said as he threw clothes out of the huge walk-in closet. "We've looked everywhere. Is this the only place he had in Atlanta?"

"Yes," she said, exasperated. "This is the only place it could be."

"Well then, it must not exist," Terrell said. "We've turned this place upside-down and all we found was an overdue phone bill, some old pictures and a dime bag of weed. I think it might be time to call Miami and tell them where you are."

"We shouldn't give up so easily," she pouted.

"I don't want to," Terrell answered. "But I don't know what else to do. There's nothing here. I think the best thing to do is to get you back to Florida before the State's Attorney finds out you violated your bond. I don't think you want to have to go back to the county jail. I've got to go to the bathroom, we need to make the call."

Terrell left the bedroom before she could say anything to make him change his mind. He went into the hall bathroom and shut the door behind him. He lifted the toilet seat and looked straight ahead. Hanging above the tank was the ugliest painting he'd ever seen. A woman with an abnormally large head and a tiny body was trapped within a series of triangles, ovals, and rectangles. Terrell was certain that it was more valuable than anything he could afford, but it was putrid. It was also crooked. He attempted to straighten the frame, but it wouldn't budge. It wasn't hung properly. He flushed the toilet, zipped up and tried to look behind the painting to see what was holding it.

"Jennifer!" he shouted excitedly. "Come here! I think I found something." The painting didn't move because it wasn't hung at all. It was on a hinge. The painting swung open to reveal a wall safe. Jennifer cautiously opened the door, her face scrunched in a look of disgust.

"Help me open this," Terrell said.

"You know," she said hesitantly. "I heard you flush, but I didn't hear you turn on the faucet. Did you wash your hands?"

"This has to be it," Terrell commented, not hearing what she said.

"That's kinda one of my pet peeves," she said a little more loudly. "I'm really going to need you to wash up before you touch that."

"What?" Terrell said.

She pointed at the sink. Terrell sighed, turned on the water and began rubbing his hands underneath.

"You really should use soap too," she pointed out. Terrell used some liquid soap scrubbed for a few moments and then dried his hands on the decorative towels.

"Better?" he asked.

"Much. Is that a safe?"

"Yeah, I think so. Do you have any clue what the combination might be?"

"Try the gate combo, 1-1-1-3-0-0," she said. Terrell punched in the numbers, but the little red light on the display did not turn green.

"That's not it."

"Are there letters on the keypad?" she asked.

"No, just numbers. Do you know his ATM pin numbers or anything?"

"I don't even think he had an ATM card. Whenever he needed cash, Clarence would just hand him some."

"I guess we're just going to have to guess. Maybe we'll get lucky," Terrell sighed. He punched in the dates of Jennifer's birthday, Optimus' birthday, Optimus' mom's birthday and every significant date Jennifer could think of. None of them worked.

"There has to be a better way to do this," Terrell said. "I don't even know how many numbers are in the combination. This could take years."

What number would Optimus choose? From what Terrell knew about him, he was sentimental. The combination would not be a random sequence of numbers. They would have some connection to him. It would be something that would never change and something that he'd never forget.

"I've got it," Terrell said with a triumphant look in his eye. "6-1-6-1-2-5," he said as he pressed the buttons. The red light blinked three times and then turned green. With smile, Terrell turned the handle and opened the safe.

"How did you figure that out?" Jennifer asked.

"It was his first hit, 'All Day Every Day'. The chorus is 61 seconds a minute, 61 minutes an hour, 25 hours a day."

Terrell peered into the dark opening of the safe and pulled items out of it. The first thing he grabbed was a large plastic envelope with First National Bank stamped across the front.

"What's that?" Jennifer asked.

"Bearer bonds I think," Terrell answered as he peered inside the envelope. He tossed the envelope on the counter and reached inside for another stack of papers.

"These look like some lyrics," Terrell said, thumbing through the sheets of legal paper. "Probably valuable, but not what we're looking for." He placed them down on top of the bonds. Next he pulled out a box of assorted jewelry. Mixed in amongst the diamond-encrusted watches and bracelets, he found a small velvet box. He opened the container, revealing a ring with the largest diamond he'd ever seen.

"Let me see that," Jennifer said. There was a small note inside the box.

"J, you and me 61-61-25, O." It was obvious that it was an engagement ring and the emotion of the moment was not lost on Terrell. He didn't know what to say, so he remained quiet as Jennifer left the room with the ring.

He found a couple of life insurance policies that named Jennifer as his beneficiary and several other assorted papers, and then he hit the jackpot. The thick envelope was stuffed into the back of the safe. He overturned it on the bathroom countertop. A stack of bound paper with a red cover fell out, followed by a CD, a stack of photographs and several letters addressed to

Felix Caldwell d.b.a. Optimus from the National Bank of Grand Cayman. Terrell picked up the stack of paper and began thumbing through it.

"Jennifer!" Terrell called out excitedly as looked at the pages. "I think you should see this!" The bound stack with the red cover was his new contract with Southside Records. The contract detailed the minutiae of the business deal between Optimus and his new label, but the important thing to Terrell was the back page. Optimus had signed and dated the agreement. He'd also obtained the signatures of two witnesses, the notary Patsy Roberson and Clarence Ferguson.

The next thing Terrell looked at was the stack of bank statements. The statements were long, and the accounts had much more money in them than Terrell was accustomed to seeing. He noticed that one of the statements had three large cash transfers highlighted. Each was for half a million dollars and there was no indication on the statement as to where the money was sent. There were a couple of letters from the bank that notified Optimus that his accounts were below the set minimums. Then Terrell found a personally addressed note from the branch manager, it read:

Dear Mr. Caldwell,

In reference to your recent inquiry concerning accounts #789526358745422 and #789526878744121. Three wire transfers, each in the amount of $500,000.00 were completed on January 14. They were routed to other off shore banking facilities, none affiliated with this branch. Your personal representative, Clarance Ferguson, authorized the transfers. If we at 1st National can be of any further assistance, please contact us.

Sincerely,

Dexter Jean

Dexter Jean
Branch Manager
1st National Bank of Grand Cayman

Terrell carefully placed the letters on top of the statements from the bank and thumbed through the stack of photographs. There were only about fifteen photos, but they told an interesting story. The pictures were of Clarence and Brian Dunn in a parking lot. The way the shots were done gave the indication that the photographer was at least 50 yards away. Brian seemed to be explaining something to Clarence in the first few shots. The next few showed the two of them looking at some papers and the last were of them shaking hands and parting ways.

"Hey Jennifer," Terrell shouted, "You really should see this." Terrell looked carefully at the miniature cassette tapes. Judging by the other items he'd found with them, he was certain that they Clarence's voice would be on them. A million questions swirled in Terrell's mind. Brian's involvement complicated matters immensely. Terrell knew that Brian was a sleaze, but he hadn't seriously considered that he was involved in framing Jennifer. AMI was paying the bills and he didn't think they'd take too kindly to being accused of conspiracy to commit murder. The pieces were falling into place, but he was still missing something.

"Jennifer," Terrell said again as he walked out into the hallway. "How well do you know Brian?" Terrell stopped in his tracks as he spotted Jennifer's body lying prone on the floor. He didn't even get a chance to wonder what happened before the butt of the shotgun came down hard on the base of his skull.

CHAPTER 21

Terrell's head hurt. It felt like it was stuffed with cotton and every sound had to be filtered before he could process it. He could hear muffled voices, but he couldn't quite figure out who they were. He concentrated and finally understood what the voices were saying.

"What'd you want me to do?" the voice asked. "They were inside when I got here. He'd already found the safe." Terrell recognized it as Clarence.

"You said that you had it under control," answered the unmistakable voice of Brian Dunn. "This is not under control."

"Calm down," Clarence replied. "This was supposed to happen at the music awards anyway. The only change is that the timetable moved."

"You idiot," Brian replied. "If those knuckleheads offed her, no one would take a second look at us. It'd just be more thug rappers killing one another. If she dies here, there's going to be an investigation. We're screwed."

"What's done is done." Clarence said. "I say we pop them both here and make it look like a murder-suicide."

"Shut up." Brian said, exasperated. "That won't work."

"It'll work," Clarence continued. "We put them in the bed together. I'll cut him up the same way I did O and then I'll shoot her in the head. I wipe the burner down and put it in her hands. Then, everyone will think that she killed him and then herself."

"No, they won't. What do you think this is, a soap opera? There's evidence all over the place that proves your little scenario didn't happen."

"What are you talking about?"

"How many things do you think you've touched since you got here?"

"I don't know, not many."

"Not many? You were rummaging around in the cabinets when I got here. All they need to find is one fingerprint of yours and they'd know it wasn't some kind of murder-suicide."

"I could wipe everything off and…"

"What about the autopsy? What are they going to think when they find that big knot you put on the back of their heads when you hit them with the shotgun."

"Uhh…"

"What? She hit him on the back of the head, dragged him back to the bed, stabbed him to death, then smacked herself in the back of the head before blowing her brains out?"

"It was just an idea."

"Yeah, a stupid idea," Brian sighed. "Ideas like that is why people like you always get caught."

"What is that supposed to mean, people like me?"

"Project monkeys," Brian spoke up. "That's what I mean by people like you. This is a damn catastrophe."

"I don't know who you think you're talking to like that," Clarence said, "but don't think I won't slice you up too."

"I'm talking to you," Brian answered. "And I'm not particularly worried about that. If anything happens to me, the tapes of our conversations will be conveniently delivered to the police. So if you're done making stupid suggestions, shut up until I figure a way out of this."

Terrell's head hung forward with his chin touching his chest. His arms were bound behind the back of the chair. He could tell from the sound of their voices that Brian and Clarence were not far from him. He tried moving his hands, but he couldn't. He cracked his eyelid and looked down at his feet. His legs were bound to the chair with several layers of gray duct tape. It was probably for the best. After all, he was a thinker, not a fighter. He could feel his neck stiffening, so he tried slowly rolling it to his left. Suddenly, a bolt of pain flashed up the cramping muscle in the side of his neck. He grimaced in pain and immediately wished he hadn't.

"Well, look who's awake," Terrell heard Brian say. He thought that maybe he could play possum for a few moments longer so he didn't move. A kick to the shin quickly dispelled that notion. Terrell opened his eyes into the faces of his captors.

"You've caused us a boatload of trouble, do you know that?" Brian asked.

"Just doing my job," Terrell groaned. He looked past Brian and saw Jennifer bound to a chair just as he was. She wasn't moving.

"What'd you do to her?" Terrell asked. The anger in his voice surprised even him.

"Isn't that sweet," Brian grinned. "You actually care about her. And all this time I thought lawyers only cared about money. Don't worry. It's just a little bump on the head."

"You know, you can still get out of this," Terrell said, thoughts racing. "She's unconscious, so she wouldn't be able to identify you."

"And let me guess," Brian interrupted. "If we let you go right now, you'll promise that you'll never say anything about it."

"No," Terrell answered, "Actually I'd call the police the second I thought you were gone. But it would be my word against yours. I'm aiding and abetting a fugitive, so my credibility's shot. There's no physical evidence and everyone knows that we didn't get along so I doubt anyone would believe me. I doubt that I could

even get you arrested. You could probably even hire Bragg &
Shuttlesworth after they fire me."

"You don't know the half of it," Brian smiled. "As tempting
as your offer sounds, I'm going to have to pass. We've got other
plans."

"So, you're just going to kill us?"

"Probably, but not right now. And not me either," Brian said.
"That's what Clarence is for. Personally, I detest violence. But you
can keep us company while we wait."

"Wait for what?"

"You'll see."

Good, Terrell thought. At least he had a few minutes to come
up with a way out of this.

"How was it?" Clarence asked suddenly.

"How was what?" Terrell responded.

"Jenny," Clarence said licking his lips. "I hope she's worth
dying for. I've been trying to get with her for three years, but
she never had the time of day for me. You didn't have a problem
though, did you? You're her hero." Clarence walked over to
Jennifer and gently stroked her head.

"Don't touch her," Terrell said.

"Don't touch her?" Clarence laughed. "I already have. Who
do you think dressed her back at that hotel? Too bad I didn't have
time for any more fun after I carved up O. But who knows?" he
smiled like a shark, "Maybe tonight will be different."

"Shut up." Terrell growled.

Clarence patted Jennifer on the thigh. "I barely had enough
time to bloody her lip before I made the noise complaint that
night. There's plenty of time now though. If you're good, maybe
I'll even let you watch."

Terrell struggled against his restraints, but it was no use. He
couldn't get free and he knew it. His wrists were bound tighter
than his ankles.

"Looks like you've struck a nerve Clarence," Brian smiled.
"You know Terrell, when I paid that photographer to get some

incriminating shots of you, I never dreamed he'd get anything as good as those roof pictures. I would have paid triple had I known he was going to catch the two of you bumping uglies."

"Why?" Terrell asked Brian. He hoped he was masking the fear in his voice.

"Why what?" Brian responded.

"Why all this?" Terrell asked again. Since he couldn't move his hands, he shrugged his shoulders to indicate the situation. "This seems pretty elaborate if all you wanted was to kill us."

"Why should I tell you?" Brian asked.

"What's it going to hurt?" Terrell asked. He would not look at Clarence, the thought of him touching Jennifer would send him into a rage and he needed to keep his wits about him. "You've already decided what you're going to do. There isn't anything that I can say that will change your mind. Besides, I'm a lawyer and we ask questions. It's a character flaw."

Brian looked at him skeptically, carefully considering his words.

"What am I going to do?" Terrell continued, "Break out of this?" He struggled with his bonds for effect. "If I'm going to die then I should at least know why."

"Don't tell him anything." Clarence said. He grabbed the shotgun that was leaning against the wall and raised the butt of the weapon as if to knock Terrell unconscious again.

"I know you want to tell me Brian," Terrell said, ignoring Clarence. "You want me to know how you outsmarted me. So humor me. Why'd you do all this?"

Before Clarence could close the distance to Terrell, Brian held up his hand to stop him.

"I'll humor you. After all, I did outsmart you, didn't I? The why is very simple," Brian explained. "Money is a fantastic motivator."

"You've already got money," Terrell pointed out. "Last I checked, you make twenty times what I do and people think I'm rich."

"I do earn a lot," Brian said. "But I've never heard anyone complain about having too much money. I'd have thought that you'd have picked up that up already."

"So AMI paid you to kill Optimus," Terrell said.

"Don't be stupid. He was the golden goose. All they cared about was continuing to use him to generate income." Brian walked over to the large front window and peeked through the curtain. "They made that very clear to me. If I lost Optimus, then I would need to find some alternate employment for myself. But they never hinted that I should kill him."

Terrell glanced across the room at Jennifer and saw her eyes open slightly. She blinked twice at him to show that she was awake and then closed them again.

"Do you have any idea who at AMI discovered Optimus?" Brian asked.

"You," Terrell guessed.

"No," Brian chuckled. "Actually, I think it was one of our summer interns. At the time, I just a low-level executive. I think I was working on some kind of vendor rebate program at the time. It was a real dead-end in the company, if you know what I mean. Anyway, this intern brought in a tape of a guy that he heard in an underground nightclub. None of the A&R executives would give him time to play it, so he left it with me. Personally, I thought it sucked. I listened to one grainy song and was about to throw the tape away when my boss came by my desk to yell at me. I forgot about what. At any rate, he heard the voice and fell in love with it."

Brian swiveled away from the window and walked back toward Terrell.

"He said it was just the sound that we were looking for and he asked me where I got that tape."

"So you told him about the intern?"

"You really are naïve," Brian laughed. "Of course not. I told him that he was a friend of mine. Then I said I was the only executive that Optimus would trust. He became my meal ticket."

"So you signed him. But Optimus was smarter than you," Terrell deduced. "That's how he was able to wriggle out of his contract."

"Yeah," Brian scowled. "Damn him. No one would've dreamed that he'd be able to meet those sales goals."

"And Optimus came to you to say he was leaving you out to dry."

"Ha," Brian laughed humorlessly. "He didn't tell me anything. He was just going to jump ship and let me read about in the newspaper. Clarence was the one that told me about it."

"Why would he do that?" Terrell asked.

"Clarence has been spying for me for years. I don't go into business without paying someone to find out all their dark little secrets. But I guess you already know that, don't you?" Brian smirked.

"I guess," Terrell answered, "But there's still something that I don't understand. I knew that Clarence was too stupid to pull off something like this on his own, but why in the world would he want to work for you?"

"What Clarence lacks in smarts he more than makes up for in greed."

"I'm about sick of you calling me stupid," Clarence said angrily.

"Shut up," Brian responded. "You are stupid. If you had any brains, we wouldn't even be here now. So sit back and shut up. You'll get your chance to take out your frustrations soon enough."

"I don't pretend to be his friend, but I pay him much more than Felix ever did. For a very reasonable price, he told me everything I could possibly want to know about his childhood buddy, including his plan to steal his master recordings from us."

"But Optimus got wise to the two of you," Terrell pressed. "He found out Clarence was passing you information."

"Eventually," Brian scoffed. "He had no idea until that fat bastard got greedy." He pointed at Clarence for effect. "There was no way I could convince Optimus to stay with AMI, so the only choice I had was to kill him. That way, at least we would retain control of his music catalog. It was supposed to look like a robbery. Some hoodlum spots him in the bathroom while his entourage is distracted, stabs him and grabs his jewelry. No fuss, no muss and nobody goes to jail. For some reason, this fool steals a million and a half dollars out of the bank account before he set up the hit. As if he wouldn't miss a million and a half dollars." Brian shook his head in total disgust.

"The letters in the safe," Terrell said. "The bank notified him about the transfers."

"Of course they did. No bank likes to lose that kind of a deposit without saying something about it. Never do business with thugs from the hood," Brain said. "Take that little piece of advice into the next life."

"So Optimus knew something was wrong," Terrell said.

"Yeah, and he didn't trust Clarence anymore. We were running out of time and there was no way Clarence was going to be able to separate him from the rest of his crew. That's when we came up with plan B. Or plan J, if you prefer."

"We?" Terrell asked. "Frankly, I doubt either of you had the smarts to put all this together. It seems a little out of your league."

"We did have a little help. He was expensive, but well worth the price. You'll get to meet him soon. He's on his way."

"I'm honored," Terrell replied.

"You should be," Brian answered. "I would imagine he'll have something quite special lined up for you."

"Well, as long as I'm waiting," Terrell responded, "Would either of you mind taking me to the bathroom? I've really got to go."

"So you can try to escape when we cut the tape around your hands." Brian laughed out loud. "Go in your clothes if you have to. It's not my chair."

Brian's complicity in telling him all about the conspiracy didn't bode well for Terrell's future. He was very afraid. He had been struggling with his bonds ever since they began talking and he couldn't get them to budge. Convincing them to loosen his bindings so that they could take him to the bathroom had been his best hope and they weren't falling for it.

"Fine," Terrell said, "Well then, how about some water? If I can't go to the bathroom, at least I shouldn't be thirsty."

"Okay," Clarence said unexpectedly. He didn't walk into the kitchen. Instead, he went down the hall to the bathroom and came back a few moments later with Dixie cup filled with cloudy water.

"Where did you get that?" Terrell asked. "I didn't hear the faucet."

"Out of the toilet," Clarence smiled. "Water's water. Drink up."

"Never mind, I'm really not that thirsty."

Clarence punched Terrell in his recently healed nose. As Terrell started to scream, Clarence splashed the water into his mouth.

"Stop it," Brian said, annoyed. "He said we weren't supposed to touch them until he got here."

"Aw, I didn't hit the little punk very hard," Clarence replied as Terrell tried to spit out the foul water. "He still looks thirsty to me. I think he wants some more."

"Leave him alone," Jennifer said from across the room.

"So the princess is awake," Brian said. "I'm glad. You know, I regret that we won't be able to continue our business relationship," he smiled. "I anticipated that you would have made me a lot of money in the future."

"Sorry to disappoint you," she scowled.

"It's okay," he replied. "I'll be fine. Just think of how much

I can make on the search for the next member of Fantasy. I'm already developing a reality show about it."

Jennifer craned her neck and spat into Brian's face.

"You pretentious bitch," he shouted and slapped her across the face.

"Touch her again, and I will kill you," Terrell said icily.

"Really?" Brian asked as he yanked her head by grabbing a handful of her hair. "Try."

Terrell had had enough and he tried to lunge at Brian. He was successful only in toppling his chair. Clarence gave him a swift kick in the chest as he lay prone on the floor.

"Calm down Romeo," Brian laughed. "She doesn't have anything to fear from me. You should save your energy for when I'm gone. Clarence isn't anywhere near the gentleman that I am."

Just then, there was a knock at the door.

With everything that had happened to Terrell, nothing could have surprised him. Nothing, except for what he saw when Brian opened the door. A short, mustached man walked into the room with a familiar step. It was a man Terrell immediately recognized as his boss, Earnest Bragg.

CHAPTER 22

"What is he doing on the floor?" Mr. Bragg shouted as he looked down on Terrell's prone body.

"He got a little wild," Clarence smirked.

"I left very specific instructions that neither of them were to be touched before I got here," Mr. Bragg said. "When I give instructions, they will be followed or you will spend the rest of your life in a very small cell. This will be the last time we have this conversation Clarence. Now pick him up and apologize."

"What?" Clarence asked.

The look on Mr. Bragg's face made it clear that his statement was not a request. Clarence righted the chair and mumbled a terse apology. Terrell was still so shocked to see Mr. Bragg that he barely could comprehend what was happening.

"We are not animals, and we do not delight in the unpleasant activities that we sometimes must perform," Mr. Bragg said as he took off his jacket and folded it neatly over his arm.

"Ms. Weston," he continued, "I'm sorry that we must be here under such circumstances. For what it's worth, none of this was ever personal, or your fault in any way. You are just a victim of poor circumstance." Jennifer rolled her eyes in disbelief, but

Terrell didn't doubt Mr. Bragg's words. As long as he'd known him, he'd never done anything for personal reasons. It was always just business to him.

"You probably think I owe you some kind of explanation." Mr. Bragg walked over to Terrell.

"No sir," Terrell answered. "If I've learned anything working at your firm, it's that you don't owe me anything."

"Well said," Mr. Bragg nodded. "You have an unlimited capacity for learning. That's one of the things that I like about you. Do you have any idea why Peter dislikes you?" His kind face seemed out of place considering the circumstances. He spoke as if the two of them were alone in the office working late.

Terrell shook his head no. He had several theories, but he wondered why Mr. Bragg was asking the question.

"He thinks you're too cerebral. Too smart for your own good, if you know what I mean."

Terrell nodded.

"He and I have a fundamental difference of opinion about our young lawyers. He sees you as weapons. He fires you at the proper target and hopes that you will annihilate whatever obstacle is in our client's path."

"And you?" Terrell asked.

"I would think you knew that by now," Mr. Bragg answered. "You're not a weapon…"

"But I am a tool," Terrell finished.

"Yes," Mr. Bragg conceded. "Do you know the difference?"

"Weapons are used for destruction," Terrell said. "But tools can be used to build."

"Excellent," Mr. Bragg said. "Sometimes Peter's right about people and sometimes I am. I have never been more right about someone than I was about you."

"You've been using me this whole time to set up Jennifer," Terrell said.

"Oh, no," Mr. Bragg said, waving his hands in protest. "You misunderstand. It was never my intention to set up anyone. If these two gentlemen had done the things I instructed them to do, no one would have gotten hurt."

"No one except for Optimus," Terrell reminded him.

"Yes, well, that was unfortunate. However, his death predates my involvement in this matter so I cannot accept responsibility for that."

Terrell looked at him skeptically.

"I suppose it would be best if I started from the beginning," Mr. Bragg explained. "This whole thing will make more sense then."

Mr. Bragg took a seat on the couch near Terrell before continuing.

"On the night of the murder, I received a call from Brian. We had done some corporate work for him before. It was as boring for us as it was lucrative, but it did have some ethically gray areas that we navigated through without a moment's hesitation. He thought we would be the perfect firm to help him, and by proxy AMI, cover their tracks. You were here alone with him for quite some time and I'm sure you were able to ferret the details from him."

Terrell nodded his head yes.

"Good work, I knew you would. He talks entirely too much."

"Hey, wait a minute. I do not talk too much." Brian interrupted.

"Yes you do, but now is not the time to argue about it. We don't have a whole lot of time, so please be quiet."

Brian folded his arms and sighed.

"As I was saying," Mr. Bragg continued. "He wanted to retain our services only to make sure nothing got traced back to him or AMI, but I had a better idea. For a substantial fee, our firm would represent Ms. Weston and AMI. That way, not only could we could closely monitor the case…"

"But you could bill Ms. Weston and AMI both for what amounted to the same work."

"Very impressive. You do understand."

"I understand you're willing to let an innocent woman rot in prison for a crime you know she didn't commit."

"No I wasn't," Mr. Bragg replied. "I was fairly certain that we would easily win an acquittal for Ms. Weston. In the beginning, I never thought she was in danger of spending any time in prison."

"How's that?" Terrell asked.

"Have you ever tried to tear open a ketchup packet from the side?" Mr. Bragg asked thoughtfully.

"No, I can't say that I have," Terrell responded.

"It is a really difficult thing to do. It's hard to get started. That's why they put those little notches on the ends. They focus your energy into one specific spot so that once the tear begins, the task becomes exponentially easier."

Terrell nodded. Mr. Bragg was fond of his little analogies.

"Criminal defense work is very similar. The prosecution puts out a lot of evidence and we try to tear it open. The trick is finding the notch in the case," he winked. "Once you do, it tears apart very quickly."

"And that's what you expected to happen in this case?"

"Expected? Hell, I knew it would. Despite their lack of planning, they actually did a better frame job than I would have thought. Still, as soon as Brian told me the details, I knew exactly where to find the notch."

Terrell racked his brain. He'd been searching for this notch for the past few months and had come up with nothing.

"They drugged Jennifer at that discothèque" Mr. Bragg continued.

"Nightclub," Brian interrupted. "Only people your age and Europeans call them discothèques."

"Fine, at that nightclub," Mr. Bragg corrected himself. "I guess my age is starting to show. At any rate, they drugged her, but they neglected to remove the glass from the crime scene. That's the notch. The forensic technicians should have discovered drug residue on the glass with her fingerprints and DNA from her saliva. At trial, we bring in a couple of experts to testify that with the drugs in her system, she couldn't have possibly had the coordination or strength to stab Mr. Caldwell and we win. It's easy as pie, right?"

Terrell came to the sickening realization of what he had done.

"I made sure someone called the detectives to inform them about the scene right after I sent you two there to take pictures of what you saw," Mr. Bragg continued. "Imagine my surprise when the police found no glass, no drugs, and no exonerating evidence. I was certain Karen was hiding it from us. Do you remember that assignment I gave you about discovery violations?"

Terrell nodded yes. Of course he remembered. He'd spent his first three weeks in the house working in it.

"I thought we'd struck gold. The fact that she was hiding it made our case even better. But even after we went through all of their evidence, we couldn't find it. That's when everything went south," he explained.

"The key piece of evidence I needed for a not guilty verdict was missing. On top of that, I couldn't make a big deal about it because I couldn't explain how I knew it existed in the first place."

"Was Joe in on it?" Terrell asked.

"Sadly, no," Mr. Bragg answered. "Joe has a troubling sense of duty and fairness. He is very good at what he does, that's the reason we keep using him. He also has a bad habit of not informing us of things until he's figured it out for himself. He didn't mention the missing glass until I dismissed you from the case."

"I'm sorry I messed things up for you. I promise I'll make it right if it's the last thing I do," Terrell said.

"No need to apologize," Mr. Bragg said. "I'm sure we'll be able to think of something to fix this."

"I wasn't talking to you," Terrell replied as he looked past Mr. Bragg to Jennifer. "I'm going to get you out of this."

"Despite the trouble you've caused," Mr. Bragg pressed on, "I must say that I am very impressed. Not only were you able to find the key piece of evidence in only one day, you were also able to make Joe like you. That's never happened before. When we dismissed you, he actually called to tell me that he'd never seen you do anything more egregious than glance at Ms. Weston's rear-end. I think he's truly going to miss you."

"I'll be sure to give him a big hug the next time I see him," Terrell said.

"I bet you will. Now, you understand the predicament you've caused me."

"Yes," Terrell answered. "The only thing that can help Jennifer is the truth and you certainly can't use that. You have a couple of murders to protect."

"Don't use that sanctimonious tone with me Terrell," Mr. Bragg said. "We've protected murderers before and I'm sure we'll do it again. I'll take rapists and thieves too, if they can pay our fee. Brian and Clarence are no worse than any other guilty clients we've had, and I take pride in representing them."

"For a lot of money," Brian mumbled.

"After it became clear to me that our drug defense wasn't going to work, Brian thought we should stop taking chances and cut our losses immediately."

"Still do," Brian chimed in. "You're still taking too many chances."

"I know exactly what I'm doing," Mr. Bragg said without taking his eyes off Terrell.

"Cut your losses?" Terrell asked. "Is that your delicate way of saying kill Jennifer?"

"Yes," Mr. Bragg answered. "The Music Awards presented a tailor made opportunity to extricate ourselves from the situation. It would have been done without undue attention being thrust upon the firm or AMI. One of those hoodlums from that rap band…"

"It's not a rap band," Terrell corrected. "Rappers don't have bands. They have entourages. You're showing your age again."

"I suppose I am," Mr. Bragg smiled with kindliness in his eyes that belied the evil of what he was saying. "A member of the entourage would pull the trigger and tragically end the life of Jennifer Weston. It would have wrapped up the entire case in a neat little bow and no one would be the wiser of why any of it really happened. Of course, I should have guessed that you would ruin that plan too. I only sent you along so that she'd have one less bodyguard. I never thought that you'd be able to get her out of there unharmed."

"Oh please," Clarence interrupted. "He didn't do anything but get beat up. You're acting like he's some kind of damn superhero."

"Shut up Clarence," Mr. Bragg said, exasperated. "If my soliloquy is bothering you so much, why don't you get the bedroom ready?"

"Fine," he answered. "At least I don't have to listen to any more of this."

"I've never seen Peter so angry," Mr. Bragg chuckled, "When Brian called to tell us that you saved Ms. Weston, I thought he was going to have an aneurysm. He wanted to fire you then."

"Mr. Foster is in on this too?" Terrell asked, shocked.

"It would have been difficult to pull off something of this magnitude without him. Once I told him how much money we were going to make, he wasn't hard to convince."

"So why didn't you get rid of me then?" Terrell asked. "I mean, I had already blown up two of your plans."

"Yes you had, but you'd also become invested in the outcome. If I was your age and I took a look into those pretty brown eyes of hers, I would have become invested in the outcome too. If I had sent you back to Tampa, you wouldn't have stopped investigating. I'd rather have you somewhere that I could keep an eye you."

"But I don't understand. You didn't fire me then, yet, you went to a lot of trouble to frame me so that you could fire me yesterday."

"I'd hoped that by keeping you close, I could protect you from yourself," Mr. Bragg shook his head. "But you really are too smart for your own good. I sent you to Tampa to dredge though some utterly dull contract work. Yet you still find a way to go to Atlanta to seek out the one person that can establish a motive for Brian to kill Mr. Caldwell."

"How'd you know?" Terrell asked. He'd thought that had been careful about hiding his plans.

"You're not the only one that's smart," Mr. Bragg answered. "You were getting too close. I had to figure out a way to get you out of Miami and keep you from any further meddling."

"Lucky for me," Brian smiled, "My source had a few pictures that would do nicely."

"I wasn't even going to fire you," Mr. Bragg explained. "After the trial blew over…"

"You mean after Jennifer got convicted or killed," Terrell corrected.

"However you want to look at it," he continued, "but after it was over, I planned on bringing you back. If you caused me this much trouble when you weren't even trying, I couldn't wait to see what would happen when I turned you loose on someone else."

"But then you had to go and kidnap Jennifer and find all this here," he gestured to the stack of papers that Terrell had discovered in the safe.

"He didn't kidnap me. I would have come all by myself," Jennifer interjected.

Mr. Bragg rolled his eyes. "The point is, once again you have ruined what was a very good and well reasoned plan. Surely, you can understand exactly what a precarious situation we find ourselves in right now."

"Of course," Terrell said. "The three of you are guilty of murder, conspiracy to commit murder, fraud, grand larceny and about 20 other crimes I can think of off the top of my head. And now you need to 'cut your losses', as you so eloquently put it."

"Yes, but not in the way that you think. As far as I'm concerned, there is only person that needs to be eliminated. It will be difficult to eliminate both of you in such a way that will not draw undue suspicion. If there is any way I can prevent your death, I will."

Mr. Bragg turned to Jennifer before continuing, "I'm afraid the same cannot be said for you. It's a shame really. My granddaughter will be devastated to hear of your untimely demise, but as I said, it's just business."

"I don't understand," said Terrell.

"It's quite simple. If your bodies are found here, people are going to want to know why. There is no good excuse for the two of you to be here except that this place contained something important. It would be far better for us if Ms. Weston met her demise back in Miami as a victim of suicide."

Terrell marveled at how coldly Mr. Bragg talked about killing Jennifer. He had always been a predator in the courtroom, but this level of callousness shocked Terrell to his core.

"A double suicide is infinitely less believable. Besides, I noticed that you managed to ditch that SUV somewhere between Miami and here. That indicates that someone saw you last night. That would make it very difficult to get our timelines correct in staging the suicide."

"That's the only reason for keeping me alive?"

"I do like you Terrell and you're worth every penny we pay you. I don't destroy that kind of asset unless I absolutely have to."

"You're too kind," Terrell said.

"Clarence, would you come in here?" Mr. Bragg called to the other room. When Clarence came back into the room, Mr. Bragg nodded toward Jennifer's bound body. Clarence walked over carrying a small knife and sliced through the tape binding her hands and feet. She immediately began struggling with him, but it was futile. He outweighed her be at least a hundred forty pounds and he easily manhandled her back to the rear bedroom.

"Where are you taking her? What are you doing?" Terrell asked frantically.

"You'll find out in a minute," Mr. Bragg said. "Brian, Peter is waiting in the bar of our hotel. I think it would be best if you were spotted there with him in about thirty minutes."

"Are you sure?" Brian asked quizzically, "I mean, I thought that we were going to…"

"I'll be fine," Mr. Bragg interrupted. "Terrell and I are old friends. I don't think I have anything to worry about from him."

Brian stood up and headed toward the door. He nodded disapprovingly as he left the apartment.

"What about your alibi?" Terrell asked. "Don't you need to leave too?"

"I don't need to leave, because I'm not here. I'm watching television in my hotel suite. Or at least that's what my wife will say if anyone ever asks her about it. Of course, she did have that extra Vicodan. It's quite possible she's been sleeping soundly all evening." Mr. Bragg replied. "But don't concern yourself with that. The question you should be asking is how are you going to you get out of this mess."

Mr. Bragg walked over to the kitchen table. He grabbed the knife that Clarence had placed there and walked back to Terrell. Terrell winced as Mr. Bragg walked behind him and made a quick slashing motion. Suddenly, his arms were free. A moment later, the tape binding his legs was also severed.

"There, now that's much better isn't it?" he asked.

"I suppose," Terrell said, rubbing his sore neck. "Are you letting me go?"

"No," Mr. Bragg answered. "But I am going to give you a choice."

"What kind of choice?"

Mr. Bragg led Terrell to the bedroom. Jennifer lay prone on the bed, arms tied to the bedposts with silk scarves. She had a thick piece of duct tape across her mouth. Her eyes looked dazed and glassy.

"What did you give her?"

"A tranquilizer. She's a fighter. She should have been unconscious by now."

"What do you want from me?" he asked.

"I want you to strangle her," Mr. Bragg replied calmly.

"What?"

"It's your only option Terrell," Mr. Bragg said. "You know far too much for us to let you go. The only way I can ensure your silence is to make sure you have a little dirt on your hands. Strangle her. She won't give you much trouble. Clarence will dispose of the body. We'll craft a story about her jumping bail and getting out of the country. I'm sure we can get a look alike to stage some sightings in Europe or South America. She'll just disappear off the face of the earth, and no one will ever know what really happened."

Terrell stood there, awed by what he was hearing. Mr. Bragg nodded to Clarence. Clarence moved toward them carrying a thick nylon rope. Terrell thought that Clarence was going to give it to him until he suddenly reared back and punched him in the lip.

"Ow!" Terrell said as he felt the metallic taste of blood flow from his lip into his mouth. "What was that for?"

"Just a little insurance," Mr. Bragg said. Clarence wiped the blood on his fist on the pillowcase near Jennifer's head. "That pillowcase will be buried with Ms. Weston's body. Should you ever have a crisis of conscience, the medical examiner will be able to tell that she died of strangulation. The DNA evidence will lead directly back to you."

Terrell rubbed his face with his hands as he desperately tried to figure out his next move. He knew that there was no way he could hurt Jennifer. He fleetingly thought of pretending to choke her, but he was sure that if he didn't finish, Clarence would.

"Time to make a decision," Mr. Bragg said.

Terrell glanced anxiously around the room and he saw his opportunity. Clarence had been carrying a pistol in his waistband. He must have pulled it out while he was tying up Jennifer because it was lying on the nightstand. Terrell couldn't believe his luck.

"Okay, okay," he said as he kneeled down on the bed. He inched closer to Jennifer and continued, "I sorry, but I don't have a choice."

He reached out as if to wrap his hands around her throat, but as he got near, he instead lunged for the pistol. He tumbled onto the floor and rolled to his feet bringing the gun to bear on a suspiciously smiling Clarence.

"I told you it would work," Mr. Bragg said confidently. "Now, wait for me to get out of here and then get rid of him."

"Wait a minute," said Terrell. "I don't think you realize that I've got a gun."

"What good is a gun with no bullets?" Mr. Bragg asked. "Do you really think we'd be so stupid as to leave a loaded weapon lying around where you could get it?"

"Yes," Terrell said. "I did actually."

"Go ahead, pull the trigger. You will see that the gun is quite empty."

Terrell pointed the gun at Clarence and squeezed the trigger. Nothing happened. Clarence smiled as he grabbed the shotgun that was leaning against the wall near him and pointed it at Terrell.

"Now we'll see if mine is loaded," Clarence chided.

"No, it has to be with the pistol." Mr. Bragg said. "It has to be one shot, close range to the temple. Don't screw it up."

"I don't understand," a befuddled Terrell asked.

"You and Ms. Weston, lovers that you are, ran away together." Mr. Bragg explained. "She likes her sex rough, as do you. Things got out of hand and you accidentally strangled her. Overcome with guilt, you took your own life. It's not the best plan I've ever had, but I think it's pretty good for short notice. The only problem was getting your fingerprints on the gun. A good CSI can tell when a print has been planted, so we needed to get the gun in your hand while you were alive. You being the hero that you are, I knew you couldn't resist trying one last time to save her."

"No one will believe that," Terrell said as he tried to think of some other way out of the situation.

"Oh, I think they will," Mr. Bragg replied. "Especially once that grainy tape of the two of you begins circulating on the Internet."

"What tape?"

"The tape Brian is fabricating. We'll use an old camera and a couple of look-alikes. It wouldn't stand up in court, but it will be enough for Jon Q. Public to believe the story."

"But…"

"The time for buts has passed," Mr. Bragg said, pulling on his coat. "For what it's worth, I'm sorry things had to end this way." Without another word, Mr. Bragg left the room and the apartment. The front door shut with a numbing finality.

Clarence kept the shotgun trained on Terrell. He was itching to use it, but managed to contain himself for a few minutes in order to let Mr. Bragg get away.

"Hey man, you know that you don't have to do this," Terrell stated.

"Shut up," Clarence said.

"No, I'm serious. There is no way they could convict you of Optimus' murder. Not with everything they have against Jennifer."

"Shut up."

"I'm just saying that this is more heat than you want. And why are you the one that has to do all the dirty work? How come Brian and Mr. Bragg don't have to stay here for…"

"I said shut up. You're not talking your way out of this. They told me that I had to use that other gun to make it look right. But you know what? They worry too much. I think I'll just use this shotgun, It's easier this way. If they're so smart they'll figure out a way to explain it."

He knew there was no way he could get to Clarence before he pulled the trigger.

"Let me ask you a question," Clarence said.

"What?"

"Do you know Lucifer?"

"What? No."

"Tell him I said what's up when you meet him."

Terrell closed his eyes and waited for the bang.

CHAPTER 23

The first thought Terrell had was that death was much more pleasant than he expected. He didn't even hear the gunshot. There was no pain. Maybe this is what it was like when you were shot in the head, he thought. It took him several seconds before he realized that pounding he heard was his heartbeat and not his angel wings.

He cautiously cracked open his eye and was surprised to see Clarence's face distended in an expression of shock and pain. His eyes bulged out from their sockets and his thick tongue pressed out between his lips. Joe had snuck up from behind and grabbed Clarence in a headlock. The crook of Joe's arm was tucked under Clarence's chin and Terrell could see Joe's muscular forearm pressing against the Clarence's carotid artery. Clarence had dropped the shotgun and was trying to pull Joe's arms away from his neck, but it was no use. His strength had already begun to fade. Clarence's eyes drooped and finally closed as his body went limp. A small trickle of saliva ran down the corner of his mouth. Joe held on for a few moments more before releasing his grip, dumping Clarence on the floor.

"Did you kill him?" Terrell asked cautiously.

"No," Joe responded. "But he'll be out for a few minutes."

"Are you going to kill me?"

Joe didn't even bother looking at Terrell.

"How'd you find us?" Terrell asked. "I mean, I know it's what you do, but how? I thought I covered my tracks pretty well."

"I followed Clarence here. As soon as I got to New York, he hopped a flight to Atlanta. I followed and here you were."

"Did you hear what…," Terrell trailed off as he thought. "Of course you did, the penetrating mike. How much did you get?"

"The walls in this place are very thin," Joe responded. "I got most of it."

"So what took you so long?" Terrell said. "He almost shot me!"

"There were three people in here. I had to wait until Brian and Mr. Bragg left before I could sneak into the apartment. Besides, no one is paying me to make sure you're safe."

"If that's your attitude, I didn't really need your help anyway," Terrell said confidently. He glanced down to make sure that he hadn't wet himself in the commotion. "I could have always used my move."

"What move?"

"The inside-out technique," Terrell said. He did several pantomime karate moves for effect, ending with a flurry of chops to the air. "If you do that technique properly, you will turn a person's entire body inside out."

"With your eyes closed?" Joe asked. "Because that's what you were doing when I got here."

"It works best if your eyes are closed," Terrell smiled.

"Do you ever shut up? Joe asked as he pulled a thin cord from his jacket and began tying Clarence's hands behind his back.

"No, not really," Terrell answered. "You saved me from getting shot in the face a second ago and I'm trying to figure out a way to say thank you. You don't seem to be the hugging type, so I figured I'd just go with a joke."

Joe nodded and Terrell thought that was the closest he was

going to get to a 'you're welcome', so he turned his attention to Jennifer. Her eyes were still unfocused. He had no idea how much sedative they'd given her. He untied her hands and propped her upright on the bed.

"Jennifer." He spoke softly. "Jennifer, are you okay?" She managed to focus on him for a moment.

"Um-huh," she nodded sleepily. "We have to… We have to… get… away…" she said before slumping into his shoulder.

"She's right. You two should get out of here. Take her to the hospital, they might have given her too much." Joe tossed a set of keys at Terrell. "Take my car."

Terrell placed his arms under Jennifer's legs and lifted her off the bed.

"What about you?" Terrell asked.

"Don't worry about me," Joe said with what could almost be described as a smile. "I'm not going anywhere for a while. I've still got a few questions and I think Clarence is going to answer them for me." Joe flipped on a lighter he pulled from his pocket. "Your firm paid me a lot of money to find out what happened. I plan on doing just that." Joe stuffed a washcloth into Clarence's mouth. "Hurry up, he'll only be out a few more seconds and I doubt someone with your delicate constitution will want to watch this."

Terrell didn't need any further incentive to leave. He heard Clarence's first muffled scream as he loaded Jennifer into the car.

***

Alicia sat in her apartment trying to get ready for her date. She wasn't taking Terrell's disappearing act very well. She couldn't believe that he hadn't tried to call her in the two days since she broke up with him. Not that she would talk to him yet, but at least she'd know that he cared. She was angry with him, but she knew she'd eventually give him another chance. She still loved him and she thought that he still loved her. However, after two days of no contact, she had to concede the possibility that maybe what the news was reporting was true. Loath as she was to admit it, Jennifer Weston was beautiful. She couldn't help but notice it when she'd tossed her Fantasy CDs in the garbage the day before. The rational part of her mind knew that any man would be attracted to her, even her Terrell.

She really didn't feel like going out with Leonard, but she'd hate herself in the morning if she spent another night waiting at home for Terrell call. She had been putting him off all summer, but now she needed some company. She tried to slide her earring into her ear, but it slipped through her fingers and bounced on the floor and rolled under the bed.

"Great," she mumbled as she reached under the bed to retrieve the earring. Then she heard a knock at the door. Leonard was early. "Coming!" she shouted as she hurried to the door.

"Good evening, my lovely senorita," Leonard said. He held a bouquet of flowers in his arm. "I brought these for you, but I'm afraid that they're not nearly as beautiful as you are."

"Thank-you," Alicia said, as she struggled not groan. On a good day, she disliked insincere flattery and today wasn't one of her good days. "Come in."

He walked through the door and into the small living room of her flat.

"I'll be ready in a minute," she told him.

"Okay. Hey, did you hear about Jennifer Weston?" Leonard asked.

Alicia had kept Terrell's involvement in the case a secret at work. With the problems they'd had over the last few months, the last thing she'd wanted to deal with was people at work trying to worm information out of her.

"No, I missed it," she said coldly.

"She got off! Apparently, her lawyer is the one that killed that guy."

"Her lawyer?" she said, cursing herself for sounding too interested. "What lawyer?"

"I'm not sure, I think it's the one that she's been hooking up with the whole time. It was on the news when I left my apartment. I only caught the end of it."

Alicia wished that she didn't care, but she did. Was Terrell in jail? Is that why she hadn't heard from him?

"Are you sure?" she asked.

"Yeah, I think he was the one. Somebody at work told me that you knew him. Is that true?"

"We went to college together," she answered. It couldn't be Terrell, she said to herself. Optimus was killed before he even knew Jennifer. At least, that's what she thought. Could they have been seeing each other for months? She told herself to stop being crazy, it couldn't be Terrell. Leonard must be mistaken.

"Could you excuse me for a moment," Alicia smiled. "I'll be right back."

"Yeah, sure," Leonard said. "Take your time, but I must confess, you already look perfect."

"Thank-you," Alicia managed a fake smile.

She dashed back to her bedroom an eagerly switched on her computer. She searched for Jennifer Weston and acquittal. The top match was the Miami television station WTLB 27. It had video clips. She clicked on the link and after what seemed like an eternity of waiting for the video player to load the face of an attractive male greeted her.

"A shocking turn of events in the Jennifer Weston case today," said anchor Juan Menendez. "As State Attorney Karen Rojas dismissed all charges against R&B singing sensation Jennifer Weston. Weston was located recovering in an Atlanta hospital after escaping home detention with her lawyer, Terrell Banks. The two are seen together here in this file footage." The station cut to the tape of Jennifer and Terrell walking arm in arm down the red carpet at the Grammy's. Alicia scowled.

"We now go to Lynn Wagoner, at the Miami-Dade courthouse."

"Thanks Hector." The screen cut to a tall brunette woman standing on the courthouse steps. "Extra officers were called in today as hundreds of fans and supporters crowded the street to catch a glimpse of Jennifer Weston exiting the courthouse." The video shifted to bouncing image of Jennifer being escorted down the crowded steps by sheriff's deputies and ushered into a waiting car. Terrell was not in the footage.

The image shifted to a split-screen of Hector and Lynn. "What can you tell us about what went on in the courtroom?" Hector asked.

"In an incredible twist, the State's Attorney announced that arrest warrants have been filed for Earnest Bragg, Peter Foster and Brian Dunn," Lynn answered.

"Aren't Earnest Bragg and Peter Foster the lead attorneys on Weston's defense team?"

"Yes Hector. They were. We have also learned that Brian Dunn is a senior level record executive for AMI, the record label of Jennifer Weston and her late boyfriend, the rapper Optimus."

"What kind of charges is the State's Attorney seeking?"

"That is unclear at the moment, however, our sources inform us that the three will be formally charged with conspiracy in connection to the murder of Optimus. We have also been told that they will be charged with a litany of offenses relating to Jennifer Weston. Some of the things being tossed around are kidnapping, racketeering, fraud and aggravated assault for their alleged roles in the kidnapping and subsequent torture of Jennifer Weston."

Alicia's mouth dropped open in shock.

"So Jennifer Weston has been completely exonerated?" Hector asked.

"That would appear to be the case. Details are sketchy at this point, but it seems as though Jennifer Weston was the target of a frame job perpetuated by her lawyers and her record label."

"What about Terrell Banks, the other member of her defense

team?" Hector asked. "Did his relationship with her set her up for this scheme?"

"I haven't seen any mention of him in the court documents filed thus far. However, I have learned that the State Attorney's office is alleging that a fourth accomplice actually performed the killing of Optimus. It is unclear at present whether that unidentified man is in fact Terrell Banks."

"Might the State Attorney be keeping his identity a secret because he's co-operating as a witness?" Hector asked.

"It wouldn't be the first time someone has cut a deal to save himself," she replied.

Leonard's shouting finally broke Alicia's concentration.

"What did you say?" she asked.

"I said you have a nice apartment," he repeated. "It's much nicer than the one they gave me."

"I'm having a little trouble hearing you! I'm doing my hair," Alicia lied. She hoped he would just be quiet. She was missing the story.

"I said!" he continued at a louder volume, "I really like your place!"

"Thanks!" she shouted back.

"Thank you Lynn," Hector said as his face filled the screen. "Joining us now via satellite," Hector continued, "to help sort out the flurry of legal activity is our legal expert Professor Douglas Crutchfield." The image shifted to a very old and crabby looking law professor.

"Professor Crutchfield, are you there?" said the anchor.

"Of course I'm here," he responded. "You asked me to be on the show, where else would I be?"

"Ah, yes," Hector plowed forward. "While all the details are not yet clear, what can you tell us about the State's decision to dismiss the charges against Jennifer Weston?"

"I can tell you it means that they have some very compelling evidence that she hasn't committed a crime," he said. "Prosecutors have an ethical duty not to move forward with a case if they feel like there is a likelihood that the defendant is in fact innocent. That is really the only reason they would dismiss the case."

"So this is a clear indication that the prosecution thinks it could not convict Weston at trial?" Hector asked with his eyebrow raised.

"Isn't that what I just said?" Professor Crutchfield answered.

"Where do you want to eat?" Alicia heard Leonard shout out again from the front room. He made her miss the anchor's reply.

"It doesn't matter," she said, not caring at that point if she ate at all.

"...I've never encountered a situation quite like this before," Professor Crutchfield continued. "We're talking about two lawyers defending a case where they were participants in the predicate felony. It violates nearly every ethical cannon I can think of. We're going out into somewhat uncharted legal waters."

"What will be the next step for the new defendants?"

"They will be arrested and booked. After that, they will have a bond setting. I think the State will want try the case as quickly as possible. They will argue that since the defendants were privy to all the pertinent information of the case, there will be no prejudice by sticking with Jennifer Weston's original trial schedule."

"I can't believe that the internship is almost over," Leonard shouted out again.

"Sorry, can't hear you. I'll talk to you in a minute!" Alicia responded.

"Thank you professor," Hector said. "Stay tuned to News 27 for the latest in this developing story." The download abruptly ended and Alicia quickly surfed around to several other websites. None of them had any additional news about Terrell. She began to feel sick to her stomach. Even if he did cheat on her, and she wasn't absolutely sure that he had, she still loved him. She couldn't bear the though of him being locked up in a jail cell somewhere.

Alicia struggled with her decision for about two seconds

before she picked up her phone and dialed Terrell's number. After a series of clicks as the network tried to locate his phone, she was transferred directly to his voicemail. She pressed the off button and plopped down on the bed. She didn't know what she should do next.

"Hey, if you want, I could…" Leonard called from the other room.

"I'll be out in a minute!" Alicia snapped. She reached under the bed and retrieved her earring, slid on her shoes and re-emerged from the room.

"Gorgeous, absolutely gorgeous," Leonard smiled as she came back into the room.

He continued talking, but Alicia didn't hear him. Her mind was 5,000 miles away. Maybe she should call Terrell's parents. They might know what happened.

"Alicia?" he said, snapping her to attention.

"Oh, I'm sorry, what did you say?"

"I said, I still don't know where you want to go."

As Alicia stood there looking at Leonard, she knew that she would not be good company for the evening. She couldn't get her mind off Terrell and what might have happened to him. She had to get rid of Leonard for both their sakes.

"You know," she started, "I'm really not feeling that well."

"You look fine," he responded.

"I was until a little while ago," she said, sounding pitiful. "But now my stomach hurts and I don't think I could eat anything."

"We could just stay here," he suggested.

"No, I think I'm going to take some medicine and go to bed," she said. She surreptitiously grabbed his arm and helped him up out of the chair. "But thank you for the flowers. They are wonderful."

"Yeah, okay," he said moving sluggishly to the door. "Are you sure there isn't anything I can get for you?"

"No, I think I'll be fine if I lay down for a little while," she said. "You're such a sweetheart for asking. We'll have to get together some other time."

"Sure," he said. "I'm going to hold you to that you know."

"Okay," she said opening the door for him.

"I guess I'll see you at work," he said. He stood there for a moment, as if he were trying to figure out whether or not he could try to kiss her. When she didn't move closer to him, he waved sheepishly and walked out the door.

Alicia's mind raced as she tried to figure out what to do. She wasn't going to be able to relax until she found out what happened to Terrell. She thought of all the possible people she could call, but she doubted any of them would have more information than she did. She decided to call the firm. At least they would know where he was.

As she dialed the first few numbers, there was a knock at the door.

"Leonard, I'm sorry, but I don't feel well," she said as she opened the door. It wasn't Leonard. It was Terrell.

He looked horrible. A scab had formed over his split lip, he was unshaven and there were droplets of dried blood on his disheveled clothes. He didn't speak; he simply took her in his arms and held her tightly.

"They said you were involved in a murder and some kind of torture and I didn't know if you were okay and…"

"I'm okay," he said reassuringly. "At least, I am now." They stood in each other's arms for an eternity. Terrell could feel the warmth of her tears soak through his shirt.

"I got scared. I thought something really bad had happened," she said when she finally let him go.

"It did," he said as he ran his finger over his split lip. "You breaking up with me is about the worst thing that I can think of."

"Stop it," she said, wiping the tears from her face. "This is serious. You don't get to joke right now."

"Who's joking?" Terrell said. "I've been punched in the face, shot at and tied up, but none of it was as bad as losing you."

"I said stop that. I was worried, but I'm still mad at you. Wait a minute. How long have you been here?" she asked.

"Cab dropped me off right as that dude got here," he said. "Let me guess. That must be that Leonard guy you've told me about."

"We..." Alicia started, but Terrell put up his hands.

"It doesn't matter. Nothing you can say would change the way I feel about you, so it doesn't matter. I must say that I am glad you made him leave. I didn't have anywhere to wait for you."

"It would have served you right if I had left. I mean, it wasn't a date to the Music Awards, but we can't all be the new boy-toy of a celebrity."

"That's not fair," Terrell said. "That music award thing was purely for work."

"Maybe, but I'm sure they didn't have to twist your arm to go. I know you liked her."

"How do you know that?" Terrell challenged.

"Give me a break Terrell," she sighed. "Just look at her. She's famous, she's rich and she's like, one of People's most beautiful people. I'm not stupid."

"From what I've seen, fame sucks and I can make my own money. She might be one of People's most beautiful people, but you're on Terrell's list of the most beautiful people. It's pretty exclusive. There's only two members."

"Two members?"

"Yeah, you're number one and I'm number two. That's why we make such a cute couple."

"Yeah, you're number two alright."

"Ha. Ha. Stop it before you ruin the mood."

"What mood? I'm glad you're okay, but we're still broken up."

"Just hear me out," he said. "I've been trying to get over here to see you for a long time."

"You haven't been trying hard enough," she said.

"Maybe not, but I've needed to tell you something for months and I'm going to do it right now before anything else stops me."

"I'm listening."

"All my life, I've planned out everything. I set these little goals and milestones and I never did anything unless it had been planned and I was ready for it."

"Yes," she replied. "I know. You are very anal."

"I've loved you for a long time Alicia. I think I loved you even before I knew you."

"Then why'd you cheat on me," Alicia asked.

"I didn't," he said "I've never even wanted to." She looked into his eyes and knew that he was telling the truth.

"There's only one person I want and it's you," he continued. "If I couldn't have you, I wouldn't want anyone else. You make me better than I am by myself and I can't spend one more moment without you."

Terrell slowly dropped to one and dug the ring out of his pocket.

"I want to give you the world," he said, "And I'm going to start with this ring. Will you be my wife? Will you let me be your husband? Will you let me love you until I'm old and gray and the only thing I can still remember is that I love you?"

EPILOGUE

The vows were exchanged, the cake was cut and the garter had been thrown. As Terrell gazed out over the dance floor watching Alicia dancing with his father, he couldn't help but smile. He hadn't imagined that she could look more beautiful than she did everyday, but somehow the team of make-up artists and hairstylists made her look like she'd stepped right out of a photo shoot. He knew that he should be mingling with the other guests, but all he really wanted to do was take a few moments to enjoy looking at his wife.

"I have to go," Terrell heard a soft voice over his shoulder. "I've got a show in DC tomorrow."

"Okay, thanks for everything Jennifer," Terrell answered as he turned around to give her a hug. "I mean it, you didn't have to do all this." She had treated them to the wedding of their dreams. At the reception, she even performed an original song she had written just for them.

"It was fun. I've never actually played a wedding before," she laughed. "Besides, now I've got some great ideas for when I get married."

"Cool. As soon as Alicia and I get back from our honeymoon,

we need to sit down and talk about those offers. I've been reviewing them and I think…"

"Later," Jennifer cut him off. "This is your wedding. We can talk about work when you get back. Have a good time."

"Fair enough, see you later." He waved as she Jennifer made her way out the side door of the reception facility. He marveled at how she had remained in the background so as not to take any attention away from the bride and groom. The media frenzy surrounding her had subsided to its normal level, but she was still very careful.

"How much did all this set you back?" Ricky asked as he gobbled a few more jumbo shrimp. His groomsmen Ricky, Wesley and Sean walked over to him. They had just exited the area where the videographer was making guest testimonials for their wedding video. Terrell could see the wedding coordinator and her assistants guiding more guests toward the area.

"Nothing," Terrell answered.

"Nothing?" Ricky asked. "This is the nicest place I've ever seen. You've got ice sculptures, a security team, like a hundred wedding assistants and an orchestra. I'm still paying bills for my wedding and all we had 100 people at the Holiday Inn."

"Jennifer picked up the tab." Terrell answered. "She didn't let us pay for anything."

"Listen to him. He calls her Jennifer like they've been friends for 10 years," Sean said.

"You're the luckiest dude I've ever met," Sean said.

"That's not luck, it's skill," Terrell replied. "And a little bit of pity."

"Pity?"

"She felt bad when she found out that the firm screwed me before Mr. Foster got arrested."

"Really?" Sean asked. "You didn't tell me that."

"Yeah," Terrell replied. "They fired me. Then the firm repossessed my house and froze all my bank accounts."

"Why did they do that?" Sean asked.

"They said that they had to make sure I wasn't involved in the murder. It sucked. They had the locks changed before I got back from Spain."

"That's cold," Ricky said.

"You're telling me. After I went through all that, Jennifer said that picking up the wedding tab was the least she could do for us."

"Alicia didn't have a problem with that?" Ricky asked. "Usually women don't get along with chicks that tried to take their men."

"I've told you a million times, that never happened. It was all a part of the frame."

"Sure it was," Wesley chided.

"Okay. It took a little convincing," Terrell admitted. "But after I told her that if Jennifer paid, there were no limits on her dream wedding, she got on board."

"I bet she did," Wesley said.

"Besides," Terrell continued, "how can Alicia be mad at her? Since she hired me as her counsel, I make more money and work less hours. The money she put into this wedding is just a drop in the bucket compared to what I'm going to get for her in the settlement with AMI and Bragg and Shuttlesworth."

"Too bad that Bragg guy got away though," Ricky said. "I read that he hopped on a plane and escaped as soon as he found out you and Jennifer were still alive."

"Yeah well, Jennifer hired someone to track him down. I have a feeling that he'll eventually get what's coming to him."

***

Earnest Bragg III was a happy man. Life was good here. He had been a wealthy man in America, but in Belize, he lived like a king. He walked into the master bedroom of the villa he'd purchased and smiled. He'd managed to transfer a great deal of his personal wealth as well as a sizable amount of the firm's money to off shore accounts before he left the country. He would live very comfortably for the rest of his life. He had left behind a wife that he'd more or less loved for 25 years, but he never wanted for company. For only a few dollars, the girls in the village were more than willing to provide female companionship to him.

He lamented that Peter wasn't able to escape as he had. Still, there wasn't anything that Peter could say that the State's attorney didn't already know. He knew that he could never go back, but that was okay. There was no way Florida was going to convince the government of Belize to extradite him. A couple of well placed bribes to the right individuals ensured that.

He peeled off his linen shirt and thought about how he should spend his evening. Maybe he could convince Izadora to have drinks with him. He liked Izadora and he knew that she liked older men. He was so wrapped up in his thoughts, that he didn't even see the bald man in the black suit sitting in the chair. He never even knew he was there.